Ulpius Felix

Warrior of Rome
By
Griff Hosker

Published by Griff Hosker 2013
Copyright © Sword Books Ltd Second Edition

A CIP catalogue record for this title is available from the British
Library.

Dedication

To the Romans, without them and their incredible efforts the world might be a totally different place.

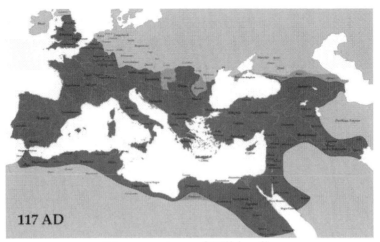

Map courtesy of Wikipedia

1

Chapter 1

Pannonia 50 AD close to the border with the Marcomanni confederation of tribes

The young warrior had always been called Wolf. It was not the name the shaman had given him at his birthing ceremony but only his mother remembered that name. His father had named him Wolf, partly because of his appetite but more for his ferocious nature, even when playing with his friends. He would never give in, even when fighting boys much older than he. The older boys learned to walk carefully around the Wolf who never seemed to mind the cuts, bruises and breaks he received. His father was proud of his son's nature and looked forward to the time when he would ride with his son to raid the neighbouring tribes. He was fated never to do so for, in the boy's tenth year his father was killed leading a raid on the Marcomanni in the lands beyond the new Roman frontier. It meant that at a young age he became the only boy in the home for his brothers had also perished in that ill-fated raid. The other men in the tribe, who survived were bitter. They resented the fact that, having been conquered by the Romans, the Romans had imposed their own laws of peace upon the warlike Pannonians. War was a way of life for the fierce warriors and they had been forced to fight further away from the lands they knew. The elders wondered if the people ought to try a different way of life.

His father had died six years earlier and the enforced responsibility made a change in Wolf. He would be as his father was; a leader and he gathered about him the young men of the tribe. They were the ones who did not want the new, peaceful way of life advocated by the wise elders. Wolf did not directly disobey the council but he and his followers took to practising in secret for the day when they would be old enough to go to war.

The chief of the tribe was Abad and he had wisely not joined in the raid which had cost so many warriors their lives. He had benefited from the absence of any rivals for the power in the tribe. He encouraged herding and farming as opposed to raiding but he watched, carefully, Wolf and his fellows as they grew into a band of warriors. It worried him for in Wolf he saw a rival. His own son was but eight years old and the sixteen year old Wolf had almost enough men following him to wrest his title from him. He spent long hours in the hut with the other members of the council working out what they should do about the threat of Wolf the warrior. In a perfect world he would do as his father had done and go on a raid and get himself killed but the Gods were not that generous and Abad was certain he was being punished for something. Perhaps the Romans, when they came to collect their taxes, might suggest a solution.

The annoyance in question was out watching the village herd. His mother had insisted that he pull his weight in the village. As much as she loved her last child she did not want him to go off, and die, leaving her a lonely widow and if that meant denting his ambitions then so be it.

Wolf sat easily on his horse with one leg cocked over the saddle. He was as the other boys, a superb rider and he did not need a saddle but he had been told that it made it easier when fighting if one used a saddle and Wolf would be a fighter. His friend, Gerjen, pulled his horse next to Wolf. The slightly older boy looked up to Wolf and tried to emulate him in all things. He wore his hair the same way with a high-top knot, his beard was braided the same way and he even had the same dagger as his friend. Wolf had not even noticed; he rarely took an interest in others. He liked Gerjen well enough but he had decided long ago that his friends would be judged on how well they fought in a battle, not the mock ones they used for training but a real one where life and death hung in the balance. Until then they were children. When he killed his first enemy, then he would be a man.

"Wolf, when will we ride to war?"

The others were even more in awe of Wolf than Gerjen and he had been chosen as the spokesperson. Wolf looked at his friend with those keen sharp eyes which reminded his friends not of a wolf but an eagle for their pierced and bore into you. "Soon. When the herd is taken into winter quarters we will ride to the next valley and blood our swords."

"Not all of us have swords like you Wolf."

Wolf grinned and a chill went through Gerjen. "We will have them when we have killed our enemies." He leaned forward, animated now by the ideas which raced inside his head. "There are two of us with swords but we all have bows. We ambush their warriors and take their weapons and their horses."

It was known that the Marcomanni had bigger horses than they did and Wolf wanted a powerful horse. There was a risk, his father had discovered that, but Wolf had had years to plan his first raid and ask those who had survived what to do. He had ridden, alone, into the land of the enemy to spy out the land and he knew their trails and their ways. He had told others he was hunting and he always returned with meat but the reality was that he was hunting men. He had found a steep sided valley with good cover for he and the other ten boys and he knew that an ambush would bring the results he desired.

"What should I tell them then?"

"Five nights from now we leave. They are not to tell anyone." His voice became chillingly threatening. "If anyone discovers what we are about then the one with the loose tongue will have me to answer to."

Gerjen was in no doubt that Wolf would carry out his threat. He wished that he could be as tough and ruthless as his friend then he too would become a great warrior.

The twelve of them were checked by Wolf as they gathered in the hills above the village. He tutted at the dull edge on one dagger. He snorted contemptuously at the paucity of arrows from another but eventually he led them off to the north at a trot. Their ponies were surefooted and each one was dark. As they rode through the tree line they became almost invisible. They had two days at least for they had said they were hunting. Wolf had told them that they were not lying for they were hunting, men. They would not be missed for the herds would be checked ready for the taxation inspection. The council of elders had learned long ago that lying to the Roman tax collector merely raised your taxes. They would not make that mistake a second time. Cooperation did bring benefits. Abad had been promised much by the collector on his last visit and he hoped soon to have a stone home like those he had seen when they had visited the city. The boys were aiming to catch some travellers unawares the following morning and

4

Wolf hoped that they would be warriors. He was determined to be a man. Had his father been alive then he would already have bloodied his sword. With no man to stand for him, he would have to stand for himself.

They rode through the night and Wolf drove them relentlessly. His faithful lieutenant Gerjen brought up the rear; goading those who lagged behind. As the first glimmer of light peered over the horizon, Wolf halted his erstwhile war band. "We are close now to the trail which crosses the Marcomanni land. We must be ruthless when we strike. This is not a game. If we are to become great warriors we need to become killers of men. If you fear to kill a man, then think of him as a beast; for in the end that is what we all are." In the half-light they could see the grin on his face and sensed his excitement which was infectious. Now that they were so close they all believed that this would be easy. "There is a trail a little way ahead. Gerjen will take half on one side and I will take half on the other. When the men pass wait until I have loosed my arrow and then take each man that you can see."

Darvas asked, "How do you know that they will come this way?"

"It is the main trail between their villages." He pointed away in the distance. "I have seen where they camp and then they ride quickly to cover the last ten miles to the village of the chief. The only thing I do not know is how many there will be. Check your arms before we leave this place."

They were all dressed in leggings with a leather shirt to give some protection. Wolf had a helmet, an old one left by his father when he had gone raiding. It was not the best protection but it was better than nothing. On his belt he had a curved dagger and the long sword, this time his grandfather's. He had left his spear behind for the bows would be a better weapon for an ambush. The others were dressed in a similar fashion but most, as yet, had no sword.

Dawn had finally broken when they arrayed themselves in two lines in the woods above the trail. The place Wolf had chosen was the perfect site for an ambush as the trail itself was below their hiding place. If the warriors tried to attack them then they would have to do it uphill. As they waited he also realised that, inadvertently, he had minimised the chances of his band shooting each other in crossfire.

It was when his own horse whinnied that he cursed himself. He should have placed a scout to warn them of the approach of their prey. It was too late to do anything about it and they would have to attack blind. It was a band of men with horses. He was so excite that he could not see the number as the large warrior at the front obscured his view. Wolf caught the glimpse of a sword which meant that they were probably, warriors. His notched an arrow as did the others. The Marcomanni deigned to wear helmets and they had cloaks about them. Wolf had seen some of them with armour and he did not know yet, what he faced. The first rider was thirty paces from him and he loosed his arrow. It flew straights and true and hit him between his shoulder blade and neck. He heard the whizz of arrows as the rest of his boys loosed their arrows. He cursed when he saw at least one horse fall. He loosed another at the warrior who tried to escape the dying beast and he struck him on the arm. He drew his own sword and roaring a war cry launched himself down the slope towards the trail. He glanced around and saw that Darvas and Panyvadi had joined him. There were still six Marcomanni warriors and four of them were unhurt. He hurled his horse, riding with his knees, at the one at the fore. He was a big, bearded warrior with many bracelets showing that he had been in battles before and won. He hurled his spear at Wolf but the youth easily evade it and, before the warrior could draw his own sword, Wolf's had bitten deep in the man's stomach. Roaring in agony he fell backwards off his horse, tumbling to the ground and taking Wolf's sword with him. Undaunted the young warrior pulled out his dagger looking for another enemy to kill.

Gerjen had continued to pour arrow after arrow at the enemy but, seeing his quiver empty, and his friend without a sword he bravely rode to his aid. He too pulled his own dagger out as another German raised his sword to strike at Wolf who was defending himself with his dagger. Gerjen did not hesitate. He threw himself from his own horse and flew like a spear towards the unguarded warrior's back. His dagger went beneath the arm and plunged into his body killing the warrior instantly. Gerjen fell to the floor and the warrior's body tumbled on top of him. He pushed him off and grabbed the weapon from his dead hand.

"Behind you!"

Wolf's cry made him turn to see the last German riding towards him, with his spear held before him. Gerjen could not evade him and he bravely held his sword before him. Wolf's arrow struck the warrior on the arm and he swerved as his reins slipped. He kicked on and the horse jumped over Gerjen, catching him a glancing blow with his fore hoof and then they were gone, heading to safety.

Wolf leapt from his horse and grabbed the semi-conscious Gerjen. "I owe you my life brother."

Gerjen tried to shake his own head but it hurt too much. "As you saved mine. I think that makes us even."

When Wolf looked around he was disappointed. There had only been four warriors and one of them had escaped. He had hoped he could return with heads adorning his saddle showing his prowess as a leader but they had had almost three times as many warriors, surprise on their side, and still one had escaped. Even worse he saw that four of his band had received wounds of one type of another. He saw Darvas binding one badly gashed arm, Kadarcs and Panyvadi looked to another two minor wounds. Gerjen rose to his feet and they went around the bodies looking for trophies of war. They had at least three fine swords and Wolf kept the best giving the other two to Gerjen to divide. He made a pile of the bracelets and daggers. When he pulled the helmets off he saw that the warriors were little older than he. One helmet fitted him and he took it, along with a shield.

"Come, the one we allowed to escape will return with others. Take what you will and bring the two horses which survive. We ride for home."

Kadarcs looked at the dead. "Are you not taking the heads? As trophies?"

When it came down to it, Wolf was not sure that he would be able to cut off a man's head and he did not wish to risk looking foolish before his band. "We have no time." He waved a hand at the weapons. "We have enough here."

They seemed relieved at that and they all roared a cheer of victory. They set off at a brisk pace back the way they had come.

Gnaeus Marcius Celsus hated this desolate, wide empty country. He and his Cavalry Turma had a huge area to patrol. The Ninth Hispana was a proud legion raised by Caesar himself but Rome had sent all but one cohort and the infantry to help subdue the new province of Britannia. The duty in this land had worn down the spirits of the few who remained. It was almost like a punishment. Although conquered, this mounted people were like a flea flicking around and annoying. Gnaeus wished that he had some of them as auxilia to relieve some of the tasks of his overworked one hundred and twenty man turma. The worst part of his duties was the escorting of the tax collectors. They were generally fat and greedy little men who insisted upon travelling in the slow and ponderous wagons making each journey an even bigger nightmare. It was for one such duty that he was returning to the fortress of Novae to begin the next round of collections.

When he reached the Praetorium one of the Tribunes was waiting for him. "Come with me Tribune. The Legate wishes a word before you begin your task."

When he entered the office he noticed a soldier, slightly older than himself seated towards the back of the office. He nodded at Gnaeus. The Legate looked up from the map he was studying. "Ah Celsus, still bitching about the patrol and the tax man?"

The Legate, Marcus Bulbus was a good natured general with white tufts of hair around a totally bald pate. This would be his last posting and when the rest of the Ninth left for Britannia he would retire to his lemon groves south of Surrentum. He was what the men called a 'sound general' which meant he did not waste their lives in useless attacks. He was also known for his sense of humour and Gnaeus did not take offence.

"Of course sir! I am a cavalryman."

Everyone laughed and the atmosphere immediately relaxed. "And that is why you are here, because you are a cavalryman." He pointed to the northern frontier of the Empire, close to the Rhenus River. "We have a couple of tribes here, the Chauci and the Frisii and they are causing a little bit of bother on the frontier.

8

As you know the divine Claudius has decided to invade Britannia and we are a little short of troops which is why we only have one cohort here and the rest are with the forces conquering Britannia." Gnaeus was intrigued; did this mean he would be in action again? "Now you cavalry fellows attached to the legions are all well and good but you are damned expensive with your armour and fine horses and the Legate commanding the force, Gnaeus Domitius Corbulo has asked for some native horsemen."

Gnaeus went from the elation of imagining that he would be leading a vexillation against barbarians to the sudden realisation that he would be a recruiting officer. "The Pannonians."

"You see Julius I told you he was quick on the uptake." He waved his hands, "Their tribe does not matter, just so long as they can ride. This is the main reason you have been chosen. You know horses and you know men. We need about a thousand in the first instance but, for the next year you will be recruiting others." He saw the disappointed look on the cavalryman's face. "If it is any consolation I think that this legion will be in action soon so regard this as a necessary evil to allow you to achieve your ends."

"Sir."

"Now then you will accompany the tax collector but I have told him that you need to be quicker than usual and he will have to ride." Gnaeus smiled. That was not so bad. "You need to be back here, with your new men within two months."

"That is a tall order sir the province is huge."

"Concentrate on those closest to the fort and work outwards."

"And who will command these barbarians. Should I find a local leader?"

"No, no. That wouldn't do. He might get ideas if we gave him a thousand men and armed them. No, no, we have an officer. Proculus."

The seated officer rose and Gnaeus could see, as he emerged from the shadows that he was at least ten years older than he with grey hair at his temples. Marius Ulpius Proculus."

Even as he took his arm Gnaeus knew that he had heard the name before but where escaped him. "Tribune Gnaeus Marcius Celsus."

9

"Proculus here will be in charge of them when they go to the land of the Rhenus. Oh and see if there are, say, six or so men who would like to volunteer for detached duty until they have fought their first action. Offer them a temporary pay grade of optio." Even as Gnaeus wondered who he could be rid of the Legate went on, "I want decent men for they will be returning to the legion and I want our Prefect here to give me a good report." Proculus gave a wry smile and inclined his head to one side. He, too, had known what the Tribune would have attempted. "Right, off you go. You will need to get acquainted. You leave today!"

As they left Marius said, "Sorry about this duty, and stealing your men. I will return them I promise."

"If you return. These Pannonians are a wild bunch and the Chauci, well I have heard of them too. Madmen, apparently. I would be worried to take my regular cavalry against them, let alone a bunch of wild barbarians who like nothing better than to take off a head or two and adorn their saddles with them."

"I have heard that but this is a chance and I intend to take it."

They walked towards the stables in silence for a while. "If you don't mind me asking, Prefect, what is your background? Even the officials in Rome do no pick out a name at random to command allies."

Proculus paused, "My father was the victim of one of Caligula's little purges. I was serving with the First Minerva as a Narrow Stripe Tribune, much as yourself, I was arrested and thrown into prison. Luckily for me Claudius came to power and I was released." He paused and looked sadly off to the west. "The rest of my family, all of them died. I suspect I am being given this assignment to be away from Rome and they hope that I will not return."

The Tribune was taken aback by the honesty of the Prefect. In the treacherous world since the death of Augustus you kept your counsel until you knew the politics of the person to whom you were speaking. "Very honest of you and sympathy for your loss."

Proculus shrugged, "The Legate said that you were an honest man and I have tired of deceit. I now speak my mind. Keeping silent when that madman was shagging his sister and his horse did no-one any good. Perhaps a little more honesty might help."

"I admire your sentiments but do not believe all that you have heard about the Divine Claudius. He is not a stammering half-wit as some would have us believe and he had spies everywhere. I would watch your tongue until you get to know people."

"I will and, as I said, I only spoke to you after the Legate spoke well of you. I wanted you to know what kind of man I am. That may help in your selection of my men."

They had reached the stables. "Decurion!"

An older cavalryman appeared from nowhere. "Sir?"

"Get the men on parade. We need to address them."

Decurion Spurius was a veteran and he was no longer surprised by commands from the young officers who ordered him around. "Sir!"

"We are going on a recruiting drive while we collect taxes and the Prefect here will command the Pannonians we recruit. We will need six volunteers to be detached from this legion to help him to train them. They will be returning to duties here when the men are trained but to compensate the men concerned I can offer a pay rise to that of an optio. If you are interested then speak with Decurion Spurius. We will of course decide which six men are chosen."

The tax collector was less than happy as he bounced along the road on the back of his horse. He was not a horseman and he liked his comfort but the Legate had been insistent. Even worse he had to do this collection quickly which was not his way. He liked to study the places he went and discern who was trying to rob the Emperor. The sooner these barbarians were recruited the better as far as he was concerned.

At the head of the column the Tribune rode next to the Prefect with the Decurion behind, listening. "What are these Pannonians like then?"

"Mad little ugly buggers who'll whip your bollocks off as soon as look at you!" The men behind laughed.

"Thank you Decurion. Very colourful I am sure. First off the Decurion is right they are ferocious fighters but the finest men on horses I have ever seen. It is as though it is not two beings but one. Did you know this is the land where the Centaurs were thought to have lived? Seeing them I can believe it. They ride with their knees and can use both hands to fight, bow, javelins, lance, and any weapon no matter what the type."

"Which begs the question how did we win?"

"I hate to say it but the legion did that. They are brave as any warrior and they hurled themselves at the legionaries who sheltered behind their shields and hammered them with ballistae. When their horses tired then they were surrounded and butchered. They only obey their chief; they do not even have a king which was another reason we won. We beat them bit by bit. Had every horsemen joined to fight us then we would have struggled." He turned to look at the Prefect. "You will have your work cut out you know. They don't know the meaning of orders; well not as far as I can see."

They rode in silence for a while and then the Tribune said, over his shoulder, have you thought of any men who might volunteer Spurius?"

The veteran gave a throaty laugh. "I can think of a few wankers I could give to the Prefect but he seems a nice chap so I will pick five who are good enough to take charge of a bunch of hairy arsed barbarians."

"I assume that this is just for one campaign?"

"That depends on how good they are. I think I am expendable; if they kill me then Caligula's work is done and if I succeed then it can be repeated. From what you say though I think they would be a valuable asset. Think of the times your hundred and twenty troopers have been the only cavalry on the field. My father said we used to have Numidians but not in our lifetime and besides I don't think the land we are going to would suit Africans from the desert. It is supposed to full of foetid swamps, forests and fogs."

"Your job gets better and better!"

By the time they were approaching Cavta, Wolf's village, they had recruited three hundred warriors. Marius and Gnaeus had still not settled on the men they would use as officers but they had whittled the list down. "We'll make our decision tonight after this village."

"What is this one like Gnaeus?"

"This is an interesting one. The warriors here like fighting so much that after the peace they took to raiding the Germans."

"The Germans! Are they mad?"

"I told you, mad as fish. They generally get the worse of it as they were outnumbered but it doesn't stop them trying. The trouble is it means there are fewer men here. Still it is the last stop on this leg and we head back tomorrow in a loop to the west. We should have good pickings there."

Abad saw the long Roman column from some distance. He glared at Wolf who defiantly faced him. "You endangered this whole village and for what," he contemptuously threw down the helmet and sword Wolf had brought proudly into the village, "this! And what of the boys who are injured following you! Wolf! You are a wolf and a lone wolf at that. Better we cast you from the village than allow you to stay here and contaminate others."

Gerjen stepped forwards, "That is not fair! We went because we wanted to go. We would be men as you were. You went on raids when you were a boy! Why not us?"

"That was in the past and times have changed. We are now ruled by Rome." He pointed at the nearing column. "This is the future. We now have civilisation and prosperity." He jabbed an angry finger at Wolf as though it was a sword. "You! Return to your mother. When the Romans have left we will decide your fate."

The other boys stood defiantly around their leader. Gerjen pointed impudently back at Abad. "If Wolf goes, then we all go!"

Wolf could not help but smile as Abad became apoplectically red in the face. "How dare you speak like that to me. I will have you whipped."

Wolf paused, "Leave it Gerjen. I am more than happy to leave the village for it is now a village of women."

His mother held back her tears as he entered the dark hut. "You are just like your father, aye and your brothers."

"You can come with me mother."

She laughed. "And do what? No my son do not worry about me. I am still the best midwife in the village. I will not starve but you are, like your father, a warrior. I should have seen it." She took the family amulet from around her neck. "Take this; it came from your father when we wed and he had it from his mother. It will keep you safe and when you touch it you will think of me."

As soon as he put it around his neck he felt different. When he looked at it, his mouth almost dropped open. "It is a wolf."

"Your appetite was not the only reason for your name. Your father was proud that you fought like a wolf for that is the family emblem. You are the Wolf!"

Wolf heard the jingling of horse furniture and wished he could see these warriors who had conquered his people. He peered around the door and saw the column of men in shining armour and red cloaks; their shields and swords gleaming in the afternoon sun. There were warriors; with armour like that a man need not fear an enemy. He had never seen so many men dressed the same way before. It was no wonder that his father and the others had been defeated by such a mighty enemy. One of the elders walked by and slammed the door shut so that he could not peer around. The red rage came and he would have thrown open the door and ripped out the man's throat had his mother not put a gentle arm around his shoulder. "Now is not the time, my son."

Abad had calmed himself by the time the tax collector and the officers had dismounted. The one he knew, the Tribune spoke, "Before we begin I have a request to make headman. We are seeking warriors for a campaign against the Chauci. We will pay and arm as many of your warriors who wish to join us." He pointed to the south. "The others we have recruited await us in their camp. I know that you do not have many warriors, but any you have…"

Abad almost leapt to his feet with joy. The gods were smiling on him. He could ingratiate himself with the Romans and be rid of all the bad apples in one fell swoop. "We have ten young warriors in the village and I am sure they would be suitable." He glanced up at his brother. "Fetch them!"

"All of them?"

Abad looked meaningfully at Wolf's hut, "All of them!"

When the ten young warriors were gathered all but Wolf wondered if they were to be punished by the Romans who seemed to be inspecting them. The one with the crested helmet came over and addressed them, haltingly in their own language. "Your headman says that you would be willing to fight for Rome for a year, for pay. But I would know what you young warriors have to say for you will be fighting far away from your home and I would not have you desert. "He stared at them all. "The penalty for desertion is death. So, who will join?"

The nine of them all looked at Wolf who said, "We will join, Roman!"

Chapter 2

As they rode from the village, none of the young warriors looked back, nor did they speak. They were the youngest of the band of Pannonians which headed south. They had received a cursory inspection by the older, scarred warriors and then ignored although their place at the rear of the column which headed across the dirty plain was clearly a mark of their status; they were the untried warriors. Wolf was offended but he knew he had to prove himself to his fellow tribesmen. His people lived separate lives and had only come together, albeit reluctantly and a little late, to fight off the Roman invader. Each clan used different weapons, horse furniture; even their style of hair and Wolf couldn't help looking enviously at the neat Roman troopers who looked identical.

"Wolf, where did they say we were going?"

The officer's words, although accurate had been hard to hear but Wolf had given the red crested Tribune his total attention. "To the west, by the sea."

Gerjen had never heard this word before. He had no concept what it meant. He looked at Wolf almost willing his leader to give him the answer but he knew he would have to risk scorn to find out the answer to his question. "What is the sea?"

Surprisingly Wolf did not heap scorn on his friend. His action in the ambush had elevated Gerjen, he was now trusted by Wolf; he had earned his respect and Wolf understood his friend's confusion. He had had to ask his mother when he had returned for his arms and clothes. "It is like a pond except you cannot see the other side and it is salty. If you drink it you drown."

"Why are we going there?"

"The Chauci, brothers of the Marcomanni, live close by and the Romans will pay us to kill them." Wolf had never been as happy in his life. Someone was going to pay him, feed him and arm him to fight and, even better, to fight his enemies; the ones who had killed his father.

As they approached the fort the three officers at the front discussed the men who had volunteered and then chosen to be the six men who would command this barbarian horde. They had only managed to recruit seven hundred Pannonians but it was a start and meant that each of the Romans would be responsible for a hundred and twenty men; Marius thought that was more than enough. He needed the troopers to know the barbarians they commanded for he knew that the big issue would be control. He had no doubt that the barbarians would fight but would they obey orders. It was one of the reasons he had wanted Roman officers rather than using the native leaders.

"So Decurion, go through the six men with your assessment of each one to give the Prefect an idea of what he can expect."

Decurion Spurius Ocella thought about what he was about to say. He had taken a long time to reach the elevated rank of Decurion and he wondered how many times he had been discussed by others. He determined to give an honest opinion of each man, regardless of how he felt about them as comrades. Sextus Vatia was an old friend and he felt safe talking about him first. "Sextus Vatia joined about ten years ago. He is reliable and follows orders. Perhaps not able to come up with a plan himself he can follow any plan you give him sir. Then there is Quintus Atinus, he is the oldest one of these and he did have a family but the fever took them. The lads confide in him. I know it isn't important but your Pannonians, when they learn to talk a decent language, will tell him things. He has that ability." He looked at the Tribune. "He is the one we will miss the most sir; he is the one they whinge to and he normally puts them straight. Now Flavius Bellatoris, he is the youngest of the ones you have and he is the one with ideas. He is quick, both with his hands and his mind. He is the best with a sword in the whole Turma. He can think his way out of problems. Seems a pleasant lad too. One final thing, he can speak the local language. Don't ask me how but he can translate for you." Marcus smiled to himself. He suspected that to Spurius they were all young lads. "Now the other three." The Tribune and Prefect exchanged a glance; the Decurion had given them the good news about the better three and now he was going to give them the bad news about the other three. "Publius Tullus. What can I say about him? He is the dullest most boring man in the whole turma but, he is organised. The lads tease him because everything is laid out neatly on his cot and his armour is always

17

polished, even when there is no inspection." The Tribune smiled, his surprise inspections were notorious for keeping the men on their toes, and obviously Publius was not worried by such inspections. "Numerius Buteo, "The Decurion gave a knowing look at his commander, "Well you know what he is like. Fucking mental!"

Marcus looked at Gnaeus, "Mental?"

"Yes, Decurion Spurius is right and we considered long and hard about this one. He seemed the best of the rest. He is brave to the point of insanity. The number of an enemy does not worry him and I have seen him charge fifty men on his own. Luckily, we have taught him to listen to the cornu and obey, albeit reluctantly."

"Thank you, that is handy to know."

"Finally, we have your bastard, Aulus Murgus. He is a bully. You will have to watch him he uses his fists more than he should but he is probably the best cavalryman you have. Tough, a good fighter, he can think and doesn't panic. Me? I hate him and others like him. There is no way I would recommend him for promotion in the regular army but," he waved a hand in the general direction of the barbarians who were following, "with a bunch of mad barbarians you might just need some steel and Aulus is just that, hard as nails."

"Thank you for your honesty Decurion and I am just sorry that you didn't volunteer. I could have used you."

The Tribune smiled, "And I couldn't do without him Marcus so there is no way you would have got him."

The Decurion muttered under his breath, "No fucking way I would sleep with a bunch of hairy arsed barbarians within slicing distance of my dick!"

The two senior officers heard and smiled. The habit of slicing off Roman soldier's manhood by barbarians was well known and accounted for the harsh treatment of any barbarian unlucky enough not to die on the battlefield.

"Well that is useful, thank you both. With your permission I will build a camp close to the gyrus and begin training straight away. You are going for more taxes and recruits?"

"Yes we will have a quick turnaround and we should be back within three weeks."

"My orders are clear. I leave in three weeks no matter how many men I have. There are other officers charged with raising bands just such as this."

"I am tempted to come with you. It might be interesting to see barbarians led by Romans."

Spurius sniffed, "Could be a disaster too sir. Imagine having a thousand barbarians on your flank. I know most of the Ninth would be a bit twitchy about that."

"I think Decurion, that this is the future. The Emperor seems intent upon conquering the known world and we have a limited number of citizens we can use. I suppose we will have to use the conquered people at some time."

"That's as may be sir but the prefect here had best sleep with a pugeo under his bed if he wants to live beyond this campaign."

The Pannonians lounged lazily near their horses watching the seven Romans who were holding some kind of meeting. They had all joined for different individual reasons but the one reason which unified them all was a desire to fight. Some of them were even casting hateful glances at others whose clans they had fought in inter clan disputes. When they were established there would be some old scores to settle. Wolf and his small group kept to themselves. Wolf was not worried about the other warriors but Darvas and some of the others were. Wolf had decided that he would not back down it trouble broke out. He was not called the Wolf for nothing.

"We do not have the time I would like to get to know you. You have all volunteered." There were a couple of looks askance at the fortress. "If anyone feels they were coerced then now is the time to go back to the legion. There will be no recriminations but if you stay then you are mine for a year and you obey my orders." He was pleased that they all stood a little straighter. Which of you is Flavius?" A diffident looking trooper held up his hand. "You speak their language?"

"Some."

"Don't be coy trooper, can you or can't you speak with these," he waved a hand behind him, "Pannonians?"

"Yes sir."

"Good. Then until they learn our language, you are designated interpreter. Stay close by me. You are all being paid at optio rate, as you know. That, of course, is less than a decurion would receive. I will try to get you Decurion pay but, in the meantime, I will address you as Decurion. It will make it simpler for all of us." They nodded their agreement. "We have three weeks to organise this horde into a functioning cavalry until which will obey orders. Regard them as new recruits with the advantage that we don't need to teach them how to ride and, apparently, how to fight. We need to do three things first. Get them to build a camp here. Secondly, sort them into six turmae, each one under your command and thirdly make sure they understand the orders to move, halt charge and retreat. We have no cornicen so we will use the standard."

A trooper held up his hand, "Yes er..."

"Sextus Vatia sir. Do we have a standard?"

"Not yet, so give it some thought and then try to find one of these warriors who might be able to carry it and use it. Now when we get to the Rhenus there will be armour and weapons for them but, until then they use their own. Just make sure that all have a sword of some type. Let me know of any deficiencies and I will see what the quartermaster here will do." The looks them men exchanged told Marius that the quartermaster was like most of that office, tight regarding every item as their own personal property. Well he would cross that bridge when he came to it. "Now Flavius we will organise them into six equal groups."

"How sir?"

"I will choose six men and then you will tell them to choose a line. Then the rest of you will count them and make sure there are one hundred and twenty in each line." The six troopers could not find fault with that and they nodded. Marius strode forward with Flavius next to him. "I intend to learn the language too so I will ask you to teach me when we have the chance. I suspect we can learn their language faster than they can learn ours."

Wolf watched as the men approached and he tensed. He was as excited as when he had led his warband to raid the Marcomanni. The younger looking Roman stepped forwards. "This is Prefect Marcus Proculus, he is your Prefect." Some of the men looked confused although Wolf had worked out what it meant. "Your new chief." They all grinned and nodded. "I am Decurion Bellatoris and these are the other Decurions." He was aware that the word Decurion would sound strange and he sighed at the confused looks; this would be a long day. "Little chiefs." Again they nodded. "When the Prefect, the chief, points to you then stand behind the Decurions, little chiefs. Put your hand up if you understand." Gradually, after small discussions all of the hands went up. He turned to Marius. "All yours now sir. They seem to understand although you are the chief and we are little chiefs at the moment."

The Prefect smiled, "Then I think after the evening meal we can begin their language lessons eh?" He walked up to one man and tapped him on the shoulder. The warrior obviously thought he had been given an honour and grinned broadly to everyone. Marius continued down the line finally touching the warrior who was standing next to Wolf.

As he returned to Flavius he said, "I would stand to the side gentlemen, this could get messy." He nodded to Flavius. "Right then Decurion, tell them where to go."

"You will all choose a line to stand behind. When I tell you to move then join one." Some of them looked confused whilst others looked confident; Flavius decided that as long as one or two went the rest would get the message. "Go!"

Wolf had worked out what this meant and he ran, yelling at the others, "Follow me!"

Used to following orders the others all ran and Wolf was behind the warrior on the end who turned and looked at him in surprise. "I hope that you are not a bum boy!"

Wolf snorted. "If I was I would choose a nicer arse than yours, don't flatter yourself."

The man laughed, "Spirit; I like that. I am Cava."

"And I am Wolf!"

"Well Wolf, in my village they called me Horse for I am hard working so we should get on eh?"

The rest soon worked out what to do and there was a mad rush to get to a line. Each Decurion walked down the line counting and, when they reached a hundred, the men were moved to another line with less numbers in it. The ones at the back were the loners anyway and most groups, like Wolf had run together.

The Prefect stood before them. He turned to Flavius, "What is well done or good in their language." Flavius told him and

Marius repeated the words. Many of the warriors smiled and nodded. He looked at the officers and counted them off, "Sextus, your turma, Quintus, Publius, Numerius, Aulus and," when he reached Wolf's line, "Flavius." As the others glanced down their own lines Marius said quietly, "You have some of the younger warriors here, thought you might appreciate that."

Flavius grinned, "Yes sir, thank you sir."

"Silence!"

Flavius repeated the command. "Decurion these are the tasks. Sextus, Quintus and Flavius; build the camp. The rest of us will construct an enclosure for their horses." As Flavius took his party off Aulus looked aghast.

"Sir, how in Hades' name will they know what to do?"

"Flavius just taught me half a dozen words. Let's see what you can pick up eh?" Aulus still looked dubious. "This is what we do Aulus and this is how you earn the extra pay."

The Prefect took off his helmet and breastplate. He pointed at the pile of wood which was nearby and then at a Pannonian. He mimed picking up. The man grinned and did so. "See. Easy."

By dint of a few words and many gestures the enclosure was built and Marius was pleased to see that the camp was nearly finished. That had been the most important lesson for the barbarians to learn. As they travelled across the country they would need to build a camp each night apart from the odd occasion when they could secure shelter in a fortress. He had been pleased by their attitude too for they had worked hard. There had been a few minor scuffles when clan rivals bumped into each other but Aulus' hands had dealt with all of them. Marius had wondered if any of the Pannonians might take umbrage and strike back but one look at the scowling Decurion had quelled any rebellious intent.

A series of wagons pulled out of the fort escorted by the Decurion, Spurius. When it reached the Prefect the veteran grinned. The Legate thought you might not have thought about preparing food yet so he sent a couple of wagons over. They'll keep you going for a week or so."

Marius looked sceptically at Spurius. "Seems very generous and I have a suspicious nature Decurion so why?"

He tapped his nose, "You have taken the majority of the barbarians who might have caused trouble. We can now send another cohort to the border and when the Tribune has all of your volunteers then he can send the second cohort."

"In that case, I would like to thank the Legate."

By the time they had eaten it was dark. Flavius struggled with some of the words the Prefect required but they managed so that the Decurions could at least pass basic orders. Each Turma would take turns at night duty and, until chosen men could be found, they would double up. That way everyone would get some sleep. Each Decurion went round and counted off ten men, pointed to a tent and said, "Your home." They would have to learn the word tent later. Technically each tent was intended to house eight men only but this way meant that they did not have to erect all of the tents at once. The Prefect was keen for them to begin training as soon as possible. After the meal they had had a lesson learning the words Prefect and Decurion. Then they learned, "Sir, yes, Sir." It was quite amusing to see grown men grinning when they learned a new word and Flavius had had to teach them, 'shut up' soon after to stop their chanting 'yes sir' over and over.

Wolf and the others were intrigued by the tent and the bedrolls they had been given. "The food I did not like," was Kadarcs main complaint. None of them had particularly liked the gruel and the bread. "Where was the meat?"

"Perhaps we hunt it?"

Wolf shook his head. "No I think that is the food we will be eating from now on. Are you hungry?" Kadarcs shook his head. "Then stop being a girl. We are warriors and we must learn to suffer hardship. But we are warriors now!"

"What do you think of our De-cu-rion?" Gerjen split it up to make sure he had said it correctly.

"Good, we must learn their language. It will make life easier. I think we have a good one. Some of the others I do not like. The Bear seems an angry man and I saw him hit the others in his… what was the word they used Gerjen?"

"I think it was tarma."

"No it sounded like that, it was turma."

"Good Darvas, yes turma. I for one cannot wait to wage war on this Chauci tribe."

"But you have never seen them."

"It doesn't matter. We are now soldiers of the Romani and we will fight their enemies. It is the honourable thing to do."

They were awake before dawn, that was their way and they left their tent to smell the morning. It was the Bear who was on duty and Aulus Murgus was not happy. He did not like missing his sleep. He roared up to the ten young men who emerged from their tent. They did not understand his words, "What the fuck are you doing out of your tent. Get back in before I rip your fucking hearts out." However they did understand the smack from the stick he held and they returned to their tent.

Gerjen rubbed his arm. "What was that about?"

"I think that the Romani will tell us when we can leave this home. They seem to like their rules."Panyvadi was the most thought of the recruits and said less than he spoke but when he did speak the others listened.

The Prefect gathered the around and, through Flavius explained the different signals. He had used a stick to represent the standard they would be using. When they all looked confused Flavius explained that, eventually it would have an animal at the top and, to honour their people, a horse tail underneath it so that when in battle they would know the rallying point. The boredom of listening to instructions and chanting their replies pales. Wolf was glad that they had Flavius for he just told them to be quiet but the others frequently used their short sticks to hit the ones who became distracted. The afternoon, however, brought its own reward, as they mounted their horses. They practised riding in columns, changing from pairs to fours to eights. They learned to wheel, although as Darvas said, they had learned to do that the second day they had mounted a horse. Gerjen nearly had them falling from their horses with laughter when he added, "And I was still on my mother's nipple that day."

When they had their first mock charge, in six lines, Wolf thought that all his dreams had come true. He was so proud when they reined in. Now they would go to war for they had shown the Prefect that they could obey orders. He was somewhat taken aback when Flavius translated his words. "The Prefect is not happy. That was not good. Some of you were not in a line and others did not stop when the command was given. They looked at each other in confusion, what did that matter? They had stopped and if one warrior was ahead of another, it just showed that he was brave. Seven days later and they had improved so that they could charge, almost in a line and they could stop, almost all at the same time. More exciting still was the fact that they many of them were issued with the long cavalry sword, which they learned, was called the spatha. For the first time Wolf regretted having the Marcomanni sword for the Roman one looked to be a better weapon. His pride could not bring him to ask for one but he looked enviously at Darvas' who proudly waved his.

It was during the second week that they were assessed for their skills. They were taken to the gyrus, which was like a second home to them. Sticks with hay for heads and boards for shields were laid out and they were given the task, in turmae, of galloping at a charge, hurling their javelins and wheeling. Wolf excelled with the javelin; he did not know that the Prefect was keeping score for each turma but he knew that he had done well. In ten charges he never missed once. When they had to charge the same targets with their swords he, like the others in his group proved to be exceptional. Perhaps it was their youth or may be their keenness to impress but whatever the reason they became identified as skilled warriors.

Flavius and the Prefect took a turn around the camp as the men cleaned their weapons. The troopers had all taken to calling, "Hail Prefect" as he passed. Flavius had tried to stop it but Marius had said, "They are speaking our language. You have succeeded. They are like the young child who first learns words and says them over and over again. No, I am pleased with their progress and yours. You also seem to have been fortunate with your turma. Those youngsters show great potential."

"They do," Flavius was proud of their keenness, "I would have chosen one of them for a chosen man but for their youth."

Marius looked askance at Flavius, "Strange coming from the youngest decurion in the ala."

Blushing he said, "Yes sir but I have been in the army for eight years. None of these have."

"So what difference does age make? They are all as inexperienced as each other." He looked at the sky. "We have another seven days and the last of our recruits should be here. Are we ready to go?"

"Another three weeks would be better but I know that the Legate needs us sooner rather than later. Yes, we should be ready. We will need spare mounts."

"Yes, I have given that some thought. Take your Turma tomorrow and see if you can buy some spares. Your men may know the best places. I have enough language now to give commands and your language will be needed for negotiation. I will get the coins from the Legate. Be back here in four days and then we can leave soon after. I am surprised we have not had more desertions." Only two men had run and they had found out that they had fled because of a blood feud. When the Tribune returned he would be given the task of hunting them down and executing them; an unpleasant but necessary task to stop other desertions.

"I think they want to fight sir. The trouble will be the journey and the temptations along the way."

"I know. That will be a bridge we shall cross when we come to it. And we need an animal symbol. The Ninth has a bull."

"Which is fine for a legion but we need something which suggests speed and aggression, something to inspire the men. I will think on it. By the time you return we may have our standard."

Wolf was excited to be riding back through his home land for he was now a Roman soldier. He looked ahead to the Decurion in his red cloak with shield and spear. One day, he knew, he would have such weapons. They were heading for the village of Cava. It was the closest to the fort and Wolf had never been there. After his first run in with the fierce warrior, Wolf had found that he got on with him. Horse, as some of the men now called him respected honesty and bravery and he saw those same qualities in Wolf. He had had sons and a wife but his village had been raided by the Marcomanni when he was tending his herd and they had been taken as slaves. That had been five years earlier and he had not found them. As soon as he heard that the Romans wanted him to fight the allies of the Marcomanni. The Chauci, he couldn't wait to volunteer. Perhaps he would, one day find his wife and sons.

The herd at Cava's old village was enormous. The flat plains around the village were perfect for the breeding of horses but, since the province became pacified, there had not been much demand for horses and the villagers had fallen on such hard times that they had done the unthinkable and eaten some of their herd. When they saw the Roman warrior returning with the column of men he wondered if the warriors they had taken would be returned. That would go hard with the village for it would be more mouths to feed over the harsh winter.

Flavius gestured Cava forwards. They dismounted and approached the headman. Horse bowed and spoke. He had been briefed by Flavius on the content but the style was left to him. "The Romans wish to buy horses, elder."

Smiling the headman nodded. This was not bad news, it was good news. "How many and what price will he pay?"

"All of them," Cava smiled at the shocked look on his former headman's face and then he added, "and a fair price. How many do we have?"

Cava knew the number as well as the elder but he wanted to see if he would be lied to. "There are twice as many as the men you have."

Cava had told Flavius that already and he nodded. Flavius held out his hand. "Thank you for your horses." As the headman took it Flavius added, "We will leave you some breeding pairs for we would buy more in the future." He smiled, a little sadly, "War is costly for horses, old one. And here is the purse of gold. "He handed over the purse. Cava had told him how much it should be and no-one was cheated.

The Pannonians were in familiar territory as they spread out in a circle and surrounded the herd. The lead stallion was lassoed and tied to the saddle of a warrior and they headed for the next village. Within two days they had sufficient and headed back to the fortress. Wolf felt honoured that the young Decurion had chosen him, as well as Cava, to be a stallion holder. He rode a little straighter and a little prouder as they head back to their camp.

That evening the Prefect called together his officers. "We leave the day after tomorrow. I want us to begin our organisation for the journey." He looked around at his officers. He had an idea now of their strengths and weaknesses. He was still unhappy about Aulus Murgus but he had to admit that while he was totally unpleasant he was efficient. The rest were as Spurius had described. "The language is no longer such a barrier. You all know enough Pannonian to communicate and I want you to teach them more of our words. When we join the army, they will need to answer to other officers."

Aulus snorted. "We need to discipline them more sir. Cut their hair and beards. Make them look like Romans."

Proculus sighed, "At the moment Decurion they are not in the Roman army. They are mercenaries which is why your enlistment with them is for one year." He leaned forwards. "It may well be that they do become an auxiliary ala but that will depend upon their performance in battle and that, gentlemen, depends on us. I daresay we will lose a couple on the way over to the Rhenus but we cannot afford to lose too many. We will be receiving arms at Vindonissa, which is the legionary fortress not far from the Rhenus. Until then we work with what we have. I hope the Tribune makes it back before we leave but we leave the day after tomorrow no matter what happens."

"Sir?"

"Yes Publius?"

"How will the new men be allocated? They will not have our language and they won't know the orders."

Smiling at the fussy but organised Decurion Marius said, "That is a valid point. We will divide them equally between the turmae and … well that brings me rather well to my next point. You will need to appoint a chosen man. You know your lads well enough by now. You need someone who can organise the men and they can be the ones who break in the new men. They should be able to speak our language better than most." Flavius smiled, he had at least six he could choose. "And now we have some assignments for you. I have secured your extra pay to the rank of Decurion." They all grinned; even Aulus for it had almost trebled their pay. "However, you will all need to earn the extra money. Flavius you will be the second in command, you speak their language and it is logical and you can also take charge of weapon training, I hear you are good with a sword. Publius, you can take over quartermaster duties and paymaster." Everyone, Publius apart, smiled at that. He loved his lists and he would enjoy the organisation of their supplies. "Quintus, Camp Commander and food. Numerius you can train up the scouts and watch the road as we travel and Aulus you can organise the sentries and discipline." Of all the tasks he had delegated the last one was the one he had the most doubts about.

"And the standard?"

"I had almost forgotten about that. Perhaps the Horse? I will see if the blacksmith at the fort can knock us one up. It might only be needed for one year anyway. You will all need a signifier, without pay of course, with the standard for each turma. And remember this first year is for us to find out what the men are like so that, when you return here, to the Ninth Hispana you will leave behind an ala with Decurion who can command. That will be your legacy."

The only one who did not look convinced by the speech was Aulus who slumped off. Publius saluted, "Sir, can I start to organise the books. We will need to know the pay scales of the men."

"Of course Publius, whatever you need." He leaned over confidentially, "I hate paperwork." The shocked look from Publius almost made Marius burst out laughing.

Flavius gathered the turma around him. He had already endeared himself to his men because he could speak their language. "You have all done very well in the short time we have worked together. It is time to reward some of you. Cava will be my chosen man and will have the rank of sesquiplicarius." They all looked blankly at him. "Second in command, corporal." Cava was liked but most but Wolf still felt slightly resentful, he wanted to be a leader. "And we need a standard bearer; someone who can guard and carry the emblem of out turma, a rallying point in battle. Wolf, that will be you." Wolf thought he would burst with pride as his friends clapped him on the back and most of the warriors seemed happy.

29

Cava smiled for he liked the youth and agreed with the Decurion; he would make a good standard bearer. "Sir, what is our standard to be?"

Flavius smiled, he had been thinking about this. "Well it seems appropriate to have the sign of the Wolf for our turma eh?"

Wolf leapt to his feet. "Sir where do we get the standard?"

"Oh that is simple signifier, you make it!"

If he thought that would have disheartened the young Pannonian he was wrong. Wolf was useless with his hands but he knew that Gerjen was a wonderful carver. "Sir, can I have permission to take Gerjen and find some wood?"

Flavius looked at the sky; it was coming on to dark. "Be back before nightfall."

Because Wolf was particular they almost fell foul of the wrath of Aulus Murgus as they galloped back into camp just before the gate was closed. The bad tempered Roman stood with his hands on his hips. "And where the fuck do you think you have been?"

Wolf held up the pieces of wood triumphantly. "The Decurion sent us to find wood for the new Turma standard Decurion."

"Well next time tell me before you leave the camp."

They both chorused, "Sir, yes sir!"

While Gerjen carved the wolf out of the piece of walnut he had found, Darvas was given the task of smoothing the ash staff which would hold it. "We need some metal to bind it."

Cava smiled at the enthusiastic young warrior. "When we are journeying we will seek a smith." He pointed at the armour of the Decurion. "They must have many men who can make metal."

Wolf's own contribution was to cut some of the horsetail from each horse in the Turma. Cava realised then that this Wolf was a deep thinker for by binding the hair to the standard it was binding the men together. It spoke well of his mind and his character. It was dark by the time it was finished but the wolf sat on top of the standard, its teeth bared, beneath if hung the horse tail which would flutter as they rode. Most of the turma had watched as it grew from the different parts and when it was lifted by Wolf they gave a cheer. Immediately they heard the voice of the Ala Police, "Shut the fuck up or you'll be shovelling shit for a week!"

Flavius came out of his ten. "I think we had better retire to bed before Decurion Murgus comes to tuck us all in!"

Chapter 3

Wolf kept looking at the standard as they prepared their horses for their last training before departure. He couldn't wait to ride behind the Decurion and the chosen man with his standard fluttering in the wind. He pictured himself defending it against the enemy. The Decurion had told them the story of the legions that had been annihilated in the Teutonberger Forest and how the standard bearer had thrown the standard of the legion to safety before dying at the hands of the barbarians. That, he decided, would be a glorious way to die.

The sound of jangling armour heralded the arrival of the tribune and the last of the recruits. There were just one hundred of them. Gnaeus stepped down as Decurion Ocella led the recruits to Flavius for distribution. The Tribune drew the Prefect to one side. "I could not get more, not in the time anyway. We will have another sweep next month but I should warn you some of these are not to be trusted."

"What do you mean? Did anything happen to make you alarmed?"

"No, it is just an itch I can't scratch and Spurius was equally disturbed. There wasn't the same buzz as we rode here. One or two seemed happy enough but some of them have a very furtive look about them."

"Thank you for your advice Gnaeus but beggars cannot be choosers. The Legate is expecting an ala and even now I am not taking him a full strength one."

"Just watch yourself. How are the troopers working out?" Marius gave him a brief account of their appointments. "Good, and as for Aulus, just send him back if there is a problem I am sure we can find another trooper to take his place. Tell me, how did you manage to get Decurion pay for them? Not that it wouldn't have pleased them I am sure."

"Simple accounting. The Imperial clerks decreed that for six hundred men we would need twenty officers and there is pay for twenty officers. When we are fully staffed we will have a problem but the chosen men are not being paid any more at the moment. I am not sure they understand the concept of pay."

"And Publius is your paymaster? Well good luck with his stiff neck. We will try to catch those deserters and I will send on the new recruits when we get them. Any idea where you will be based?"

"Tungri or Castra Vetera. It depends upon the Legate."

Gnaeus took the Prefect's arm. "Well may Mithras watch over you. I think you will need all the help you can get."

"And thank you Gnaeus. You have helped me more than you needed to."

"Let us just say that my family almost fell foul of Caligula..."

Neither Cava nor Flavius were happy at the allocation of the new men. Some of them did not appear to have embraced the Roman army as an opportunity. One in particular, Sura, made Cava suspicious. He wondered if he was judging him on his looks, for he had a long scar down one cheek which gave him an evil look to start with but there was something else which he could not put his finger on. Neither officer nor chosen man had the chance to do anything about it for the prefect was keen for them to head west and join the army. Wolf was excited beyond words as he sat proudly behind the Decurion, next to Cava, with the standard in his hand. He had seen the other standards and they were crude by comparison with the excellent handiwork of Gerjen. The Prefect had not brought out the ala standard yet as he had neither standard bearer nor reason to use it but he was pleased that his auxiliaries had taken to the idea so readily. He smiled when he saw Wolf holding a wolf. He was a warrior to watch and for all the right reasons. He had warned his officers about the new men and Aulus had growled, "I'll smell out the bad 'uns sir. They won't want to cross me twice!" Marius wondered if he had misjudged the sour looking trooper.

The mountains which were a thin grey line in the distance grew day by day as they trekked west. Prefect Proculus ensured that they changed horses each day to maximise the distance they could travel. They learned to build a camp quickly, especially as the new recruits soon learned that the sooner the camp was erected the sooner they would be fed. Wolf enjoyed travelling at the head of the turma and he found that he could speak the Roman language quicker than the others. Cava already had a good knowledge of the words he would need and Wolf listened to their conversations and he improved as quickly as Cava. It enabled him to understand the Roman officers when they spoke with each other and it made him understand their motives and their actions. They were not so different from him; they too had volunteered to get away from some farm, or some town or some father. He discovered that they signed on for twenty-five years and had taken an oath. As none of his comrades had done that he wondered how they were different. He would happily take an oath and sign on for twenty-five years. He had seen nothing in this army that he didn't like. It was as though he had found his destiny, just when things were at their darkest.

They followed the course of the Danubius and camped as close to any forts they found as they could. It meant they were safer and the Prefect was able to pick up snippets of information about their route and any dangers they might encounter. The Pannonians were not used to mountains as high these nor valleys that were quite so deep. The metalled roads wound close to the river and their hooves echoed on the mountainside. Wolf could not help asking a question, "Decurion, who built these roads?"

"Romans of course, Wolf, soldiers like us."

"Do we have to build roads?"

"No Wolf the legions do that. My Legion, the Ninth Hispana, built some of the roads in your land and they will build more." He pointed south, to their left. "Behind those mountains is a pass which takes you to Rome. Had this been winter we would have travelled through the northern part of that land but the journey would have been much longer. This is harder but quicker."

"Good for the quicker we are there the quicker I can collect heads."

"We do not collect heads Wolf."

"Then how do your friends know you are a great warrior?"

In answer Flavius turned in his saddle and pointed to a shiny metal disc. "This is a phalerae. It is an honour given to me by my general for bravery."

"Ah like a battle armband."

"Just so."

"But who decides if you get one?"

"Any superior officer who sees you doing something brave or heroic or something which helps the ala." He nodded to Cava,

"The chosen man here could tell me if, say Darvas, did something brave."

Wolf sniffed, "If Darvas could get a phalera then it must be easy and I will have armour covered with them. I will armour of phalera!"

Flavius laughed, "They are not that easy and you do not know what your comrades are capable of until they are in battle. You do not know yet Wolf."

"I have killed Marcomanni!"

"A raid? Ambush?" Wolf nodded. "It is harder to be brave when you face many enemies who are trying to kill you, especially when you have to stand there and take it."

"Why not run and then attack again?"

"Because sometimes it is important to stand and to die. That is one way we measure bravery. When you have to defend the standard, you will have a choice, use a shield or a sword, but you cannot use both and hold the standard. Have you thought how you will do that?"

"No, I have not Decurion. You have given me much to think on." Horse smiled at the serious expression on Wolf's face as he pondered the problem.

When they reached the auxiliary fort at Teurnia the Camp Prefect rode out with the Cohort Prefect. He drew Marius to one side. "We need your help Prefect." He pointed north. "Yesterday a convoy of grain wagons was captured by some Marcomanni bandits. I sent half a cohort after them but they were badly mauled. They are holed up in an old oppidum ten miles up the valley."

The Prefect pointed at the Pannonians. "These are recruits. They are not even trained yet. It is impossible for them to attack a hill fort."

The Spanish Prefect smiled, "We would not dream of asking you to assault the hill. That is the job of my men but the Marcomanni have horses and when we attacked yesterday they used their horses to escape to the oppidum. If you place your men to the north of the oppidum then you will close the door on their avenue of escape. You will only need two hundred men."

Marius was not convinced but the Prefect suddenly became serious. "If it is easier then I can give you a written order."

"In that case we will but I will need one of your men as liaison."

"I will send one to you and he will give you your written orders and your instructions."

Flavius watched the Prefect returning and saw the disturbed look on his face, even from forty paces away. "Problem sir?"

"It looks like we may have to put some of the men into action sooner rather than later. Decurion Murgus! Decurion Vatia!" The two officers galloped up. "Decurion Vatia, take charge of the ala. Make a camp this side of the fort. Decurion Murgus, Bellatoris, have your men give their spare equipment to the other turmae. We are going to fight the Marcomanni."

"But sir, the men are only half trained and we haven't seen them fight."

"I know Aulus but we have been given orders." He pointed up the valley. "There is an oppidum there with Marcomanni in it. The Spanish cohort will attack the hill and our job is to stop them escaping with the grain wagons."

The two officers both knew the impossibility of their task but both had been in the army long enough to know that orders were followed no matter how ridiculous. The liaison officer galloped up. "Here are your orders, sir." Proculus inclined his head. "Oh you are to take your men along the road and station them eight hundred paces from the north wall of the oppidum, sir."

"Thank you optio, my mind reading act needs work these days. Flavius I'll lead with your turma. Aulus bring up the rear and watch our arse." He nodded in the direction of Wolf. "We might just get the chance to use that wonderful standard of yours."

Wolf heard it and swelled with pride. He changed the standard to his left hand and slid the sword in and out of its scabbard. He had not had time to practise fighting one handed, it looked like he would soon find out how to do it the hard way.

The road they rode along was not Roman made but was a worn and dusty track. They could see it had been churned up by hooves. The cohort of Spanish Auxiliaries was up ahead, tramping along the road. As they past them Wolf could not help but admire their armour. He suddenly felt naked in his leather jerking and old helmet. The Spanish Prefect pointed up to the oppidum as they rode next to him and then pointed up the road. "With luck Prefect your men will not be needed."

Wolf turned in his saddle to watch the auxiliaries turn on command and begin to make their way up to the oppidum. "Head forward Wolf. Nothing to see there." Wolf's head snapped around, how had the Decurion known what he was doing? He risked a furtive sidelong glance at the oppidum. It looked impregnable; the sides were steep, there were two towers and a ditch. The Spanish would be slaughtered!

"Here sir."

"Thank you optio. Halt! First turma turn right. Decurion Murgus take your turma to our left."

The two turmae formed an oblique line with their left flank resting close to the woods and their right flank half way across the road. The only escape possible for the Germans was either through the woods, in which case they would lose their wagons or back to the fort. Marius was gambling they would lose the wagons rather than risk their lives. They had a grandstand view as the Spanish Cohort lumbered up the hill. The straight line occasionally halted and when it moved on Wolf could see the red splotch which marked the place a soldier had fallen. As the lines progressed up the hill the blotches became more frequent. To the recruits it seemed impossible that the infantry could reach the top and there was no way that they could take it and then suddenly they were at the gates and a cluster of men gathered around the entrance to the fort. They had hardly been there for more than a couple of heartbeats when the side gate opened and the Marcomanni and their wagons erupted through the gate. The infantry reacted quickly. While the cluster of men at the oppidum continued to break it down the rest double timed it to the other gate and began hurling their javelins. A good javelin thrower himself Wolf was impressed by the casualties that they inflicted.

His role as an observer was ended by the Prefect's command. "Prepare javelins and stand firm." The order was repeated by Flavius and Murgus.

Wolf could see the wagons and the fifty riders making like an arrow for the road. They were heading directly for him. Cava was next to him. "I would take your sword out son, you might need it!"

Wolf blushed when he realised he had forgotten to arm himself. He took it out and waited for the heavy horde of horsemen to hit their line. If he had been at home in the same situation he would have turned and attacked the enemy from the side but the Prefect sat astride his horse patiently waiting. When the first enemy was forty paces away he ordered, "First twenty troopers, loose." Flavius yelled the order in Pannonian to make sure they all understood. The ragged volley, plus a couple of others thrown by excited troopers flew through the air. Not all struck but, hitting the horses as they did, they made the first two wagons crash and hit two of the riders. "Turma, loose!" The rest of the line threw their javelins and even more men fell. To his horror Wolf saw a wedge of warriors making straight for him. He could not know that they were heading for the two officers who, with Cava were either side of him. Cava and Flavius engaged one man each while the Prefect fought two. The last of them raised his axe to hack down on Wolf. Instinctively he nudged his horse to the left and blocked the blow with his sword. His arm felt as though it had been struck by an iron bar. He saw the axe go back and he kicked the horse forward thrusting with his sword as he did so. Even as the blade went into the throat of the screaming warrior Wolf caught a movement out of the corner of his eye. Another German was heading for him. He aimed the head of the standard at the charging warrior and was amazed when he rode directly into the heavy wooden Wolf.

Prefect Proculus looked down the line and could see that the men had not broken and the Germans had turned into the exultant Spanish who fell upon them and slaughtered them where they stood. The Prefect left the line and rode forwards with Flavius. "Well done Pannonians you have your first victory." The two turmae cheered madly, "Chosen man Cava, check the casualties." He looked wryly at Wolf, "And signifier, check your improvised spear and see what damage has been caused."

Gerjen and the rest of his friends gathered around. "You did it Wolf. You killed your first warrior."

"I thought he was going to gut you."

"So did I Panyvadi. So did I."

As they rode back to the fort they saw the crosses being erected and the few survivors being crucified. Cava asked the Decurion, "I thought they would have been sold as slaves?"

"No Cava. This is more effective. It warns others not to risk the wrath of Rome. When we fight the Chauci we will capture slaves and sell them but this is a small-scale battle on the frontier and the Prefect wants to save his men's lives not make them rich." He dropped back and rode next to Wolf. That was bravely done Wolf. It takes courage to stand like that armed with just a sword. I think we shall see if you can be the first to get some mail, it looks like you will need it."

The Turma was elated with their success. A couple of men had been wounded but no one had died and they had defeated their hated enemy. Wolf took the ribbing from his friends in good part and he had learned that he was not being mocked. The Wolf standard had not been damaged but its carrier was determined to make it more robust when they next found a smith; he wanted Gerjen to put metal bands around the top to protect it and a spike on the end. Panyvadi laughed, "What? Are you going to make a lance?"

"Until I learn how to fight without the shields which you will all have then I need to protect myself as much as possible."

Darvas shook his head, "We have no shields."

Gerjen leapt to his friend's defence, "But we can move position he has to stay near to the Decurion with the standard and we need to protect him. Let us take an oath on the standard."

The boys who had joined with him and whom he had led gathered around the standard and all placed their hands upon it. Panyvadi was the thoughtful one and, as they all looked at each other he began to speak quietly, "I swear to protect this standard and my friend Wolf with my life." The rest nodded eagerly and each one repeated it.

Wolf was touched, more than his friends could know. He had led them before but not really understood them or even, Gerjen apart, liked them. Now that he was no longer their leader he saw a different side to them and their friendship had become more precious.

"If it isn't the Roman officer's bum boy and his arse lickers!"

39

Wolf and the others leapt to their feet angrily. It was Sura and some of the other new men who had joined the turma. "Take that back or feel my blade!"

Sura laughed contemptuously. "Why should I fear a boy who cannot even take the head of a warrior he managed to kill," he turned to his cronies and spread his hands, "how I will never know." He turned back, all humour gone. "Any time you fancy your chances boy and I will be ready."

Before Wolf could reply Horse's voice came out of the dark. "If you don't get back to your tent you will have to face me, Sura, and I am no boy."

The scarred man stormed off with his men. Cava walked up to Wolf. "I could have handled him Horse. I am the standard bearer and I need no protection."

The huge warrior known as Horse put his arm around Wolf's shoulders. "All of us need protection Wolf but Sura is a particularly bad man. Keep away from him. He will get himself into trouble soon enough. Now get some sleep. We climb the mountains tomorrow and that will be hard work."

Mollified Wolf and his friends went into their tent. Cava looked at the backs of the departing Sura. He wondered whether he ought to mention it to the Roman officer. He enjoyed being the chosen man but he did not know the boundaries of the post. Was he above the men or one of the men? He had never been a chief but he had led men in wars. There you took command because men followed you here, in this Roman army, it seemed you were selected. It would take some getting used to.

When they completed the next leg of their journey there was a spring in the step of the men of the two turmae which had fought. The Prefect noticed that even the sour faced Murgus had the hint of a smile upon his face and did not appear quite so bad tempered. Marius had been pleased with the performance of his men. They had obeyed orders. He had worried that they would not stand but follow their instincts and retire and then charge at the enemy and when the enemy had fled he had feared that they would follow them headlong. He had not wanted to blood them so early but he had learned much. It also showed him that they needed arming in the Roman way, sooner rather than later; the lack of shields, helmets and armour could have proved disastrous if they had faced a greater force.

The legionary fortress at Vindonissa had not yet been turned into a stone bastion against the barbarians who lived across the river but even as it was, largely wood and earth it was a monumental structure. The Sixteenth Gallica legion had to keep a keen eye across the river to foil the frequent raids of the barbarians who were keen to profit from the burgeoning empire. Marius took Publius with him to procure their equipment when he went to meet with the Legate. Inside the fort had the half empty look of a deserted home. Publius was taken to the warehouse where their equipment was kept while the sentry took Marius to the Praetorium. The Camp Prefect apologised to Marius. "We only have one cohort in the fortress at the moment. The Legate has taken the others on a punitive raid across the river." He shrugged, "We have to do it periodically, sort of thin the enemy numbers out. I believe you will be further north and east?"

"Yes we are part of Legate Corbulo's army."

The Camp Prefect had been a centurion and this would be his last posting before retirement. He looked up at the Prefect who seemed relatively young for his rank. "Castra Vetera then. How are these barbarians you command then?" He saw Marius' reaction at the term. "No offence meant Prefect but I have a reason. You see I fought against the Pannonians, I was with the Ninth. Years ago now but I remember them as wild and uncontrolled."

Marius relaxed a little. "I thought that too but we had to help some auxiliaries out in the mountains and their discipline surprised me. I think being in one unit helps but they seem to be responding, well most of them."

"Have you met Legate Corbulo yet?"

"No I was briefed in Rome. I have never met the man."

"Well a word of advice, he is s stickler for rules and he likes discipline and neatness. He is a good general but he likes everything polished and bright. He believes that a smart soldier fights better."

"I can't argue with that but I suspect you are telling me this because my Pannonians won't fit the bill."

Shrugging the veteran added, "When they are in uniform they might look a little better but if the Legate holds a parade then watch out for criticism if they don't sit straight enough on their horses."

"Surely it is how they fight that counts."

"Oh I would agree with that but, as I said, the Legate believes that a neat parade ground leads to a better soldier. And he sent these orders for you." He handed him a leather tube and Marius took it out to read the new instructions.

When he had read it he looked up. "Interesting. It seems that your assessment of the Legate is an accurate one. They are all to take an oath and be organised along regular lines. A nightmare for me. We will need to organise smaller turmae than the ones we have and more officers."

"If you want my advice don't promote until you have seen your men in battle. Just use the chosen man principle." He shrugged, "It works."

"Thank you that is good advice and it puts my decision off for a while."

"I have been in this army for almost twenty-five years; you pick up little tricks over that time. Anyway, is there anything else that you need?"

"Do you have a blacksmith we could use? We have some standards but we didn't have enough time to finish them."

"Help yourself and if you would like to join me tonight I can promise you better fare than you are used to."

Although Marius did not want to leave his men he realised that the Camp Prefect had information which could be useful. Forewarned was forearmed. "I would be delighted."

Publius met the Prefect at the gate. "I have found the uniforms. I thought that I would use my turma to bring them to the camp. The Quartermaster says we can borrow some carts."

"Good you stay here and I will send them along with your chosen man."

The camp was already taking shape for they were used to it. After the turma had been sent into the fortress Marius summoned Flavius and Cava. "The Camp Prefect says that we can use the smithy in the fortress but before we let your men go in I need your opinion on something." Cava wondered why he was there. "We need a vexillarius. How about that Wolf of yours?"

"He is brave enough and he handled himself well in the mountains. Yes I agree. What do you think Chosen Man?"

Cava was a little dubious for he thought he was a little young for what seemed an important post, to carry the ala standard into battle, but he could not deny the young man the opportunity to better himself. "He will do a good job sir. He is a good warrior."

"Excellent. Bring him along then."

Wolf thought he was in trouble when Cava took him to meet the Prefect and he had a terrified look on his face. Marius saw it and smiled. "Don't worry trooper, you are not in trouble, in fact just the opposite. We would like you to become the ala vexillarius. What do you say to that? It would of course mean more money and you would be attached to me and my staff." He shrugged, "At the moment my only staff, but that will change."

"I am honoured sir but…"

"Come on Wolf, out with it."

"Well if it is all the same to you I would like to stay with the turma."

The Prefect looked nonplussed but Cava and Flavius exchanged a knowing look. "I didn't expect that trooper and of course you don't need to accept but do you mind explaining to me why. I am curious."

"Firstly, sir I would love to serve with you but my comrades took an oath to protect the wolf standard and, well I think it is fate that wants me to carry it. Don't get me wrong sir. I would like to be promoted but that will come in time, if I am good enough."

"A good answer. Thank you for your honesty. If you want to go with Cava here you can use the fortress smithy to put some iron on that precious standard of yours." When they had gone Marius turned to Flavius. "Remarkably mature for one so young. He will go far will that one. It speaks well of you too Flavius that they would rather stay with you."

"I'm sure he meant no disrespect sir."

Marius waved away the apology. "Don't worry about me. I think this is a good thing. We need to build up loyalty in the ala

43

and this is the first sign that we are heading in the right direction."

"With that in mind sir, those last recruits, well they are causing trouble. Nothing major but I noticed when we fought the Marcomanni the new ones hung back a little."

"Yes I know and you are not the only Decurion who has mentioned that. What we need is another officer so that we could put all the bad apples in one basket." He shrugged. "For the moment, just keep an eye on them and try to bring them into the fold as it were."

Publius did not issue the new arms and armour until the following morning. After talking with the Camp Prefect, Marius had decided to spend an extra day at the fortress to organise his men more effectively. The comments about Legate Corbulo had worried him and he wanted them to be as prepared as possible. The men were like excited children as they lined up next to the carts which were being used as points of distribution. Punctilious Publius gave the equipment out piecemeal. Leggings first, then the caligae, followed by the mail shirt and finally the helmet. While those carts were returned to the fortress he went around each turmae to check that it all fitted and they all had the correct equipment. Then he gave out the long spatha and scabbard and finally the scuta and javelins. Marius had worried about Publius but he had shown that he was the perfect choice for his role.

Knowing how excited they were the Prefect allowed a short time for them all to admire each other and to use the polished helmet to try to see what they looked like and then he ordered them to attention. "You now look a little more like Roman soldiers. Good but you still behave like the Marcomanni." He knew he was insulting them and it was deliberate. "We will be joining the army in the next seven days and the General will want a smart looking ala. You look smart but we need to make you to look like an organised ala. Each of your turma will be divided up into four turmae. Each of those will have a chosen man. Your officers will choose them. This will allow us to organise the ala better and when that is done you will all swear an oath to Rome."

The troopers all looked at each other. An oath was a serious matter and not to be taken lightly. Wolf and his friends were already oath takers and Cava knew it would not be a problem for them but he watched Sura and his band; they seemed a little put out. Cava would watch time during the ceremony and gauge their true feelings. Flavius beckoned Cava over to him. "I will keep Wolf and his oath takers with me as the first Turma. I think it will be better for them. We need another six to join them. Make them older men. I want you to take Sura and his malcontents as the Second Turma. I know it is asking much but I am sure you will be able to handle them. That leaves us with two more chosen men to find. Any idea?"

"Well I would have said Wolf, he is a good lad, but you are probably right and this way we have at least one turma that we can depend on."

"Don't depress me. They will all be dependable."

Cava looked over at the surly Sura. "I am not sure about that."

Wolf was proud that he was in what he thought was the most honourable turma, that commanded by a Roman but he wondered if he would regret his decision to cling on to the standard. He fingered the token given to him by his mother and knew that it was ordained by some spirit of his people. He was still Pannonian but, increasingly he felt Roman.

When they rode out the next day the Prefect sat astride his horse watching them pass by. They all looked like Roman soldiers now. Some of them had balked at losing their old weapons and helmets and Marius knew that somehow, they would have secreted them somewhere but it did not matter for they would become more Roman with each step which took them from their homeland. He remembered the Roman official who had explained his new role to him and who had explained their police. "You see Prefect by taking these new allies away from their homeland we do two things; we eradicate a threat to us and we use that threat to subjugate those who will be our new allies. You are from Rome but many of the legionaries come from other parts of Italy and they were once allies. It is a system which works."

He now saw that he had told the men a lie when he said they would only be needed for a year; they had signed on and taken the oath and although they did not know it, they would be in the army for twenty-five years. He would need to tell them that at some point but he would wait until they had all been blooded.

Chapter 4

Legate Gnaeus Domitius Corbulo was not a happy man. He had two legions at his disposal the Fifth Alaudae, known as 'The Larks', and the Fifteenth Primigenia but he still did not have either enough men or the right men to subjugate the Chauci and the Frisii. The terrain did not suit the legions. He needed more auxiliaries. The Batavi were a treacherous people who seemed to be able to cross water as though it wasn't there. Their horsemen and foot soldiers were all accomplished swimmers and crossed the Rhenus with impunity. He had six auxiliary cohorts but what he needed was more cavalry and he was waiting for the new ala to arrive. He was not a patient man and, with winter approaching, he knew that, if they did not arrive soon then he would have to wait until the following year to finally conquer Germania Inferior. He wished he was with his friend Aulus Plautius in Britannia. From what he had heard that was a better battlefield than the marshes and forests of this part of the world.

The aide knocked on the door and waited until the Legate said, "Enter."

Making sure he saluted correctly the immaculately turned out young officer said, "The gate house reports a column of Roman cavalry approaching."

"Good, about time. I will go to watch them ride in. That's how you assess a unit by the way they march!"

As soon as he had seen the huge fortress in the distance, with the camps clustered around it Marius had ordered his men to sit up and to ride in pairs. He now knew that the Legate would be watching them as they rode in and he was determined not to give him any cause for displeasure. He had pushed the ala on to reach it before dark and he had succeeded but the horses were lathered and looked tired. He sighed to himself. There were some things he could not control. Riding along the road flanked by the camps Marius realised that the best spots had already been taken; at first glance it looked like they would be a little too close to the river for his liking. He saw auxiliary infantry recognising Gauls and Spaniards but he could see no cavalry. He knew that meant even more pressure on his untried ala.

Entering the gate, he saw, immediately, the glowering face of the Legate flanked by his aide and Camp Prefect. He saw the Legate speak to his aide who scurried off. Halting before the Legate Marius resisted the urge to turn and watch his men line up behind him but he had faith in the officers. They had proved themselves time and again on the journey from the east; he could trust them, even Murgus. When there was silence behind him he saluted and said, "First Pannonian Ala, Prefect Marius Ulpius Proculus commanding."

There was silenced and the Legate approached Marius and then walked behind him to inspect the lines of troopers. After what seemed an age he returned to his post, now rejoined by his aide. "Commanding what Prefect? A rabble? A mob? A horde? What?"

Marius was confused and he risked a glance behind. The men were sitting straight. Their faces were forward and their armour was new. What had he to complain about? "I am sorry sir, I am confused. They are Pannonians…"

"They were Pannonians. Now they are Roman soldiers and they will look like them. I want the facial hair removing and their hair cut appropriately."

Marius heard the murmuring from behind him and he roared, "Silence in the ranks!"

"But sir their hair is part of their identity. I thought auxiliaries were allowed a little leeway in such matters."

Corbulo pointed an imperious finger at Marius. "Prefect, join me in the Praetorium." As he passed the Campo Prefect Marius saw the slightest shake of the head and he followed the smug looking aide up the steps to the office. As soon as the door was closed an angry Legate turned on Marius. "I do not argue with junior officers in front of the men. This is my army and I say that your men will shave and have their hair cut and I will hear no more about leeway. What other Legates allow is their business but I will have discipline!" He was shorter than the Prefect and when he approached him with wagging finger he had to look up at the cavalryman. Proculus thought it must have looked ridiculous. "I know about you and your family. I know how lucky you were and I will be watching you. One mistake Prefect and your luck will run out. We have no time to shear all

of your animals tonight but as a mark of our intent the camp
tonsor is expecting your first men as an example to the rest."

There was no arguing with such a martinet and Marius saluted
and left. His men were as he had left them. He went to Flavius,
"Have the First Turma remain behind. Chosen Man Cava, join
them. Sextus take the rest of the ala and build a camp. I will join
you shortly."

Wolf and Cava exchanged a look while the rest of the turma
were just confused at the turn of events. Why had they been
selected? Neither of the leaders thought it boded well and when
the Prefect spoke with them they knew that it was not good news.
"I am sorry lads but one turma is going to be shaved tonight. You
are the First Turma and you have shown yourselves to be loyal. I
know it is hard but…"

The Legate's voice boomed from the top of the steps. "Just give
the order Prefect. Now!"

His eyes pleading Marius mounted his horse, "Follow me." He
set off behind the smug aide. He hoped that they would follow but
there was no guarantee.

Behind him he heard Cava say, "Come on lads. At least this
way we'll get rid of the lice and we don't want the fat bastard
upset do we?" Marius smiled, Cava had spoken in their own
language and no-one else would understand. The sound of the
hooves on the parade ground told him that they had obeyed his
orders and he breathed a sigh of relief. The tonsor was waiting
eagerly. He was a legionary who earned extra money and the
thought of shearing the barbarians appealed to him. He stood at
his door as they dismounted. They waited for Flavius and the
Prefect. Wolf asked, "Why must we have our hair cut sir? It will
not make us better warriors."

"The General thinks it will."

"Come on then ladies, do not be shy."

Cava walked up to the legionary. Cava was a big, well-built
warrior and he had learned enough of the Roman words, thanks to
Aulus Murgus to make himself understood. "Listen to me any
blood and we will see yours too now cut mine first!"

He sat himself down and said a mental prayer to the gods of his
family to forgive him. Wolf and the others watched as the hair
was swiftly cut. They had never seen hair cut before and did not

48

know how quick it could be. Cava changed before their eyes. When the tonsor put soap on his face and took the sharp blade they were tempted to rush forward and stop their comrade being tortured. Flavius saw the movement. "It is fine lads; it just makes the shaving easier." They had all seen the officers shaving themselves but they had just used water and a sharpened dagger.

The shaving took longer but when his face was dried they did not recognise Cava and Gerjen almost tried to run out, but the Prefect restrained him. "He is still the same Cava, just a little cleaner. Tell them Cava."

The Chosen Man gave a half smile and rubbed his hand around his face. "Well I feel lighter anyway but this feels cold. It doesn't hurt lads and I will watch this prick in case he gets sloppy." He then glared at the legionary, knelt down and picked up the hair.

"What the fuck…"

Cava stood and put his face close to the soldier. "A prick like you will not understand but I will bury this and when I go to meet my ancestors it will be waiting!"

Soon they all looked the same and they stared at each other as though trying to reassure themselves that they were the same men. Each clutched the precious hair which had cascaded to the floor. "Well done. You have shown yourselves to be brave warriors. When we ride back into camp do so proudly."

"But sir what if the men laugh at us?"

"Ignore them for by this time tomorrow they will all look the same."

As they left and the legionary began to clean up he looked after them and shook his head. "Bloody barbarians! They'll be back to collecting heads next."

Riding back in the darkening evening they all felt naked, as though they had no clothes on. They had to ride through the other camps before they saw the sign of the bull at their gates. The whole of the ala, officers included watched in silence as the seventeen shorn men rode in to their camps. Panyvadi's fears had been groundless as even Sura and his cronies stared in horror at the vision of their future. As the ala went back to their duties Flavius turned to Marius. "I don't think it will be easy in

49

the morning sir. I saw some very belligerent looks. It's a shame, all that good work undone because the Legate wants them to look like his legionaries."

Marius held up a warning hand. "Be careful with your tongue Flavius. This Legate regards any criticism as treason. Let us see what the morning brings and deal with it as best we can."

Wolf and his turma went straight into their tents. The last thing they wanted was to be stared at. Gerjen shook his head. "I thought it was good to join the Romans but I do not like this. I feel as though someone has taken my face from me and given me another's."

Darvas laughed, "I never knew you were such a pretty boy Gerjen."

Gerjen leapt at Darvas with his dagger in his hand. Wolf smashed his own hand down on to the back of Gerjen's making him drop it. "Stop this now! You have both taken two oaths, one to the standard and one to Rome. That means that we do whatever we are ordered to. It is as simple as that. We may not like everything we do but did we like everything at home? Is this not a better life? Here we serve the wolf, "he pointed at the standard in the corner, "and that is enough. The Decurion told me that Rome was founded by two boys who were suckled by a wolf. Is this not a sign? I do not like this bare and itchy face and I miss my hair hanging down but I will get used to it. We all will."

Sura and the other disenchanted Pannonians whispered in the dark. "I am not having my hair cut. I will look like a woman. These Romans all smell like women and I do not wish to stay in their army."

"But where will you go?"

Sura pointed beyond the tent walls to the north. "We will cross the river and join the tribes who fight the Romans. We came to fight and to kill. We can continue to fight the Romans." He ran his hand down his scarred face. "I still remember the Roman who did this to me and I will have my revenge. Are you with me?"

There was a murmur of ayes and one lone voice said. "I will stay. I like this Roman army. May the Allfather be with you."

Sura turned to the man who crouched at the rear of the tent. Smiling he put his left hand on his shoulder and murmured, "And may you be with the Allfather soon." The pugeo sliced across the man's windpipe and he died silently.

Sura and his men slipped out of the tent. While his warriors slipped to the entrance of the camp and the guards, Sura sought the others who did not like the Romans. Twenty warriors made their way to the entrance where Quintus was on duty. The smiling Decurion spoke to the two men on guard at the entrance and then went on his patrol around the other sentries positioned in the middle of each wall. As soon as he had disappeared the twenty eight men with Sura surged forward and overpowered the two young guards who died as silently as the single protestor had done. The night was silent as they crept towards the horse lines. There were three sentries there and one of them managed to cry out before being silenced.

Quintus heard the cry and, knowing how close they were to the river shouted, "To arms! To arms!"

Sura and his men were, first and foremost Pannonians which meant they needed no saddles. They each grabbed a handful of mane and hauled themselves onto the backs of the horses. They kicked on across the open ground to the Rhenus, dark and menacing in the distance. They did not pause at the river but leapt in and let their horses swim, frantically across. By the time Quintus and the other guards had reached the horse lines all that they could see was the vague shape of dark bodies slipping across the water.

Marius and the other officers saw the dead bodies and their first reaction was that the Chauci had come across the river to steal horses. As they checked the bodies of the dead Flavius glanced up and saw the troopers emerging, armed from their tents. He pointed to an empty area of tents. "Sir, there are no men in those tents, perhaps they have been killed."

"You and Publius check them. Sextus, have the men line up outside their tents. We will have a roll call."

Soldiers from the other camps began to arrive, having heard the commotion. "Whoever it was has fled across the river!"

The other officers nodded. "We will double the guards around our camps. It is too dark to pursue them across the river. What damage have they done?"

"At least five men killed and a number of horses stolen."

Flavius came back; his face displaying his anger. "It was not Chauci. It was Sura and his men. They have murdered one man."

"Damn the Legate and his orders. This is the hair cutting isn't it?"

Decurion Murgus shook his head, "No sir. These buggers would have run at some point. In a way it is better that it was now rather than later. This way the bad apples have all gone and good riddance to them."

"The trouble is Aulus that they know our commands and our orders. They may come back to haunt us."

The next day the ala was paraded by Prefect Proculus. The First \Turma stood out as different with their shaved faces and short hair but Marius was in no mood for truculence from anyone. He had yet to make his report to the Legate but he knew his superior would not be pleased. He could afford no more arguments about the tonsor.

"Last night six of our comrades were murdered by Sura and thirty other warriors. I do not know why they ran but I suspect they were not happy about the loss of their hair. But they took an oath."He paused as the word 'oath' echoed around the camp. "You all took an oath. You will all have you faces shaved today and your hair cut because you are my men and you obey my orders. If any of you cannot obey that order then leave now. I do not want you in my ala."

The officers looked at each other with a worried look on their face. With the mood of their men the Pannonian ala could cease to exist if they chose to leave. They watched as the men peered at the warriors around them.

Cava stepped forwards. "Sir the First Turma have obeyed the order. While the rest make up their mind shall we see to the horses? We all want to stay in this army."

Smiling, Marius said, "Carry on Decurion Cava!"

The men of the First Turma proudly marched out and Wolf murmured to Cava. "Did I hear right? Are you a Decurion now?"

"Unless he made a mistake I guess so. We'll find out soon enough."

Prefect Proculus waited until the turma had exited the camp. "Well? Any man who wishes to leave, step forwards." Not a man moved. They all kept their faces forward. "Good. Then the second

Turma will march to the fortress followed by the other turmae in order. Carry on Decurion Murgus."

As the men marched off Flavius stood next to the Prefect. "That was close sir. I thought they would have all left."

"I think they were waiting for one man to do it first. Thanks to Cava they had the model of what to do. "

"Did you mean to promote him?"

"Not necessarily today but we need officers who can lead. I only have six of you and that is not enough is it? I just thought it would make the point that we reward loyalty. You take over here while I go and face the wrath of the Legate."

"I don't envy you."

"Well at least once I have received my bollocking we can go no lower. The only way is up."

"I have no idea why you have been sent here Prefect. As far as I can see you are more of a liability than an asset. I do not have a full ala. Your men are disobedient and now, I find, murderers who have swelled the ranks of the very enemy they were sent to fight. Have I omitted anything?"

Marius kept a stony face, as much as he wanted to punch the smug faced aide who grinned at him from behind the Legate's back he would have to take his medicine silently and bite back any retort. "No sir."

The Legate seemed satisfied with the acceptance of his censure. "And they are being shorn?"

"Even as we speak sir."

"Good! Then you can begin your patrols. Your men are to patrol this side of the river from here to the coast and then up the river towards Novaesium. I want early warning of any movement by the Chauci. I want to launch a raid next week to destroy their capital and I do not want them to be aware of our preparation. Clear?"

"Yes sir."

As he left the office the Camp Prefect, Gaius Bassus was waiting for him. "Do you mind if I walk with you?"

"I would be delighted although I feel very much like a leper at the moment."

"Oh don't worry about the Legate. He is a good general once you get used to his funny little ways." Marius stopped and gave him a puzzled look. Bassus shrugged and smiled, "Well eccentric then. The important point is that you are the only cavalry and when we attack next week your men will have to swim the river and protect the pontoon bridge my engineers are constructing."

"I wondered how we would get across."

"The Gallic cohort will be ferried across by the Classis Germania and once they are there then your job will be easier but you will have to cross the river while they are harassing you. It will be hard."

"Unless we go at night while they aren't watching."

"That is a little risky isn't it?"

"I would have said yes but for the fact that thirty of my men did it last night to escape us."

"I heard."

"I suspect we will never live it down."

"It will be forgotten quickly once you perform on the battlefield. So you could do it at night then?"

"First we will need to practise swimming. We will be wearing armour and we have never done it."

"Why not see the Navarchus; if he placed his ships downstream they could rescue any of your man swept away."

"Would he do that?"

"His priority is the protection of his ships. This is their main base. By destroying the Chauci base his ships are safer."

"Why didn't the Legate explain that to me?"

"I told you he is eccentric; a brilliant general but he only rates the legions. You auxiliaries are still barbarians." He glanced up as the third turma rode out looking glum and without their hair. "Believe it or not that will help to convince him that they are Romans."

"Thank you for that Camp Prefect."

"Gaius, please, and we are all on the same side. I for one was glad to see you and your lads arrive. This is not the country for my men."

Wolf felt better now that the rest of the ala had been shaved. He was getting used to the lack of hair but his face felt itchy. He was riding behind Flavius as the three turmae headed along the river to the next Roman fort of Novaesium. He had never seen such a wide river. Even the Danubius which they had seen for many

54

miles was but half its width. He could see the smoke from the fires of settlements across the river and he wondered how they would get across. It seemed strange, to him, that they had not built the camp on the opposite bank.

Their journey to the fortress was uneventful. Flavius rode up to the gate and reported to the optio there, and then turned to return on the second leg of the patrol, the journey home. "Sir?"

"Yes Wolf?"

"Is that all we do now sir. Ride along the river."

"Are you bored then?"

"Well I thought that we were needed here to fight the Chauci."

"Have you seen any?"

"Well no sir."

"Then fighting them is a little hard but we will have a diversion on the way back I assure you. You will not be bored for long."

They were halfway back when the Decurion halted them. "Right lads. We are going to do some training here." They all looked around and wondered why he had chosen the flat part of the river bank for training. "We are going to have a swimming lesson."

Gerjen blurted out. "But sir, we'll drown."

"Why?"

"We can't swim."

Flavius raised his voice so that they could all hear him. "At home how did your horses get across rivers?"

"They jumped in and swam sir."

"Well done Darvas. And did they drown?"

"No sir."

"Then let us see how it is done eh?" Flavius had never swum either but the Prefect had assured him that they needed to learn and learn quickly. He nudged his horse forwards and walked it into the river. He could see the current and he headed his horse up stream. As soon as he felt the motion of the horse become smoother, as its hooves left the river bed, he grabbed a handful of mane and the reins and lay flat along the back of the horse. He found, to his surprise that he still floated, despite the metal he was carrying. He pulled the reins in his right hand the horse began to turn, gratefully, back to the river bank. As it slipped up

55

the slippery mud the Decurion almost fell but managed to right himself and save his dignity.

"Well then. How does that look?"

He could see them smiling. "Yes sir, I think we could do that."

"Good, well you and Gerjen can be the first to try. Do just as I did, and complete one loop. It is just for you to get the feel of it." Wolf warily nudged his horse forwards and Gerjen followed. Once they found that they did not sink their faces brightened. The river was cold and that appeared to be the only problem.

Later as they rode back to camp, all chattering excitedly about the experience Wolf nudged his horse, Blackie, next to the Decurion. "So sir, is that hew we are going to attack the Chauci? Swim across the river?"

Flavius gave the young standard bearer an appraising look. Since Cava had been given his own turma he found himself relying on Wolf more and more. He was bright for Publius had taken much longer to work out what the Prefect had intended. "Between you and I Wolf yes, but keep it to yourself."

"Of course sir."

Flavius looked at the standard. "Have you worked out how you are going to fight with that then Wolf?"

"Yes sir. When we were in the camp the other day I saw a Legion aquilifer and he had a small shield in his left hand. I thought that would give me some protection."

"And save you using the standard like a lance."

"Yes sir. Sorry about that, I just forgot what I was holding."

"Don't forget that when we fight you will have to give commands from me with the standard. We do not use the buccina of the legions. The men need to look to you to know my orders."

"I know sir. I won't let you down."

"I never thought for a moment that you would."

Sura and his men had largely survived the crossing of the Rhenus. When they reached the other bank they found that there were four of their number missing. It was an acceptable loss. As dawn broke they smelled the fires of the villages which were dotted along the bank. This was the tricky part. They wore no helmets but still retained the armour and swords of the ala. Sura was relying on the fact that their hair made them look less Roman to give them the chance to speak with the warriors of the Chauci.

He had contemplated just hiding out in the forests but winter was approaching and he wanted the safety of a hut to survive the snows. They rode, nervously in single file towards the nearest smoke. Sura was no coward and he took the lead; half expecting an arrow from the forest to be his only warning of the Chauci. He saw the lightening of the trees and knew that there would be a clearing ahead. He saw the warriors charge from their walled village. "Keep your hands away from your weapons." He spread his arms wide and hope that the universal sign for peace would keep them safe.

They were surrounded and each of the deserters found themselves with two spears at their throats. Sura tried Pannonian first, "We have left the Romans to fight with you."

The blank look from the two warriors told him that they did not understand him. He tried the same in Marcomanni and they showed that they understood a word or two although which two, Sura did not know. It did, however, appear to make their captors relax and they were led into the village. They were thrown unceremoniously into a hut and left there for some hours.

Finally, after they had begun to fear the worst, the door was opened and a sour looking guard prodded them out with his spear. Outside they found some well armed and armoured warriors. Three of them had the torcs of chiefs around their necks. Their tattooed bodies showed many battle scars and on their arms they wore the amulets which measured their success in battles. Sura was in no doubt that they were chiefs. A slave was brought out. Sura knew he was a slave for he had an iron collar about his neck. One of the chiefs spoke with him and the man then spoke in Pannonian.

"Chief Herrmann wants to know what Pannonians are doing this far from home."

Sura was desperate to find out the slave's story but something told him he had to gain the trust of the Chief first. "We were recruited by the Romans and the rest of our brothers are across the river. We deserted and wish to fight the Romans."

The slave translated and then gave the Chief's question. "Why did you desert?"

"They were going to cut our hair."

When that was translated there was a ripple of conversation and a look of horror on the faces of the chiefs. "And your brothers submitted to this?"

"Yes they did!"

The look of outrage on the faces of the Chauci told Sura that they had probably been accepted. The chiefs spoke for a while and then the slave said, "Chief says you may join the warband but you must take an oath and at the first sign of treachery you will be burned alive."

Sura nodded his agreement. "We will take any oath which lets us kill Romans!"

Chapter 5

Prefect Proculus first met the other Prefects and the Navarchus the day before the attack was to take place. He was intimidated as he knew they had all heard about the deaths and the desertion but he could do nothing about that. Bassus was quite right, they could only clear their name in battle and he had suggested the swimming plan to the Legate having first enlisted the support of the Navarchus. The aide still had the smug smile which made Marius want to punch him and when he spoke in the high-pitched equestrian voice it made the Prefect dislike him even more.

"I am the Legate's aide, Decimus Livius Bucco." His name made Marius smile, a fool by name, a fool by nature. "When the Legate has briefed each of you I will issue your orders. If there are any deficiencies in equipment then I need a list, in writing by the end of the briefing."

The Legate stood. "We are going to engage in a punitive campaign against the Chauci. I will be using '*The Larks*' for this. The Prefect of the Fifth Alaudae kept his gaze steadfastly on the map. They will be crossing my pontoon bridge. To secure the crossing the First Pannonian Ala will swim the river tonight with the Classis Germania provide support and when the bridgehead is secured the Second Gallic Cohort will be ferried by ships to protect the engineers." Every face turned to look at Proculus. They had heard of the ala but not yet seen the commander who had volunteered to swim the mighty Rhenus at night. It seemed foolhardy, some said suicidal. The Prefects of the Gauls and the Legion did not care what happened to the ala so long as the bridgehead was secured. "If I may have your full attention gentlemen!" All of them knew the Legate's ways and every head swivelled back to the map. "Once the Legion is across the ala will scout the village which is five miles from our crossing point and will prevent the enemy from escaping. The Gallic Cohort will guard the bridgehead and the legion will assault the village and destroy it. Some slaves would be useful but I want every warrior dead!" He paused to let his words sink in. "Any questions?"

Marius was about to ask one when a nudge in the ribs from Bassus silenced him. The aide then squeaked, "Any deficiencies?" No-one spoke. "Good then good luck."

Gaius said quietly, "Sorry about that but the Legate regards any questions as impertinent. I just saved you being embarrassed. What was your question?"

"What is the terrain like around the village? My men are used to plains."

"Ah, that would have been a good question then but I suspect the legate would have had an even lower opinion of you had you asked it. It is thick forests. They are thicker next to the river."

"So if I take my ala further from the river we will have an easier passage?"

"Yes and you should avoid detection that way although there is a road."

"Thank you Gaius."

"Just be careful Marius."

"Tell me Gaius why are you so kind to me."

"I knew your father. He was a tribune when I was an optio and he was a good man. He didn't deserve to die in the way he did."

It was strange the way Fate tied so many men's lives together. He had not known the Prefect but now they had a bond which had made them instant friends and, as the only ally he had, he was invaluable.

The Navarchus had embarked the Gauls and then, as darkness had fallen rowed his ships downstream and moored them end to end across the river. Marius was grateful; he knew it meant more work for the crews as they would have to row against the current to land the Gauls. The engineers were busily building the pontoon bridge as Marius stepped into the icy river. They had all practised swimming but it still felt strange to be doing it at night time when you could not see the opposite bank. They all knew that they had to swim diagonally across the river to counteract the effects of the current. He did not turn to see if his men followed, he knew they would. Flavius and the First Turma followed and Aulus Murgus would bring up the rear; that would ensure that none lagged behind as they would not like to risk the wrath of the Decurion. The opposite bank appeared dark and threatening and, as he risked a glance downstream he saw that the ships were becoming alarmingly close. He pulled on the reins to turn his horse's head further upstream.

A few paces further back Wolf was struggling to hold the standard and the hunk of mane. He too kept jerking his reins to the right as he had seen both Flavius and the Prefect drifting further towards the moored fleet. He was becoming more than a little worried. He dare not lose the standard for such a dire event would ensure disaster, but nor did he wish to lose his grip on the horse for then the waters would swallow him and he would never reach heaven. He whispered in his horse's ear. "Come on Blackie, the sooner we are out of this river the better. I have an apple for you. Come on boy!"

Perhaps it was his encouragement or the fact that, without a full sized shield he was lighter, but whatever the reason it was Wolf who first felt the hooves of his horse find purchase on the river bed and he gave a silent prayer of thanks to the Allfather. Even as he stepped ashore he was on the alert and he drew his sword. It seemed strangely quiet but he could see nothing. He turned to watch the rest of the ala swimming towards him. Gerjen joined him and Cava. Cava grinned, "Well lads, with us three here the bridgehead is safe eh?"

Soon others dragged their wet and bedraggled bodies ashore. Neither Flavius nor the Prefect had arrived and Cava took charge. "Wolf stay here with the standard. The rest of you spread out a hundred paces from here. Keep watch."

It seemed to take forever for the ala to reach the other bank and the first sliver of light appeared on the Eastern horizon before they all managed it. When Flavius reached Wolf he saw that they were a hundred paces further downstream than they needed to be. "Right men, follow Wolf." With the standard held high Flavius led the ala north to the right place. "Spread out and wait for the Prefect." As they did so he grinned at Wolf. "Quite the little swimmer eh Wolf?"

"To be honest sir I was just shitting myself. I wouldn't want to do that too often. In all my fourteen summers I was never so afraid."

"Fourteen summers? Surely you are older than that?"

"In my clan you only count your age from the day you can ride a horse without falling off. That was fourteen summers ago. This was harder and I do not look forward to crossing it again."

"Well don't worry. When we go back we go across a bridge. It might be moving a little but we will be dry."

Marius rode up having finished further downstream than any others. "Flavius do a head count and see how many we are missing." When Aulus arrived Marius asked, "Any behind you Decurion?"

His sour faced grinned in the light of dawn. "I think I scared them more than the river but I did see a couple being picked up by the ships."

"We are about twenty short sir. Decurion Cava has secured the road."

"Good. Form a skirmish line a hundred paces from the river and we will just wait for the Gauls to arrive."

They watched the huge warships begin to turn and then row up the river towards them. They could now see the engineers frantically building their bridge. When the auxiliaries were unloaded the fleet would anchor next to the bridge to prevent it being swept downstream. The first few centuries had clambered ashore when a trooper galloped in. "Sir Decurion Cava sent me. There are riders approaching."

"Decurion Vatia, take your turma and reinforce Cava. Buteo, Murgus, form a line behind Vatia's men."

"I am glad now that we came in the dark Flavius. At least this end is secure and the Gauls are here now."

Some sheepish troopers arrived. "Sorry sir, we lost the horses."

"Can't be helped. You men stay here and when the legion is across go back across the river and fetch your spare mounts. You can scout for the Gauls."

The Gallic Prefect landed. He looked around. "I think we have enough men here to hold now. You had better get started around the village."

"There are Chauci riders approaching."

"We have landed now so I am not worried."

"The men who were rescued will fetch their horses and they can scout for you."

"Thanks."

Marcus led the column quickly forwards towards the road. The light was much better and he could see the defensive line. When he reached it Aulus said. "Decurion Cava has taken his turma and chased after the scouts but I don't think he will catch them."

"Right. Flavius, Numerius. Take your turmae down the road. I will take the rest to the north. When you reach the village leave some men to guard the road until the Larks arrive and take the rest around the village to cut it off. I will meet you there."

"Sir!"

"Gerjen, take Darvas and scout a hundred paces ahead. I would like to be forewarned of any enemies."

The cold wet tunic under the armour felt uncomfortable but the troopers soon forgot about it as they rode through land that, for the first time, was not Roman. Their only friends were behind them and, behind every tree could lurk an enemy. They were Pannonians and used to the plains. Trees were frightening for they held the spirits of dead souls who had committed great crimes. Wolf gripped the standard tightly and felt the reassuring metal of his new shield which would protect his left hand. He had made sure that he had put the shield around his hand as soon as he had prepared for this day. He looked up at the Wolf which now had a metal band around the shaft and a small sharp spike on the top. Gerjen had used some elderberries to stain the wolf's teeth so that it looked more ferocious. Wolf had honed both his spatha and his pugeo so that they were razor sharp. He had proved it to himself by shaving his own face. None of the ala would suffer the humiliation of the legionary tonsor again. If they were to be clean shaven they would do it themselves. The nicks and cuts were testament to their lack of skill but they would learn.

Suddenly Gerjen galloped down the road. "Riders!"

Darvas followed and they fell alongside Wolf as Flavius ordered. "Stand to!"

Every javelin was pointed forwards and every shield held tightly to their bodies as they heard the galloping hooves. They were relieved to see Cava but as he approached he shouted, "Chauci! Behind us!"

"Numerius put your men in the woods. First turma and Third turma prepare to receive cavalry."

Every trooper held his javelin ready to hurl. The Chauci had sent forty men after the patrol and they galloped headlong along the trail. Flavius watched as their eyes opened in surprise at the fifty men who faced them. Flavius knew he could not wait until they were close for they would flee and he shouted, "Loose," as soon as they were within throwing distance. The first horses and men tumbled to the ground and the ones behind crashed into them. Numerius and his men poured their missiles into their flank and the survivors fled.

"Kadarcs, dispose of any wounded." The young trooper leapt from his mount and quickly slit the throats of any who showed signs of movement. He then put all the wounded horses out of their misery. The former was easier than the latter.

"Gerjen back on point. Any casualties Decurion?"

"Just two. They surprised us. They had sentries in the trees."

"You had better join Gerjen then and show him where they are."

They made the ambush point without further incident and then approached carefully. They saw the clearing and the village ahead. The villagers had been warned and Flavius could see the spears of the men on its walls. "Decurion Numerius. Guard this road. Decurion Cava bring your men and we will skirt the woods."

Marius and Flavius had hoped that they would be able to avoid detection but their red leggings marked them clearly in the woods and Flavius knew that they would be observed. It could not be helped. Wolf looked at the fort as they negotiated the woods. It was bigger than their own village and had higher walls. He wondered how the legion would assault it. It took them some time to circumnavigate its circumference and they saw the other gate was open. Flavius could see riders at the gate. They were escaping. "First turma follow me."

Wolf raised the standard and they set off at a gallop, leaving the security of the forest to try to cut off the five riders who rode from the beleaguered village. Flavius was a good rider but not in the class of the men he lead. "Panyvadi, Gerjen take the men and stop them!"

64

Whooping a war cry the rest of the turma left Wolf and
Flavius to hurtle after the five warriors who looked in horror at
the twenty men who were catching them. They could have
turned and returned to the village but they were brave men who
had been given orders by the chief. They had to get to Armin's
oppidum and they tried. It was in vain. Gerjen and the others did
not use their javelins but hacked the fleeing warriors from their
saddles with their swords. By the time Flavius and Wolf
reached them they had finished off the wounded and were
leading the five horses. "Well done. Let's get to the other side
of the clearing."

Wolf felt envious of his friend's achievements. They had been
bloodied in battle. He began to regret being the standard bearer
and having to stay by the Decurion. By the time Cava joined
them they heard the Prefect and the rest of the ala approach.
Flavius reported their actions and they waited for the assault to
begin. The sun had almost reached its zenith when Numerius
arrived with his turma. "The Prefect sent us. Said we would be
more use here. They were just starting the attack."

As they listened they could hear the collective moan and the
sound of screams and the clash of iron. It was maddening to be
able to hear but not see their friends and comrades; were they
winning? The soon discovered that the Larks were indeed
winning when the gates opened and the villagers fled. "Flavius
take your three turmae and charge them. The rest we stop them
here. Warriors die. Try to take prisoners."

Flavius turned to Wolf and the others. "Charge!" Wolf raised
and lowered the standard and they galloped forwards. The
villagers were mainly the women and children but there were
some warriors and boy slingers with them. Ignoring the women
and children who would be captured by the rest of the ala the
troopers went for those with weapons. Wolf saw a slinger
aiming at Gerjen and he sliced down with his sword. The boy's
head burst open like a ripe plum. Gerjen himself threw his
javelin into the chest of a warrior who was trying to rally the
warriors. "Head for the gate!"

Keeping as close as he could to the Decurion Wolf galloped
towards the gate which was now thronged with those trying to
escape. Wolf had no chance to discriminate between those with

and those without weapons; he hacked to the left and right of Blackie's head and all died. Then they were in the village and Flavius could see the legionaries had broken in. "Wolf signal rally."

Wolf turned and raised the standard three times. The slinger on the walls had watched the Romans enter and he aimed at the warrior with the wolf. The stone struck Wolf in the right eye; it disappeared in a bloody eruption. Even as Wolf felt the shooting pain Darvas had thrown his javelin to end the life of the brave slinger while the rest had circled Wolf and the Decurion with a protective wall of shields. Through his good eye Wolf saw Flavius' concerned face. "Are you.."

Wolf grinned through the pain. "I am fine sir. Just got a headache."

Gerjen looked concerned. "Well it looks a mess."

"I can't see anything but it hurts a little."

"Just hang on Wolf we have almost won. Pannonians charge those warriors." A line of warriors had formed a wedge and were advancing towards the legionaries. The troopers charged into the unprotected backs and they died to a man as the ruthless Fifth legion hacked and slashed their way to meet the auxiliaries. The Centurion grinned up at Flavius. "Neatly done Decurion." Then he saw Wolf. "What a fucking mess! Capsarius!" The medical legionary trotted forwards. "See to the lad."

"Gerjen, take the standard."

"But sir I am fine!"

"That is an order Wolf," then he added in a gentler voice. "Just until you have had medical attention.

As he stepped from the horse the capsarius took a water skin and a piece of cloth from his bag. He took off Wolf's helmet and gave it to a waiting Darvas. He was a big man but remarkably gentle. "This will sting a little but I have to clean it out." The pain was excruciating but Wolf was a warrior and he gritted his teeth. "Good lad, nearly finished. He bandaged it up. "There you are son. We'll have the doctor look at it when we are back in camp."

"When will I see again?"

"I am sorry son. There is no eye in there. It is just an empty socket. You only have one eye now."

66

Wolf suddenly felt his legs go. It was unfair. He had not even had the chance to defend himself and he had lost an eye. He was no longer whole. Would he be pensioned off? Sent home?

"Steady son!"

"Will I have to leave the army?"

The capsarius put his arm around his shoulder. "I don't think they would be daft enough to get rid of a brave bugger like you. You'll just have to learn to cope with one eye."

Wolf looked up as Flavius dismounted. "That was a brave thing you did. Many men would have fallen but you did your duty, Wolf. You are the heart of this turma and do not fear. Your time with the Pannonians is not yet over."

Riding back, once more with the standard in his left hand Wolf experienced increasingly frequent waves of pain. He could not believe that such pain could be endured but he was determined that he would. If they thought that he was hurt they might take the standard from him. The Prefect was at the rear escorting the prisoners but Flavius and his turmae had suffered injuries, wounds and death and Marius wanted them across the bridge as soon as possible. Behind them the flames from the burning village sent plumes of black smoke high in the sky. The raid had taken the Chauci unawares but they now knew that the Romans had crossed the river.

When they reached the river The Gauls asked them about the attack. "Their warriors could not stand against the legion."

The huge First Spear looked up at Flavius, "There's not many who can."

"How is the bridge?"

The Gaul grinned, "Moves up and down a bit too much for my liking but the Fifth got across without a problem."

They heard the tramp of feet as the legionaries tramped down the road. They nodded at the auxiliaries and just tramped across the bridge. Wolf's pain was forgotten as he watched the alarming motion of the bridges. It looked as though it would tip them all off but miraculously it did not. Flavius saw Wolf's look of terror. "Don't worry Wolf; Roman engineers are the best in the world. The bridges are all short ones so that they do pitch and toss but it means they are less likely to break up. If you notice the soldiers are only marching in half centuries so that there are fewer men on each one. We will do it with half turma. We will not get a ducking, trust me."

By the time the legion had crossed Marius reached it with the prisoners. The Gallic Prefect said, "I'll send a couple of centuries over with them. You'll have your hands full with your horses. Besides, as soon as you lads have finished, this thing will be covered in horseshit!"

One of the optios returned across the bridge. "Legate's compliments and he wants the ala to cover the withdrawal." He looked at the Gallic Prefect. "He said to bring your men over now sir."

The Gaul looked in disbelief. "All we have done optio is sit on our arses while these have been doing the fighting."

The optio looked embarrassed. "Sorry sir, he was insistent."

Under his breath he murmured, "Prick." He put his arm out. "Sorry about this Prefect."

Marius gave a rueful smile. "We'll be along soon enough."

"Right First Spear, the sooner we are over the sooner these lads can follow."

The last Gaul had just reached halfway when a rider galloped in. "Sir. Decurion Murgus; compliments and there is a warband of Chauci on our tails."

Marius cursed the Legate. "Publius, get the wounded over. Turmae four and five form a defensive line. As soon as the wounded are clear we start to pull out. Flavius go and warn the Navarchus that the Chauci are coming. Ask him to have his ballistae ready." He looked at Wolf. "Go on son. You are wounded. Over the bridge now! That is an order!"

"Sorry sir. I am the standard bearer and I leave when my Decurion leaves."

Marius shook his head. He would have left as soon as he had the opportunity. "Ready javelins." He shouted loudly," When I give the command to retreat I want you all over the bridge, even if there are too many of us. We sink or swim together."

They heard the screams and the clash of metal. There were the sounds of men dying as the two forces crashed together. Flavius came back. "He said he will but the Legate has ordered the bridge to be destroyed rather than let the enemy cross."

"Shit! Decurions Cava and Tullus, get your men over. The two Decurions looked like they were going to argue. "No arguments! Go."

Murgus and the remnants of his turma appeared. The Decurion was bleeding heavily from a wounded arm. "Thousands of the bastards sir! Couldn't hold them."

"Well done Aulus. Get your men over. Don't argue just go!"

They heard the clatter and whoosh as the sailors fired their bolts and the first Chauci were hurled from their mounts. "Decurion Vatia, one volley of javelins and then over the bridge."

The turma charged the enemy and hurled their missiles. As they returned Wolf saw empty saddles. The clattering of the hooves on the bridge meant that they had saved at least half of the ala. There were just a hundred and fifty men left but Wolf could see that they would be outnumbered. Suddenly a band appeared from their left and Wolf recognised Sura. "Sura, you traitorous bastard."

"See you lost an eye you little arse licker!"

The deserter galloped directly at Marius who was busy organising the turma of Decurion Quintus Atinus across the bridge. Wolf saw the javelin pulled back and he galloped forwards and thrust the wolf standard at Sura who was not expecting the wounded warrior to fight. The sharp spike drove into his left side and the shocked deserter fell from his horse. The bolts had slowed the attack down and given them some respite. Suddenly they heard the voice of the Navarchus. "Prefect we are destroying the bridge get across now!"

"Retreat!"

Wolf had the only standard left and he lowered it to the horizontal as the last turma, his, fled across the bridge. He waited until he saw Flavius retreat and joined him. As soon as they reached the bridge they felt it move away from the bank as the ships began to back oars. They rode as hard as they could but by the time Wolf, Flavius and the Prefect had reached the middle the integrity of the temporary structure had reached breaking point and the wooden bridge disintegrated. It cracked and the water began to seep between the wood. For a brief moment it seemed to hold the weight of men and horses and

69

then it went. Suddenly Wolf found himself in the icy river, clinging on to the mane of his horse and the standard. Blackie had been ridden all day and was tired. "Come on boy. One last effort. We are half way there."

He felt the horse try to pull away but he also felt the current pulling him downstream towards the sea. The ships were still keeping the barbarians back with their bolts and there were no ships to catch men who were lost. It was too dark to see the others and Wolf knew that he had to save himself. He suddenly realised, somewhat dispassionately, that he had felt no pain from his damaged eye socket since he had entered the water. That was a blessing at least. It gave him the strength to kick with his own legs and he found that they were a little closer to the shore. He kicked again hard and then felt Blackie slow up as its hooves found purchase on the river bed. He kept kicking until his exhausted horse dragged them both wearily to the shore. "Thanks boy! There will be apples. Lots of them."

At the remains of the bridgehead Sextus Vatia took charge. "You troopers who have just landed, get off your horses and get in the water. Drag these poor buggers in."

The Gallic Prefect turned to his men. "Come on, let's get our comrades out of this shit hole."

Soon there were three or four men pulling in the survivors who were beyond exhaustion. The last two were the Prefect and Flavius. Marius looked at Vatia and the Gallic Prefect. "Thank you. We owe you."

The Gaul said, "No, thank you. You have been badly treated."

Just then Gerjen ran up to Flavius. "Sir, where is Wolf?"

They all realised that the standard bearer had not been pulled ashore. They all began shouting his name and searching out over the river. It was some time before they gave up. The Navarchus brought the fleet over. He leaned over the side. "Sorry about that Prefect but I had my orders and the Legate is not a man to be crossed."

"Did you see any more men when you were coming over?"

He shook his head. "None living."

All the exultation after their victory was now gone and they were all left with a sour taste in their mouths. It would take a roll call to find the extent of their casualties but Marius knew that they

70

had lost many and none more valuable than Wolf. They trudged back to the camp feeling as down as it was possible to be. Decurion Tullus had organised food and his men had begun making hot food. The exhausted men who had had to swim across the river were grateful to feel the warmth seep into their bodies. There was no talk, no singing and no banter. The men were numbed. Their victory felt like a defeat and Marius and his officers sat around a fire staring into the flickering flames. Publius coughed. "Er sir? There are one hundred and five missing men. We have twenty wounded. They should all survive. We lost thirty horses." That, in itself, was a miracle. Many horses had lost their riders but joined the swim across the river with the rest of the herd. But men were harder to replace.

Marius stood up, angrily, "I am going to give the Legate a piece of my mind!"

Flavius stood and placed a hand on his chest. "And what good will that do sir? The Legate doesn't strike me as the kind of man to take insolence of that order lying down. Where would that leave us eh? The Pannonians would be sent back home, without their hair and their honour and we would be shipped back to the Ninth. No sir. The whole army knows what a prick the Legate is. The Larks were singing the praises of the ala and the Gauls are as angry as we are. You know how this army works sir. Shit always rises to the top."

Marius forced a smile, "Which doesn't say much for me then does it?"

"No sir…"

"I am only joking Flavius and you are right. But we brought these lads on a long journey and they deserve better than this."

Cava said quietly, "I am the only true Pannonian on this river bank and those men who died, they are in the Otherworld now. They died fighting and they died with their honour intact. There are none of them who would regret their deaths. They are warriors. They died a warrior's death."

"What drowning in the river like poor Wolf?"

"You mean I died?" The pale figure of Wolf, leading a shattered and exhausted Blackie stepped into the firelight. "Funny, this doesn't feel like death." And then his one remaining eye went up into his head and he collapsed.

They all raced to him. Sextus put his hand on his neck, "He is still alive. I feel his heart beat. Get a blanket for him."

Cava shouted. "Pannonians, the Wolf lives!"

In his office Corbulo jumped when he heard the roar from the river. He turned to his aide. "Is that the barbarians?"

The aide raced out and came back. "Yes sir, it is our barbarians, they are cheering."

The Legate would never understand these barbarians who fought a different way from the Romans; even when they fought on the Roman side!

Chapter 6

The Legate was pleased with the raid. His precious legionaries had survived intact and the only losses had been the ones he could easily afford, the barbarians. Appius Verres, his aide, was also pleased for he hated barbarians more than his general. They smelled foul and they were uncouth. They were good for one thing and that was dying for the Empire. "Have the Prefects make me a list of soldiers who deserve a phalerae."

"Even the barbarians?"

"The Emperor says they will become citizens of the Empire, Appius, and the laws apply to them."

A malicious look spread over the aide's face like blood from an open wound. "But surely if they are citizens they should have Roman names. Certainly, the Gauls do."

Corbulo smiled, he liked the young aide who attended to his every need, "True, Appius, but they have been in the Empire since the first Caesar. These Pannonians are recent additions."

"They have had their heads shorn; now we give them a Roman name and then they can have a phalera."

Corbulo thought about that. It would make life easier than trying to get your tongue around their horrific names. "Good. Send for Prefect Proculus and I will tell him."

The ala was busy cleaning armour and looking to their horses. Wolf had insisted that he do as the others were doing but the Prefect took him to see the doctor in the legionary camp. To ensure that he did not run away Marius stayed there. The Greek doctor removed the dressing and it was only then that the Prefect could see the extent of the damage. The rock had not been a round pebble but had rough edges and the bruising and scarring ran down Wolf's cheek. There was no eye, just an angry red socket. The doctor cleaned it up. You are lucky." He used the Latin word Felix and Wolf looked at Marius for an explanation.

"The doctor says you are Felix, lucky."

"Why is that doctor?"

"Two reasons, firstly the stone stopped before it entered your head fully." He picked up a skull and showed him the eye sockets, "It is the brain behind these holes. Had it not stopped you would be dead."

"And the other reason?"

"You had a good capsarius. He cleaned the wound well and there is no pestilence within. However, I will have to sew your eye shut or it will fester and you could die."

Wolf nodded. Marius had been about to leave and speak with the Legate as he had been ordered but instead he said, "I will stay with you." He gave a wan smile. "It is the least I can do for the warrior who saved my life."

As the doctor prepared the cat gut Wolf said, "I did not think you had seen sir."

"I didn't but Gerjen told me. You saved me from Sura and I am grateful. Your men love you, you know?"

"I know." He shrugged, "It has always been so."

"Are you ready?"

"Yes doctor."

"I would use ice to numb the pain but we have none." He gave him a piece of wood. "Bite down on this."

Marius gave his hand to Wolf. "Squeeze hard on this. I have found that helps alleviate the pain."

Marius saw Wolf wince as the needle went into his eyelid. In Wolf's head, for he had his good eye closed, he was trying to see his mother back at the village but the searing heat of the needle made him want to cry. He was determined he would not. The doctor was, like all Greek doctors, highly skilled and he carefully placed the needle as close to the eye socket as he could. It would hurt the boy but many small stitches would help it to heal and to make it look better.

"Tell me doctor, how will this affect Wolf?"

"Eventually he will compensate for the loss of sight but for the next few months he will be vulnerable on his right side."

"It will make defending himself difficult then?"

Wolf heard the words and made the connection. "I am not leaving the army sir!"

Smiling Marius said, "No one said that but Wolf I am afraid that you would not be able to defend the standard, would you?"

74

Wolf hated the thought of not carrying the standard but he understood the Prefect's words. "I suppose Gerjen could carry it until I am better."

"Well we could do that anyway but I have a mind to promote you."

"Promote me sir?"

"Yes Wolf, not the pay grade of an aquilifer but Decurion Bellatoris' Chosen Man. It makes sense, the men follow you and the Decurion thinks highly of you."

Wolf had forgotten the pain of the stitches. He loved being standard bearer but he would be a leader! "Thank you, sir. I think that would be the best for the turma."

The doctor put the last stitch in and stepped away smiling. "Finished! Now I will mix some medicine for you to take away the pain."

"Wolf while the doctor does that I will see the Legate. Wait for me here."

"Yes sir." Wolf looked around the doctor's room. It was filled with amphorae and dishes. He watched the busy little doctor with a mortar and pestle grinding up white seeds. "Can I look around sir?"

"Of course but do not touch anything. We have poisons here."

As he wandered he asked, "Why do you have poisons? You are a shaman are you not? You heal people."

"Shaman eh? I have not heard that word in a long time. Some poisons, given in a mild dose make a person go close to death and sleep. Sometimes that is what the body needs."

"And if you give too much?"

"Then you try to save them by grinding charcoal and mixing it with water."

Wolf had always been interested in medicine and he had a curious mind. "Which poisons?"

"Oh any poison. It makes the patient vomit and the residue acts like a filter. Sometimes it does not work but it is always available." He poured the white liquid he had made into a small amphora. "There, drink a little of this each night. I have given you enough for seven nights."

"Thank you doctor."

The doctor looked closely at Wolf. "I meant what I said you are lucky but you are also clever. You will make a good leader."

"How do you know?" Wolf hoped that this man, the cleverest he had ever met, knew something he did not.

"You ask questions and you are logical." Wolf did not understand the Greek word and had a puzzled expression. "It means you can take emotion out of your plans. You want to remain standard bearer, I could see that, and yet you knew that it made sense to allow another to carry it. That is logical. Thinking with the heart is dangerous. The Gods gave us minds and we should use them. A word of advice, do not lose your temper. It gets you nowhere and once you have lost it, how do you regain it? Better not to lose it than look for it. Here," he picked up a metal bowl the size of a small shield; it was highly polished, "see yourself as others see you."

Wolf saw himself for the first time and he gasped in horror at the bruised side of his face. "I am ugly!"

The doctor laughed and went to his drawer. "Your eye will heal and there are many women who will say that you are handsome," almost under his breath he added, "and many men too. Here wear this." He tied a leather patch over the offending eye and Wolf sighed with relief. It did not look so fearsome. "You may keep this but I suspect that you will, eventually not wear it." He shrugged, "It is up to you."

Wolf took the patch and put it on. It felt strange. He could bear the pain and he could bear the scar. They had both been earned as a warrior. He was truly a warrior now.

"Ready Wolf?" The Prefect's voice sounded from outside.

"Coming sir; thank you doctor." He placed the bowl down and clasped the doctor's arm like a soldier.

The doctor was bemused. "Thank you, er, Wolf." As the boy left the doctor reflected that many so called civilised Romans would not have behaved with such dignity as that barbarian. He had admired his stoic attitude whilst being stitched. He was also intrigued by the questions. That trooper was one to watch.

As they rode back to their camp the Prefect was distracted. He heard Wolf ask something and realised he had not been listening. "Sorry Wolf I am far away. That patch looks good. What did you ask?"

"I wondered sir, what the Legate wanted."

"Tell me Wolf, how do you and the others feel about your names?"

"Our names sir?"

"Yes, Gerjen for example, would he object if he were not called Gerjen but, say, a Roman name such as mine."

"But he is Gerjen, if you change his name, he will still be Gerjen." Wolf could not understand the question. The Romans had different names for the trees and the plants but the plant remained the same whatever it was called.

"Were you born and named Wolf?"

He grinned, "No sir, it was because of my appetite. My mother named me Mada."

"So you had a name chosen for you?"

"Yes sir. I am sorry sir but where is this going?"

They were passing the Gallic camp and the auxiliaries shouted and grinned at them. Marius raised his arm in salute. "Those Gauls all have Roman names and yet they were born with Gallic names."

Wolf could now see where the questions were heading. "The Legate wishes us to take Roman names. Is that what you are saying sir?"

"In a nutshell yes."

Wolf wondered about names. He would always be a wolf in his head. He had the wolf token around his neck but he was also Chosen Man and he answered to that. "How do Roman names work?"

"You have a Praenomina, mine is Marius then you have a Nomen, like a family name, mine is Ulpius and sometimes, especially when you become Roman you have a Cognomen which says something about you, mine is Proculus and it means born during a father's absence."

"So you were born when your father was away?"

His curious mind could not help coming up with more questions. It was like talking to an inquisitive child. "No Wolf that goes back some time in my family's history."

"I think we could ask the men and many would do it sir. It still keeps you as you were and your own name is in your heart anyway."

"Would you do it?"

"What is Roman for Wolf sir?"

"Lupus."

He nodded and rolled the name around in his head. "A family name, that would be hard, what is yours sir?"

"Ulpius."

"So I could be Lupus Ulpius. I like that."

Marius smiled, this would work. "And of course the doctor gave you your name."

"Did he sir, what is that? One eye?"

"No, Felix, lucky. Lupus Ulpius Felix."

Wolf grinned, "That sounds Roman and I like it. I do not know about the others but if it helps I will be the first Pannonian with a Roman name."

Flavius was waiting for them when they rode in. "How did it go sir?"

"Er, Felix, bring your turma to the command tent please." Wolf walked off grinning.

"Felix?" Flavius was totally confused both at the name and Wolf's reaction.

"Let me explain." He looked at the departing warrior, "That one is interesting let me tell you." He then explained about the Legate's need for roman names and the discussion with Wolf. "I took the liberty of offering him Chosen Man. I realise that is your prerogative."

"I totally agree with you, sir. He is the perfect choice but how did you get him to agree to give up the standard?"

"It is his eye. For a while he will not function as efficiently on that side. At least if he has a shield he can turn to defend himself. He took it well."

They heard the murmur of voices outside of the tent. They saw the turma lined up. Wolf was holding the standard and grinning at Marius. It was as though the two of them were sharing a joke. "Fist turma reporting as ordered sir."

"Thank you Lupus Ulpius Felix."

The Decurion joined with the turma in looking at the two men who seemed to know something they did not. "You have a new Chosen Man, Sesquiplicarius Felix. Gerjen would you accept the post of aquilifer?"

"Yes sir!" He beamed with pride.

"Now you may have noticed that Wolf here has a new name. It is a Roman name. That is because he is to be awarded a phalera for his bravery." It was the turn of Wolf to look surprised. "The Prefect has ordered that only those men with Roman names can be awarded a phalera." He took a deep breath. "Gerjen and Kadarcs you showed great courage yesterday and I have recommended that you also receive a phalera."

"And you want to know will we change our names sir?"

"Yes Gerjen. I want to know if the First Turma will be, once again, the pathfinders for the ala, and take on this duty."

They all looked at Wolf who nodded forcefully. "Then, yes sir I will."

The ceremony was held in the main camp. Only those honoured were present. There were three from the ala and eight from the Fifth Alaudae. The Gallic Prefect had told Marius that they deserved more but Marius was pleased that, at least they had some recognition.

The aide, Appius, had a sour look on his face as he handed the shiny piece of metal to the Legate who managed to look down his nose as he, reluctantly handed them to the Pannonians. "Decurion Casco Petronius Paterculus."

Cava stepped forwards and took his medal, "Thank you Legate."

"Sesquiplicarius Lupus," the Legate wrinkled his nose at the choice of name, "Ulpius Felix."

Wolf did not care, "Thank you sir."

"Aquilifer Serjenus Ulpius Lupus."

Gerjen shyly took it and murmured, "Thank you General."

Gerjen had wanted the same family name as his friend, as did the others in the turma but Cava still felt he owed much to Flavius and he took his family name. The rest of the ala was interested in the idea but not all took the plunge. Wolf knew that they would come around for he had noticed that they were becoming more Roman each day. They used the language easily although there were new words, such as Felix, which caused some confusion. Some of them had even been persuaded to visit the newly built baths. Their patrols, as winter drew on, taught them to use their new equipment more efficiently and the cloaks, which had been seen as cumbersome at first, were grateful used to keep out the biting winds and give them some protection from the biting snow showers. The Legate still had a low opinion of the ala but it gradually improved as they captured Chauci who tried to infiltrate the camps to sabotage and terrorise the Roman invader. Their camp was the one closest to the danger area and, under the watchful eye of Aulus Murgus they became vigilant in the extreme.

As the first signs of spring arrived Decurion Paterculus was on patrol when he saw the column of men trotting towards him. He recognised the Tribune from the Ninth, Gnaeus Marcius Celsus. "Sir, what brings you over here?"

Celsus waved his arm behind him, "More recruits for you." He seemed to see the Pannonians for the first time. "I almost did not recognise you." He waved his hand before his face. "What happened?"

"The Legate disapproved and we now have Roman names, "he shrugged, "you get used to it. You have a long journey back then sir."

"No Decurion, we are to rejoin the rest of the legion in Britannia." He pointed to the river. We sail from here. We have the foot sloggers with us."

"The Prefect will be glad to see you sir. If you will excuse me I have a patrol to finish." As they rode down the line of new recruits Cava and the rest of the troopers wondered had they ever looked that way. Their hair hung lank down their shoulders or in a pony tail and their moustaches and beards were festooned with bones." They would change as he had.

The Tribune decided not to accept the invitation to dine with the Legate, much to his obvious annoyance. As he said to Flavius and Marius as he joined the ala's officers in their quarters, "I will be serving in Britannia. The last thing I need is to have to watch my manners. I prefer eating with barbarians. Much more my style!"

"I thought Britannia was pacified."

"No Prefect. This character Caractacus is causing all sorts of problems. We are joining the rest of our legion to put an end to him. The Eight has replaced us in Pannonia. These six hundred recruits may well be the last ones you get for a while. All the ones who wanted to fight have fled north to join the Marcomanni."

Cava almost spat out his food, "But they are our enemies!"

"They are now seen as allies."

Marius pointed across the river. "Some of the last recruits, the ones you were worried about, they deserted and joined the Chauci so I suppose we can understand it."

"You'll be campaigning again in the summer then?"

"I suppose so but until we actually build forts on the other side of the river we will never have true peace."

They watched their friends in the Ninth sail away. It was not the last they would see of them but the next time they did would be the Ninth's darkest hour. Marius had his work cut out assimilating the new men. "Flavius, I think we merit a Decurion Princeps now. That will be you. You can take charge of the training of the new recruits. I am going to Promote Felix to the post of Decurion."

"Good he will do well."

"We will make Casca the Decurion of the First Turma and move Felix and the rest of your old turma into Turma two. Now we need other officers who would you recommend?"

"Most of Felix's men."

"We can't take them all but how about taking Quadratus, Cicurinus and Paullus?" Darvas, Kadarcs and Panyvadi had shown themselves to be highly self reliant and efficient.

"They will hate it but they will be good officers and we can spread some of the new men in the other turmae." They had learned not to separate and isolate new men. Sura had been a salutary lesson to them.

The Legate, however, did not give them time to settle in the new men. The Prefects and tribunes were ordered to the Praetorium where Appius waited with written orders for each of them. "Gentlemen we have been asked to teach the Frisii a lesson. They have been raiding the ships taking supplies to Britannia. The Classis Britannica is busy supporting the fighting in the west and the Navarchus tells me that he cannot control the pirates on his own. We need to destroy their ships and their towns."

The Gallic Prefect, Arminius, came from the north coast of Gaul and understood the nature of the people. "But sir, if you destroy their ships they will starve, they are a sea going people."

"Then perhaps the lesson will be a good one. Do not raid Rome! This time we will be ferried by ship. The disaster of the bridge will not be repeated and besides the Rhenus is wider near the Frisii land. The ships will tow barges with the horses of the cavalry. The Fifth will remain here and we will use the First and Second Cohorts of the Fifteenth. This sort of work is best performed by auxiliaries." Marius and Arminius exchanged a knowing look. It meant they were expendable.

Deep in the forests north of the river, Herrmann and his chiefs were seated around a fire with Sura. The winter had been a sombre one; the attack on the village had cost two of the chief's sons their lives; the abortive attempt to prevent the evacuation of the slaves had cost many brave warriors and the tribe wanted revenge. Herrmann was a cautious and wise chief. He had lost too many men to be able to launch the attack he wished but he needed to send a message to the Romans that the incident was not forgotten.

"You fought with the Romans. What do they fear?"

Sura had acquitted himself well in the battle but his wound had been grievous and he still found difficulty in breathing. The warrior called Wolf would pay for that but it had given him much time to think about the correct way to wage war against his former enemies. "They think they are secure behind their river and behind their ditches and ramparts. If we could make them fear us at night then they would begin to weaken." There were nods around the fire for that suggested a few brave and reckless men rather than risking the heart of the tribe. "We need to tempt them across the river again but this time, we must ambush them." He told them the story he had heard about the Teutonberger massacre and they seemed impressed.

Herrmann nodded. "They are good plans. We have not the numbers yet to ambush them but you, Sura, the Pannonian, take your men and a hundred of my warriors. Cross the river and make them fear us/"

"I will do as you command."

The voyage across the Rhenus was frightening for those in the ala who had had to swim after their last battle and for the recruits it was another ordeal on top of the horror of the hair being torn, as they felt it, from their bodies. Wolf, or Decurion Felix, as he was getting used to, was eager. This would be the first time he had led his men into battle. He knew twenty of them but there were ten recruits and he hoped that he had trained them well. He knew that they had all been intrigued by his wound; many men's wounds remained hidden but his was there every time he looked at them. He deigned to use the patch and the scar had reddened and then turned white. He knew from Decurion Casca that he looked frightening. He hoped that his enemies were as fearful as his men. He had chosen to keep his men on the barges with the horses rather than travelling in relative comfort on the biremes and triremes of the Classis Germania. As he said to his men, "The horses are our most valuable weapon; we travel with them to protect them."

The low marshy shore loomed ahead as the trireme pulling them swung around so that the ungainly barge was side on to the reeds. "Get those ramps over!"

His turma worked well, led by those warriors who had followed him from their homeland. They led the shaking beasts into the land of the Frisii. By the time the other turmae came for their horses the Second Turma was mounted and in skirmish order. "Well done Felix. Take your men in a five mile circuit. Tell us what is out there."

"Yes Prefect. Second Turma, follow me."

The Prefect couldn't get over the change in Wolf. Since his promotion and the wound he had become a different officer. No longer reckless he was efficient and organised. He marvelled at the change. If losing an eye could guarantee such a change he would order them all to be so blinded. He looked at the sea of reeds before him. His men and horses would need to become fish or frogs to survive here. "Come on get those horses ashore."

Wolf turned to his chosen man, Gaius. "Send Lucius and Titus ahead to scout." He hated having to use his old companions all the time but he knew he could rely on them. The new troopers were keen but he feared to use them. He was always looking for a safer occasion in which to test them. So far he had not found one and now that they were so close to the Frisii, it seemed almost foolhardy to do so.

The two troopers galloped off and wildfowl took to the air. Had they had bows then they could have had meat for the pot. They rode through the fens until he felt solid ground beneath Blackie's hooves. He halted the column to give them time to rest. "Gaius, make sure they all take a drink." Gaius gave him a look which suggested that he was trying to teach his grandmother to suck eggs. "I know the old hands know what to do but some of these are still fresh faced." He looked at the nicked chins and cheeks, "Literally, fresh faced."

Grinning, Gaius rode off, "Yes sir!"

Wolf took a swig from his own water bottle. He had been tempted to bring some of the wine they had acquired. He knew that the Gallic Centurions and Optios did, but much as he enjoyed the taste he knew that it made him less alert and in enemy territory that could cost you your life. Suddenly, about four hundred paces from their left a pair of wild fowl noisily fluttered into the air. He could see Titus and Lucius well to the right and knew it was not them. As quietly as possible he said, "Gaius. There are men in the reeds. Warn the men and on my command I want a line abreast. Do it quietly."

Gaius knew Wolf from their village and he went around each of the men quietly giving them clear instructions. Now would be the time when Decurion Ulpius Felix would see the mettle of his men. He checked that his shield was tight, loosened his spatha and held the javelin in his right hand. He would now see if the Greek doctor spoke true; he would find out if his left eye was working harder. He glanced at Gaius who nodded. He turned to Spurius the standard bearer, "Signal the charge!"

The standard pointed forwards and Decurion Lupus Ulpius Felix led his men into battle for the first time. Titus and Lucius had seen the movement and they galloped to join the right-hand side of the line. The first arrow almost struck Wolf but he sensed rather than saw it and inclined his head to one side; it flew over his head. He instinctively pulled his shield to cover his precious left eye and aimed Blackie at the place from whence the arrow had come. The ground was relatively firm and Blackie was

84

surefooted. Wolf looked ahead for the sight of a target. He had covered almost three hundred paces when they flushed their quarry. A dozen men stood and loosed a volley of arrows. Hoping that they would miss his mount the Decurion hoisted his shield to take the impact. He heard the crack as three of them hit his scutum. The red crest atop his helmet marked him as a leader and that meant he was the primary target; that suited Wolf. Their quarry turned and ran; it was a foolish move as the horses could move faster. He hurled his javelin at the nearest man and had the satisfaction of seeing it strike him squarely in the back. The escape route of the barbarians was being cut off by the approach of Titus and Lucius. Wolf threw the second of his three javelins and he aimed for the lower back of the man ahead. He struck him in the thigh. His last javelin hit another in the back and he drew his sword. It was not needed. "Don't finish them off. We need prisoners!"

The Tribune of the Fifteenth had built his camp flanked by the Pannonian and Gallic camp. The fleet was lying offshore with all the artillery aimed at the marshy banks of the river. As soon as the scouts were in they could begin to plan their route to the strongholds. The Tribune was no Corbulo and respected the abilities of the auxilia. They had decided that they would send out the ala as a screen with the legion and the Gauls as two long columns. It would make travelling as swift and as safe as possible. The three men were still finalising their plans when the sentry shouted. "Riders coming in."

In this part of the world it did not pay to be complacent and take things for granted. Every soldier grabbed his weapons until Marius yelled, "It is my men."

One prisoner was being tugged by a rope while another was draped, heavily bleeding across the saddle of Decurion Ulpius Felix. "Well done Wolf. Any casualties?"

"No Prefect. There are ten dead Frisii out there. They tried an ambush." He grinned. "They failed."

"Good, leave them with us and you get your men sorted in the camp."

Wolf rode back to the camp feeling pleased with the new men. They had performed well and obeyed every order. The only down side was that one of his javelins had broken and he would have to get another from Publius who seemed to regard every piece of equipment as his own.

The next morning the ala spread out in a line eight hundred warriors long. There were twenty five turmae and they were well led. The prisoners had told them that the Frisii were gathered close to the coast in a low lying hill fort and that their king was Gannascus. Tribune Rufius Longus felt that they should strike quickly before their allies, the Chauci could come to aid them.

Cava and his men were on point. Like Wolf Cava trusted his men and found that he enjoyed this life in the Roman army. Unlike some of the other officers he also liked the detached duty of scout. It felt more like being a Pannonian on a raid. It was his sharp eyes which spotted the spiral of smoke which marked the hill fort. The low lying land made it quite obvious to Cava that the hill fort was no obstacle and only rose thirty or so paces from the land. He sent a man back with the news and then closed on the Frisii stronghold.

The Tribune, in turn, sent a messenger back to the fleet to join them on the seaward side of the fort. He hoped that they could cow them into submission but the prisoners had said that Gannascus had ambitions to invade the Roman lands; he would want his moment of glory. By the time they reached the fort it was too late to attack and they all built secure camps. Flavius took Marius to one side. "I will bet a week's pay that they attack us tonight!"

"No takers there Flavius. Have half the men on guard tonight. Use Aulus to take charge. Rest turmae one through six and we'll use them tomorrow. We won't be needed for the assault."

"You can see that Corbulo isn't here or we would have been sent to take it on the backs of our horses."

"That sounds cynical Flavius." He lowered his voice, "Don't let the men hear those kinds of opinion eh?"

"Of course not sir."

The third turma were on duty that night and every trooper was alert to danger. They might wear the Roman armour and look Roman but they all had Pannonian instincts. Metellus, who had been Mabad when he rode the plains, sniffed the air. There was the smell of the sea and the pines but there was something else, a sour smell of unwashed bodies. He half smiled to himself, a year ago and that would have been him but now he took occasional baths; not as many as the regular Roman troops but enough to make him aware of others. "Decurion, there is someone out there!"

Cava's neck had been prickling and Metellus' words merely confirmed it. "Third turma stand to. Drusus, wake the Decurion Princeps."

The thirty troopers checked the straps on their scuta and held their javelin above their head. The other two were jabbed into the ground, ready for a second volley should it become necessary. "What is it Decurion?"

"There are men out there sir. Can't see them but I know they are there."

Just then a duck took noisy flight. Flavius grinned, "I think you are right. I'll bring the others." He pointed to the ditch. "Keep your eyes closer to the fort."

Cava knew that Flavius was an old hand at sentry duty and he heeded his advice. Within moments he had spotted the pale face glimpsed for a but moment. He tracked where he thought it would reappear, "Steady lads they are twenty paces from the ditch." As soon as he detected the movement he hurled his javelin and was rewarded with a scream as the Frisii fell. Suddenly the ditch was filled with howling warriors wielding axes and swords. Orders would have been superfluous and he and his men hurled their javelins at the approaching men. He was aware of the gaps on either side being filled as the other troopers joined them. His last javelin thrown he drew his spatha as a Frisii warrior tried to haul himself up using the bodies of his dead comrades as a ladder. He was a brave man and Cava hoped he would find his way to the Allfather as he thrust the length of the blade through his open, screaming mouth.

The ala's troopers were just spectators, as Marius had predicted, for the assault. The failed attack on the ala's camp had taken the heart out of the Frisii who were quickly subjugated. The Gallic Prefect had not needed to worry about their livelihoods for, when the boats were destroyed and the fort dismantled the people were herded aboard ships and sent to the slave markets of Rome. The Frisii threat was over.

Chapter 7

Decurion Felix stopped wearing the patch as summer approached. It itched and sweated when he wore it and he only received strange looks for the first few days. Soon they all came to ignore it and see beyond the disfigurement and recognise their old comrade beneath. The new recruits had been assimilated and with almost a thousand men the ala was as full as it would ever be. There would be fewer Pannonians making the journey west. The Decurion had been told by Flavius that a second ala was being raised for action in the east. Any new recruits would have to come from the land around them. Wolf couldn't see that they would ever be able to trust the Frisii and Batavi who had been conquered. Flavius had laughed, "In your father's time the Pannonians fought against my legion and yet now his son fights with me. Times change, Wolf, as we all do."

He still couldn't see it himself. He was happy however; he had become used to not fighting alongside his old friends. There were still a couple of the men he had led in his turma but his core had been picked clean to provide officers and sesquiplicarii for the rest of the turmae. He enjoyed the patrols but he missed the action. He could not wait for the proposed autumn invasion of the Chauci land. He was a warrior and that was what warriors did.

Sura and the forty men he had brought with him laid up in the woods to the west of the camps. They had made their way through the Roman lines at night to wait during the day in the quieter hinterland where the Roman gaze was not so vigilant. He had brought his deserters and fifteen Chauci youth who wished to be blooded. Sura had already chosen his target, the Fifth Legion whose camp was close to the fortress. There they would feel secure, protected, as they were, by the fort on one side and the two auxiliary camps on the other. Tonight, they would visit their terror on the camp and then flee south, not back to the river as the Romans would expect but to Tungri and the other settlements where they would continue their raid. Sura had promised Herrmann a summer of destruction and he would deliver a summer that the province would never forget.

The third century had drawn the night time duty for the third consecutive night. They were all looking forwards to the next ten days when they would just have the drills and the practice and not have to endure the boring and pointless sentry duty. Centurion Julius Cuneo was getting close to his pension. Retirement loomed and he had already earmarked an inn in Cisalpine Gaul. He had passed through it many times in his twenty-five years and knew that he could make much money from the legions who passed through that land. Every night he filled his head with the ideas and the profits. He pictured the comely women who would work for him and whom he would bed. He envisaged his old comrades sharing an amphora of wine, slightly discounted of course, and talking of old campaigns. He had been lucky in his twenty-four years. It had been fifteen years since he had had to fight. When they had assaulted the Chauci village the previous year he and his century had been in the second wave and the Pannonian charge had meant that it was without danger. He had been lucky.

His tired ears thought they heard a noise and he glanced over the rampart but could see nothing. He smiled to himself, he was getting old and hearing things. When he smelled the unwashed body close to him and felt the hand cover his mouth his hand went to his gladius, but too late his life blood and his dreams of retirement were dripping in pools at his dead feet. The rest of the century on the north wall were all despatched silently. The raiders took their heads and slipped them over the wall. While the ten warriors outside placed the gruesome trophies on the spears placed there earlier, the rest descended and opened the gates. The attention of the other sentries was to the river and they did not see the warriors as they took the burning torches and threw them at the tents. The raiders had left by the open gate before the sudden flaring of the tents drew their attention. "Fire! To arms!"

The legion centurions reacted the quickest and leapt from their tents, half-dressed but with a gladius in hand. First Spear took charge, "Get a chain of buckets. Marcus, get your century and reinforce the sentries on the walls. I'll have the dozy buggers backs laid bare for allowing this."

"First Spear, the south gate is open."

"Shit! Centurion Flaccus. Get your century to the south gate and check on the sentries." He suspected that any who should have been punished were now dead. The Tribunes and the Legate of the fifth arrived, half-dressed and looking annoyed. Legate Julius Salvius Labeo knew that First Spear was a competent officer and he went directly to him. "Well Gnaeus?"

In answer he pointed to the open gate. "Someone got in and out of the fort and set fire to these tents."

"And the sentries?"

Just then a grim-faced Centurion Flaccus arrived. "Sir the sentries are all dead, including the centurion."

"Any sign of the perpetrators?"

"No Prefect but…"

"Out with it man!"

"They have no heads."

By the time dawn broke a short while later the fires had been doused and the whole legion stood to arms. As the mist cleared it became obvious where the missing heads were as the grim line of severed heads stared back at them.

When Marius arrived at the Praetorium he noticed that the normally smug expression on Bucco's face had disappeared and he had a distinctly green look about him. The Prefect allowed himself a smug smile of his own. They had heard about the attack on the camp and he knew that every one of the Legate's staff would be sleeping less soundly for a while.

The Legate stood and addressed them all. "As you may have heard some barbarians entered the camp of the Fifth last night and killed some of the sentries. The atrocity will not go unpunished. We are going to begin our campaign against the Chauci and this time we will destroy all of their river side bases and send them back to their forests. The two legions and the Gauls will cross by two pontoon bridges which are being built. I have asked the Sixteenth Gallica at Colonia Claudia Ara Agrippinensium to build a pontoon bridge there. The Pannonian ala will pursue last night's raiders and then cross the river at Colonia Claudia." He then looked directly at Marius. "Your main role will be to close the bag. We will be driving along the northern bank of the Rhenus and you will use your ala to prevent the refugees escaping. We will all then return here via the temporary bridge at Colonia

Claudia for the engineers will have dismantled the two other bridges." He gave a grim smile, "as we are only leaving one cohort here it would not do to give our enemies the chance to cross the river and destroy all our good work eh?"

Labeo stood, "Who will command sir?"

"I will. It is time my staff and I saw some action. Planning these campaigns is all very well but I need to be on hand in case all does not go as expected."

Marius put his hand before his mouth to stop himself from laughing as the aide, Bucco, visibly went green as he heard the news. As he left he knew that it would be almost impossible to find whoever had killed the legionaries. He would spend no more than a day at the most. It was just a day's ride to the nearest legion and he could be in position with most of the ala.

"Flavius you will be with me and the main body. Detach the Second and Third to try to pick up the trail of the men who got inside the fort."

"Do you think Wolf and Cava will find them?"

"I doubt it but the Legate is insistent that we try. Personally, I think it is more important to reach the other side of the Rhenus. The army will be across within two days. I am hoping that the Legate of the Sixteenth has good security at the bridge or we could all be in the shit if the Chauci use that as a means of invading us.

Surprisingly Cava's Chosen Man, Drusus, found their trail quite quickly. "They are Pannonians sir." He held up a bone. It was from a raven and was the type that many Pannonians used to decorate their hair. The strands of hair showed that it had had human contact.

Wolf joined the two men and scoured the ground. "Looks to be about thirty men and they headed south."

"Away from the river."

"Exactly."

Cava turned to one of his troopers. "Tell the Prefect we have found the trail and it is heading south. We will follow and meet him at the bridge."

This was the first time that they had had detached duty and they were travelling light. The carts with the spare equipment and food was with the ala. The two officers had already been enjoying the freedom and now that they might be within sniffing distance of Sura they were even keener.

The huge numbers of carrion birds which noisily squawked into the sky was the first warning that the village had suffered a disaster. "Decurion, Take your men around the village and approach from the south."

The sixty troopers closed with the village and, as soon as they reached the first buildings they saw the bodies. All had been slaughtered, men, women and children. From the position of the legs it was obvious that all the females had been raped, some of them while they were dead. There were the bodies of three raiders, one Pannonian and two Chauci which showed that the men had, at least, put up a fight. Cava recognised the dead deserter. "Gyak!" He spat at the dead body. "Useless sly little bastard he got what he deserved."

"Sir. There are hoof tracks. They are mounted!"

"Decurion! Get your men. It looks like they have horses."

The tracks were clear and easy to follow. They rode hard for they could see that the deserters and raiders were heading for the very place they were, Colonia Claudia! "Well at least the Sixteenth should be able to stop them."

Wolf looked at Gaius, his Chosen Man "Not true. They are more likely to have guards and sentries on the north bank. The ones on the south will not be expecting to be attacked and remember Sura and his men have Roman armour."

"But they have long hair!"

"The Sixteenth have never seen us, have they?"

The optio at the pontoon bridge saw the auxiliary cavalry riding up and saw the four men with ropes around their necks. "Go and find the centurion. It looks like those cavalry we were expecting have got here early and they have prisoners." As the legionary trotted off to the main camp the optio turned to the second soldier. "Rough looking buggers, aren't they?"

"Where are their shields sir?"

The keen-eyed sentry had noticed that although they looked like auxiliaries they looked even less formally attired than others. "You are right. Stand to."

The eight men held their spears before them. Sura saw that the game was up and the twenty five men charged the contubernium.

The Pannonians threw their javelins and then drew their swords. Two of the legionaries fell to the missiles whilst another two, including the optio died from the wicked sword blows. Then they were on the bridge. The remaining four hurled their spears at the horsemen as they passed. Three fell to their deaths in the icy river whilst a fourth dripped blood from his calf. The guards at the other side of the river heard the noise and formed a double line, one faced the bridge whilst the other kept watch on the forests. The pontoon bridge was without sides and Sura had no intention of charging the forty men at the end of the bridge. The raiders leapt, with their mounts, from the bridge when they were just thirty paces from the wall of steel. Their terrified horses were swept downstream, away from the Romans the survivors all struggled to the bank. Sura turned to laugh at the Romans who stood impotently on the bridge. "Just to let you know Romans that Sura of the Tecteri clan will return and your heads will adorn my saddle!" His men whooped their own insults and the raiders headed back to the Chauci stronghold of Herrmann. They had fulfilled their mission and the Romans had learned fear.

Cava and Wolf reached the bridge shortly before the ala. The Tribune and First Spear of the Fifteenth were there too with two centuries of their men. Decurion Casca Petronius Paterculus of the First Pannonian Ala, sir." He gestured at the bodies covered by their cloaks. "I see the raiders got here before us."

First Spear growled, "My men said they were dressed like you." There was a threat implicit in his voice.

"First Spear!" admonished the Tribune. "The optio was a young officer, well thought of."

"Sorry for your loss. Did they have long hair and only basic weapons?" First Spear looked at the legionary who nodded. "They were some recruits who deserted a year ago. they also killed twenty men of the Fifteenth. We are going after them."

The Tribune nodded, "They headed south."

"You are Pannonians too eh? Well bring back their fucking heads!"

"Sorry First Spear, it's only barbarians who do that. We are Romans now." He gave a lopsided smile.

First Spear nodded and gave a grim look. "Well as a favour to me, bring the bodies back and I will take their heads!"

"Consider it done." He glanced over his shoulder. "Tell our Prefect that we are in pursuit. Come on Wolf. They have a head start."

Sura and his men had slowed up once they reached the safety of the forest. Two of them carried wounds. "Bandage them if you can or..." The threat was not an idle one. Two of the Chauci who had been wounded by the villagers had had their throats slit when they could not keep up. Sura dismounted and lifted the hoof of the nag he had stolen. The horses were not the best and could not compare with the horses of home but they had, at least enabled them to escape. Herrmann would be delighted with the news of the bridge. It meant that the Romans were coming over. He had recognised that the camp at the bridge only contained one legion. Herrmann had five times that numbers. Sura contemplated sending a rider to the stronghold but he wanted the glory of that himself. He could see himself rising in the ranks of the Chauci and this could be his first toe hold.

The javelin struck the deserter next to Sura and he fell at his leader's feet his face looking shocked. Sura's first reaction was to see which of his men had done it and then he knew, it was the ala. "Defend yourselves!"

Cava rode his horse directly at Sura. His turma spread out behind him like a wedge. Wolf and his turma tumbled in from the side away from the river and it was Wolf's turma which met the fleeing raiders. They had all dismounted and were facing the men they had betrayed, the men who were armed and armoured far better than they. Rather than risking their javelins striking their friends Wolf and his men slashed down with their long swords, leaning low in the saddle to reach out. Sura saw Cava and tried to run. One of the Chauci had mounted his horse and was fleeing. "Wait for me!"

The Chauci cast a contemptuous glance behind him just as Cava's sword sliced down to split the deserter's back in two. "That is how oath breakers die!" Sura collapsed to the ground and, his eyes still open though death was close he reached out for his sword, but a hand span away. Cava leapt from his horse and kicked it away. The last thing the deserter heard, as death and darkness took him was, "You are a murderer, you do not deserve a warrior's death."

Marius had ordered the camp to be built at the northern end of the bridge. "We can leave it up with the carts inside and a turma to guard it. You never know Flavius; we may have to return here in a hurry."

"Riders!"

The ala and the men of the Fifteenth on Guard duty all took a defensive position. They were in the land of their enemies. It did not pay to be careless. They relaxed when they heard Cava's voice, Decurion Casca Petronius Paterculus returning from patrol."

First Spear had been checking that the sentries on the southern end had been briefed when he heard the call. His caligae rattled the bridge as he strode over, vine staff in hand. He reached the camp of the ala just as the Decurion was reporting. "One man escaped, I believe he was a Chauci. The rest are here," he pointed to the string of horses with the bloody bodies on them. There was a question in the Prefect's eye. Cava saw First Spear and grinned, "I brought them back for First Spear. He wanted a present."

"Thank you, Decurion, I am in your debt. You idle buggers, get over here!" The sentries ran over. "Yes, First Spear?"

"Get that baggage from the horses and lay them in a line." He took his gladius from its scabbard and as Sura's mangled body fell to the ground he lifted the head and slice it from the body. He turned to the white-faced young legionary next to him. "Pick up the head."

Soon there were just the bodies left on the ground. He stomped back to the bridge and, taking one of the sentry's spears, jabbed it into the earth. He took Sura's head and stuck it on the end. Soon the sides of the entrance to the bridge were decorated with the heads. "Now throw the bodies in the Rhenus. We'll see if Herrmann likes the sight of his dead, headless men." Nodding to the cavalrymen he said, "Evening gentlemen." He looked up at Wolf and Cava. "When this is over, you lads are more than welcome to come and have a wet with me and the other centurions. A sort of thank you."

By the time the clatter of his hobnails had disappeared into the darkness Cava and Wolf had finished their report. Flavius nodded at the departing centurion. "You seem to have made a friend there."

Wolf shook his head. "If you had been here when we arrived you wouldn't have thought so. He was really pissed off, believe me."

"It is a pity that one got away."

"I am not so sure Flavius, it might help the Legate. The Chauci will think we are invading from this side. Of course it means we will have to face the whole Chauci nation."

"How many warriors is that then sir?"

"Well Decurion Lupus Ulpius Felix, at the last estimate it was more than thirty thousand."

Leaving a reluctant Publius to guard the camp with his turma the rest of the ala left the camp and headed south towards the Chauci stronghold. Decurion Numerius Buteo had developed over the last two years into a much wiser and far less foolhardy warrior. In addition he had become one of the best leaders of scouts and he and his handpicked turma ranged a mile ahead of the main columns which were split into two groups half a mile apart. The Prefect had reasoned, when he had briefed the officers, that this way any Chauci scouts who avoided Numerius' men would report a larger army and Herrmann would be fooled into thinking he had the main army ahead.

Deep in the forests Herrmann received the survivor's account of the events across the river and at the bridge. He had been wise to use Sura and, even though his ally was dead, even in death he had served him. If the Romans came south through the forests they would be ambushed. It was how Arminius had slaughtered Varus and his legions. They would use the trees, their allies to defeat them. Herrmann had seen how effective the legionaries could be on a flat battlefield but in the forests, where they would be outnumbered, they would not be able to use their solid ranks. He turned to his chiefs. "Bring all the people here, to this stronghold. We will leave the old men and the boys to guard them. Send the riders north to scout this Roman army and see if it has left its camp yet. Bring all the warriors to me, here. We will give the

Romans a lesson which they will never forget, we are not the women of the Frisii, we are the Chauci!"

By the next dawn thirty thousand warriors were spreading towards the bridge at Colonia Claudia. Their riders were rapidly racing through the forests looking for sign of the enemy. They all moved quickly for they were not laden down as the legionaries were with heavy armour, caligae, scutum, helmets, swords and javelins. Each man carried just his own weapons; some had bows, others had spears and shields, axes and shields or swords and shields. Some just had a sword and axe or a hammer. The keys to their success were their speed and ferocity.

Numerius had dismounted his men and they were walking through the forests keeping their profile as low as possible. They had ridden hard to get deep into the forest and then slowed down. One of the horses whinnied and the Decurion held up his hand. His men halted and each drew out his javelin. They had learned that, to be a good scout, you needed patience and stillness. They had both and were rewarded when the first Chauci scouts galloped into view. Numerius and his men had worked on hand signals and they had no need for words. The javelins left the hands of half of the turma and the first scouts fell to a silent death as their horses raced on. Quickly mounting the turma rode to where the Chauci lay dead. Two were briefly alive but the pugeo to the throat ended their pain. There were more Chauci scouts in the second band. These were the warriors who had travelled the furthest. There were thirty of them that they could see but Numerius estimated that there must be more on the flanks. This time the javelins emptied many saddles but not all and at least eight warriors rode back to their king. This time, when they mounted, Numerius took them away from the river, north; he would take his patrol in a long loop around the advancing Chauci. He waved to a trooper, "Ride back to the Prefect. Tell him there are scouts from the Chauci army and we will try to find out their position."

Back with the column the ala was gingerly making its way through the thick, heavy undergrowth. It was dark in the forest and the trees had high crowns of leaves. Marius knew that he would not have much warning of the approach of the enemy and he was relying on Numerius and the skills of his men. The trooper pulled up smartly next to him and relayed the Decurion's message. "Serjenus, signal halt." Gerjen raised and lowered the standard. The ala had all taken to the wolf standard and the bull insignia still remained wrapped in a cart. The Wolf was lucky and why tempt fate?

"Flavius, stick Wolf out front as a screen. We need early warning. Spread the rest out as lines, two men deep."

Wolf waved his men forwards and they edged towards the unseen enemy, still an unknown quantity. Wolf was aware that this was the first time he had been given the responsibility of being the vanguard and he relished it. He would not let Flavius and Marius down. He was proud to be a Roman warrior and, perversely, proud of his wounded eye. He found it did not stop him from fighting effectively and he even found that he sensed enemies from his right before he saw them. He did not know how but he suspected it was the power of the wolf token he carried. When they reached the line of dead bodies which marked the first ambush he halted his line and waved left and right. His turma spread out with Gaius, his chosen man at the furthest extremity. He would move forward when they were ready but he would only do so cautiously.

Far to the south the Chauci riders who were sent to bring in the last of the villagers brought disturbing news to Herrmann. "Great King, the Romani are coming from the south. They have the legions and the Gallic traitors."

He had been fooled by the bridge to the north! It was typical Roman cunning. "We will withdraw to the stronghold. Leave the warband of Brennus here to watch for the Romans from the bridge and take all the rest to the south. Every horseman must hide himself in the forests to the south. We can still ambush them."

Numerius reached Wolf before the Prefect. "Better halt here Wolf, there is a warband up ahead and they are waiting in ambush. I'll report to the Prefect. We have found them!"

"How many?"

He shrugged. "We counted as many as we could but it must be more than twenty thousand."

Night had fallen by the time Marius reached his vanguard. "Do we make camp sir?"

"I know we should Flavius but," he waved his hands at the trees, "this isn't the place for it. No Numerius has spotted their advanced guards and we know where they are. They are waiting for us. We will let half of the ala sleep while the other half watch and swap over after a couple of hours. I want to attack before dawn when they are cold and sleepy, having watched for us and I want to send in four turmae on foot. Let's spread a little terror in their direction eh?"

Flavius led the four turmae, Cava's, Numerius' and Wolf's. Aulus grumbled that old one eye got all the best missions but even he had to admit that they were the most effective turmae for cut throat work. They left four men from each turma holding their horses and, with just shield and swords slipped forwards. The rest of the ala were mounted and waiting with the horse holders. They had no buccina and Marius would have to rely on the noise of death to launch his attack. Numerius had told the Prefect that the enemy were fortifying the stronghold. It would be bloody work for the legions but at least it meant it would not be women and children they would be fighting but warriors.

Wolf thought he would have been more tired but he found that he was alert and every sense tingles as they slipped silently through the forest, each man watching the ground to avoid the twigs and broken branches. In the night the crack of a breaking piece of wood sounded like a crack of thunder. They moved slowly watching for the soft shapes of men hiding behind the hard outlines of the trees. Tiberius next to him tapped his shoulder and pointed. They could see the first sentry. Tiberius laid his sword and shield down and drew his pugeo which was wickedly sharp. He slid up behind the warrior and, with his hand over his mouth slit his throat and then rested the body against the tree as though he was sleeping. With his sword and shield recovered they crept further forward. Suddenly there were more bodies lying with their throats cut as Wolf found himself amongst those killed by the men on his left. He was beginning to think they would get through the Chauci lines unseen when there was a scream to his right and Spurius, the standard bearer received a sword to his leg. Titus despatched the warrior but the damage was done and the barbarians were awake. They now had to hold the line until they were reinforced. "Second Turma, shield wall!" His men fell in before the wounded Spurius.

Lucius was busy tying a bandage around the gushing wound. "Sorry sir!"

"Don't worry Spurius; we got further than I thought we would."

The barbarians threw themselves at the Romans. A bearded warrior with a bare chest and armed with a double handed axe hurled himself at Wolf, aiming the fearsome weapon at the red crest which marked him as an officer. The Decurion thrust his shield up and felt his hole arm go numb as the blade sliced a chunk out of the wood. The gladius is a stabbing weapon but the spatha held in Wolf's right hand swept around in a long arc and slicing through the left arm of the warrior. It did not stop at the bone but crunched through it. The warrior was brave but with no tendons his left hand lost the grip on the axe. As Felix pulled back his sword for a second blow he punched with the boss of his shield and the wounded warrior fell backwards. The spatha pierced his neck and Ulpius Felix looked for his next enemy. There were many of them and they were like a wasps' nest which has been disturbed. They threw themselves at the invaders. A shield wall needs integrity to hold and they had that integrity. Each trooper defended the one to their left. They were no longer the wild barbarians of the plains, they fought for their comrades and with a discipline which the Chauci, brave though they were, could not match. Suddenly they heard and felt the thunder of hooves as the rest of the ala slashed into the flanks of the wild warband.

Flavius' voice roared out, "Now push them back!"

Each trooper roared his own war cry and they punched and slashed with their swords. They were not as effective as a gladius would have been and were intended to be used on horseback but their long reached matched the axes of their enemies and soon they were climbing over the piles of the dead. "Vexillation halt!"

Flavius halted them when it became obvious that the enemy were fleeing; the few survivors were pursued by the whooping ala. The men of the four turmae took to despatching the dead and tending to the wounded.

The Prefect sought out Aulus who had been itching for some chance to have half of the honour of the others. "Aulus take your turma and circle the enemy, find the Legate and report to him."

"Yes sir. Right you fannies of the sixth disengage and follow me."

The men of the turma had come to like and respect the foul mouthed disciplinarian. "Sir, yes sir!" chorused through the forest.

To the south of the stronghold the men of the Gallic cohort had learned to respect the axes of the barbarians and, as Wolf had found out discovered that their lighter shields were no match for the sharp blades. Decimus Bucco was terrified for the Legate insisted upon keeping as close to the forward cohorts as possible. The shield and sword he had seemed inadequate somehow for the brutal world he found himself in and the sword lessons paid for by his senator father were nothing like the combats he had witnessed. The Legate turned to him. Tell the Legate of the Fifth to bring up his men. It is time we gave the auxiliaries some respite."

Delighted to be away from the death and the blood the aide raced to the legion which trudged along. "Sir, the Legate says can you take your men forward and relieve the Gauls."

"Thank you son. First Spear? Take the First cohort forward."

"About fucking time too. "First cohort. Column of fours! Double time!"

The steel behemoth moved surprisingly quickly and reached the Gallic line before Decimus had reached the Legate. "First century. Form line." The double century quickly formed a deadly shield wall."

The Legate turned to the signifier. "Sound fall back for the Gauls."

The Gallic Prefect was pleased to hear the recall; he had lost too many men already. "Disengage!"

As the Gauls fell back and slipped through the Firth which opened ranks, the Chauci thought they were retreating and that they had won. They roared forwards screaming their war cries. They ran straight into the spears of the elite First Century. Fist spear stood to the right of the line with just his gladius and shield. "Like lambs to the slaughter. Remember lads, no prisoners! Gut the bastards!" The roar told him that they were getting revenge for the attack on their comrades and they were getting it with relish! The Chauci attack soon faltered and they fell back. As they neared the stronghold Herrmann emerged with his last ten thousand warriors, his reserves who were both fresh and ferocious.

Corbulo saw in an instant that he could deploy his two legions in the classic style side by side. He turned to the cavalrymen next to him. "I want the two legions next to each other and tell the Gallic Prefect to split his men and defend the flanks of the legions."

The highly trained legions quickly deployed although the Prefect was less than happy about having to move his men so far. They had just made it when the huge warband struck. This time they had built up momentum and they hit in a solid mass. They may not have been shoulder to shoulder but they had weight, bulk and most importantly, anger. The front ranks of the two legions were forced back a few paces. Bucco was almost cowering, terrified behind the legate but he could hear the centurions urging the men to stand. Their voices and their hectoring worked and the lines stabilised. It now became a battle between two lines. The Romans had their shields for protection and they stabbed through any gap to gut, slash and hamstring the Chauci but the barbarians had weight of numbers and weight of weapons. The warriors who wielded the two handed hammers shatter shields and arms, causing gaps to appear. The Roman lines began, inexorably to move backwards. The Chauci who had retreated now rejoined their comrades and the numbers were swollen. Gradually the Gauls on the flanks began to take casualties and were squeezed in.

Corbulo himself began to worry that he might lose the battle when suddenly a wail of despair came from the Chauci right flank the Gauls managed to push their enemies back. "What is it Tribune?"

The Tribune who was taller peered in the distance and then turned with a joyous expression on his face. "It is the ala, they have charged the flank."

Marius and his ala were in two long lines and savagely slashing and hacking into the backs of the Chauci. They had nowhere to go and were hemmed in by the Gauls, their fellows and the legions.

They could not turn and fight and they were slaughtered by the troopers who could not believe that they had got so close before they were detected. The legionaries felt the easing of pressure and the centurions roared their orders, "Push!"

The Chauci tried to hold but, as the ones at the back, who could, fled it was like a dam being burst and all semblance of order went. The Roman lines kept coming forwards scything down any brave enough to stand. Corbulo punched his fist with glee. "We have them! Now Germania Inferior is safe!"

By the time the prisoners had been tied to each other and the wounded despatched, the men of the ala were exhausted. They had been victorious but it had been at a cost. Thirty of their troopers lay dead whilst another five would never fight again. They could fight, as Wolf did without an eye but arms and legs were more vital to a soldier than the ability to see. Even Corbulo was forced to grudgingly praise the efforts of the ala although he did so with ill grace.

"I believe my orders were to catch any refugees who fled north weren't they Prefect?"

The Gallic Prefect and the Legate of the Fifth both rolled their eyes but Marius shrugged, "Technically sir we obeyed orders. We had the stronghold surrounded but I took the opportunity of aiding my auxiliary brothers."

"For which we are in your debt Prefect."

Corbulo sniffed, "Well I suppose we had better start back for Colonia Claudia. Oh I forgot to mention that is to be my new headquarters. Much better than the disease ridden one we left. The Fifteenth will remain here with me."

If he thought the other three commanders would be upset he did not see the smiles as he left with the green faced Bucco.

Chapter 8

Decurion Lupus Ulpius Felix looked back on the last two years with satisfaction. Since the Legate had shifted his headquarters up the river to Colonia Claudia life had become much easier for the ala. The Fifth, the Gauls and the Pannonians worked well together having shared in the hardest fighting against the Chauci. Without the Legate's beady eye they were able to interpret his orders in creative ways. They used the appropriate skills for the task so that when they were asked to finally subjugate the Frisii the auxiliaries cleared the enemy whilst the Legion built the forts and then the Gauls took over the garrisons. The land of the Frisii was pacified within months and with barely a casualty on each side. The Navarchus was happy to ferry over the ala to conduct long ranging patrols in the land which took them as far as the borders to the north. Had he known, the Emperor Claudius would have been happy that the Empire and its influence was expanding north. The Emperor, however, had his own problems. The rumours which reached the frontier was that there were many plots against Claudius' life and many enemies had been purged. To Wolf it did not matter, he was happy performing his job. He missed the action which had been so intense a bare two years ago but he had settled into a routine with his men.

Felix had learned the lessons of the various combats he had fought. All of the officers had noticed that the spatha was only a useful weapon whilst mounted and on foot could become more difficult to use. The ala began to learn how to fight on foot. In this the Gauls proved most useful as they were magnificent swordsmen. Wolf became close to one of the centurions, Vexus Cilo. The Second Turma had managed to rescue Cilo and his men from a Chauci ambush the previous year and a friendship had formed.

"The problem with this Roman equipment Lupus, is that it is made for one purpose. In my case the gladius is a stabbing weapon. It works well in a shield wall, the way the legions fight but sometimes we don't fight like that which is why my men have a longer sword we can use. Why don't you carry a gladius as well?"

"The weight Vexus."

The Gaul had laughed, "You have a bloody great horse don't you? Put a scabbard on the saddle for your spatha and carry a gladius on your baldric."

When he found it worked, he then spent hours with the centurion honing his skills with the short Spanish sword. It required different skills. "You see you need to stab with this. It is short so you can strike upwards and it is wider than your spatha so when you cut it causes nasty injuries, far worse than your long swords. Remember most of these barbarians have no armour. When we fight men with armour it is much harder."

Ulpius Felix had laughed. "It doesn't seem that long ago we were the barbarians, what was it Decurion Spurius called us, 'hairy arsed barbarians'? Well he was right. If I rode into my village they wouldn't recognise me."

"You never go back. I did once and it was hard. The filth and the dirt… you get used to clean clothes, baths, water you can drink. And when you do go back the ones who remain look at you as though you are a leper or someone who has betrayed them. No we have made our beds now."

"Well I am happier here than I was at home."

The ala would have happily finished their tour in Germania Inferior had events in Britannia not caused a huge change and upheaval. Caractacus had been captured after the Queen of the Brigante had handed him over to her allies. Her protection had been ensured but her husband, Venutius had tried to take over her throne and the ala was needed to bolster the troops which were stretched too thinly across the new wild frontier. The Legate did not bring the orders himself but sent the unpopular Bucco. Marius had remembered his look at the battle and now, the smug self satisfied look was gone when the aide faced the three Prefects and Legate Labeo. He looked less self assured and was more hesitant.

"The Legate is pleased with the work you have done and it is now time for the Fist Pannonians to aid Governor Gallus and subjugate Britannia. You will sail with the Classis Germania to

Rutupiae and then travel north to Lindum where you will support the Ninth Hispana in their new campaign."

As soon as he had scurried away Labeo voiced the opinion of all of them, "Prick! We'll be sorry to see you go Marius and we will miss your horsemen."

"I know sir. It seems a mistake to take away the only cavalry in this region but at least we will be working with the Ninth and six of my officers served with them."

The Gallic Prefect was less sure. "Without your horse we can patrol less of the land and without the patrols who knows what the bastards are up to?" When the Batavi revolted some years later the Gaul's words were proved prophetic; not that it did him much good as his body was hacked to pieces as he defended his standard.

As they sailed west they were all sharing a mixture at regret in leaving somewhere they had become comfortable mixed with the excitement of action and the pleasure of being reunited with some old friends. The journey across the Oceanus Germanicus was short but it was far from pleasant. None of the Pannonians had ever seen the sea before and the storm clouds on the day they left meant that they felt as though they were sailing towards the end of the world. The pitching of the ships made them all ill, much to the delight of the marines and sailors on board. As they sailed past the white cliffs which marked the river and the entrance to the port of Rutupiae they all vowed that they would die in Britannia rather than risk the voyage back; sadly their wish came true. The fort at Rutupiae was the strongest in Britannia and they had to spend a night there for their horses to recover and for Marius to be briefed by the Camp Prefect. There were maps to be copied and equipment to be replaced. This was further north than Germania and the Prefect had a wicked smile when he issued the extra blankets. "Believe me Prefect. Your men will need these. I have never been in such a cold country and you will be further north. It either snows or rains almost every day!"

Marius spent the latter part of the day briefing all of the officers. "We head towards Londinium here along the Via Claudia. It will the busiest road we travel along but there are plenty of places along it to gather any supplies we need. From Londinium we head north. The Via Claudia travels west and we go on the road they are calling Fossa Lindum but the Prefect told me the soldiers call it the Via Hades." He gave a wry smile. "I think we can work out what that will be like."

"What about the tribes then sir?"

"Well most of them are happy little bunnies with villas and baths. In fact the Iceni king, Prasutagus, is a big fan of ours, just like Cartimandua. Once we get to Lindum then we can expect trouble. The Brigantes have a Queen, Cartimandua, she is an ally of the Emperor. Met him apparently and she likes all things Rome. Her husband, Venutius, sees himself, according to the Prefect as the new Caractacus. You know the hero who will rid his land of the Romans. He is busy trying to remove his wife and then raise the Brigantes against us."

"What sort of troops do they have over here?"

"Much like the Gauls. They like long swords, they don't wear much armour, they have horses but they are a bit small and ,oh yes, you will like this they still use chariots and some of them have scythes along the wheels."

Decurion Aulus Murgus snorted, "If they are anything like the ones we encountered in the east they are easy to avoid. They can't turn and they won't have armour to protect them. Bring them on!"

The officers all laughed. They had grown into each other and accepted the foibles and character traits of their peers. "We shouldn't have any problems until we reach Lindum. That is the end of the province although, as I said, the Brigantes are our allies and their land is a buffer for us."

"Who is further north sir?"

"Good question Felix. The Carvetii, that is the tribe of Venutius and after that they are the Pictii. Blue painted barbarians who terrify even the natives."

"Just like being at home then?"

"Except that we don't speak their language. I know the lads did well with learning Roman but we need to speak with the Brigante. The Prefect suggested we hire a Brigante scout who can teach us the language."

The Prefect was right and they made excellent time as they travelled north. They camped north of Londinium which gave

Marius and Flavius the opportunity of observing the land through which they travelled. "It looks like flat farmland."

"It does sir. I am surprised that they haven't sent us here earlier. It is perfect cavalry country. Better than the swamps of Germania."

"I think Corbulo hung on to us as long as possible. Despite what he said to our faces I heard he took all the credit for our successes."

"He was a prick."

"When you have survived in this army as long as I have you will find out that good senior officers are few and far between. Apparently even Caesar was a bit of a bastard and he could waste men's lives needlessly."

"Aye but at least he fought with his men."

"True. I don't think Corbulo was a coward. He never flinched when the Chauci got close to him."

Back in the camp Gerjen and Wolf were comparing the land of Britannia with Germania and Pannonia. "I tell you what Wolf, it is green. Have you ever seen such a green country? And the farms?"

Gerjen had grown up since becoming aquilifer. He was not a leader but he was fiercely loyal and, for him, the standard represented his friend Wolf. When Wolf had lost his eye Gerjen had prayed that he would not have to leave the army; he did not know what he would do without his friend.

"But the towns Gerjen. They look like proper towns and we have only been here for ten years. The Romans conquered our land over fifty years ago and it hasn't changed. I guess the people here must like the idea of Rome. Perhaps our job will be an easy one again."

Sextus Vatia wandered over, having heard them. "I heard that the tribes in the south already had much trade with Rome and they had their ideas. They didn't take much conversion not the tribes to the west, I have heard they still have druids."

Wolf shook his head, "Vexus told me about them. They are like our shaman but armed to the teeth and he said that they had them in Gaul. They used to sacrifice any prisoners they got to their gods. Sometimes they put their prisoners in wicker baskets and burned them alive." He shivered. "Vexus was a brave warrior but he was scared shitless of the druids."

"They are so tough that there are two legions the Twentieth and the Second trying to contain them. The Ninth have the rest of the country to control. I don't think this will be as easy as the fight against the Frisii."

"Yeah but at least we can ride here. I haven't seen a hill yet."

"Me neither and look to the east, the land is so flat it looks like you could walk back to Germania."

It was, indeed, a monotonously flat horizon and featureless land which oozed east and the next day it became, if anything, even more monotonous. Wolf was slightly disappointed. This had all the signs of being a boring posting where they would be policemen rather than warriors. He brightened up when, four days later they reached Lindum, the fortress of the Ninth. It was a frontier camp with no sign of stone to be seen anywhere. The ditches were deep and the sentries keen eyed. "That looks a good spot for a camp Flavius. I will see if there are any familiar faces in the fort and find out our orders."

The Camp Prefect was a new man for the old one had retired with Bulbus. He had every indication that he had been a centurion who was seeing out his time in a comfortable job although from the scars on his arms he had been a brave man. "Appius Graccus. I remember when you picked your men up in Pannonia. I take it they survived?"

"Yes we had some interesting times but I wouldn't swap them."

"Well you have come at the right time. We have a new Legate Quintus Petillius Cerialis. His brother Caesius Nasica was the one who defeated Venutius last year. He is out with the Tribune and the First Cohort doing a patrol of the region. Visiting Stanwyck to meet the Queen."

"The Queen?"

"Cartimandua. She is the real power in this land. Her support means we didn't have to fight the Brigante. They are a real threat but, so long as she rules then we won't need to fight them but it is a huge land and your lads are going to have to cover a huge area. That is why you were summoned. You will be the only cavalry. The other auxiliary force is the First Tungrians.

They came from the land you were just stationed in, close to the Rhenus."

"Thank you for that update. It will help. I have my Decurion Princeps building a camp."

"The Legate will tell you where you will be based; I suspect it won't be here. We have few soldiers in the fort. Most are spread out in smaller forts. We just need to control them here. They are peaceful, generally. Anything else I can do for you?"

Marius smiled; the Camp Prefect was dismissing him, politely of course. "Well I wondered if you had a Brigante we could use as a scout and translator."

"Not sure, but there is a Decurion in the infirmary who might be able to help. He worked with some of the scouts in the campaign. Decurion Spurius Ocella."

Marius brightened. "Spurius? I know him."

"Good that will make things easier."

Spurius was lying in a bed with a bandaged leg. Marius heard him complaining before he reached the room; the orderly was being berated by the sharp-tongued veteran. "I told you before dick head. I don't want the gnat's piss the locals drink I want a decent amphora of wine from home. If you can't get it then some of the muck from Gaul will do."

"Still making friends and influencing people I see."

The orderly gratefully fled and Spurius smiled. "Still alive then sir? I take it the bastards didn't knife you then?"

"No Decurion. They turned out to be good lads. They did well."

"Must be the training sir." His grim face softened. "I'm glad sir. The Tribune told me your story...there are some bastards out there."

"How is the Tribune?"

"Happier here. We gave the Brigante a good kicking and this is lovely cavalry country. The grass is good for the horses not that stuff in Pannonia. He is with the new Legate."

"What happened to you?"

"One of the Legate's aides, a bit of a dickhead if you ask me, well this Gaius Cresens sees a Brigante and instead of waiting for the order to attack he leaps straight towards him. His horse crashed into mine and I broke my leg." He raised his voice. "And

110

I thought I would have a nice rest here but the dick heads can't even get some decent wine."

"Don't worry, I'll send over Decurion Vatia with one later."

The invalid's face brightened. "They still in then?"

"Aye, all of them. They'll see you later. Now I need a scout and the Prefect thought that you might be able to help."

He nodded, "He'll mean Osgar. A good lad. He can run all day and keep up with the horses but the new legate didn't take to him. He said we didn't need the locals; couldn't trust 'em." He leaned over, "You can trust this lad, believe me."

"Your recommendation is enough for me. Where will I find him?"

"He has a hut by the stream about a mile north of the fort. He likes hunting. Tell him I sent you."

"He can speak our language?"

"Aye, not well but he can understand most words. But the most important thing is he is like a bloodhound; can track over rocks, through water. How he does it I have no idea."

The camp was taking shape when he returned. "Flavius take charge. When they have finished let Sextus and Quintus go to the fort with an amphora of that wine we brought. Spurius Ocella is in the infirmary and is pissed off." He lowered his voice. "See if he can find out about this new general and the other officers. We are going to be working closely with them. It would be handy if they were as accommodating as the Fifth."

"Yes sir."

"Can you spare Wolf?"

"Yes sir why?"

"Thought he could come with me to meet our new scout. I'd like him to get a little more responsibility. When the older lads, Quintus, Publius and Aulus retire we will need another senior decurion. Can you think of anyone better?"

"No sir I reckon if you cut him he would bleed First Ala. But isn't it a long time of retirement?"

"Publius keeps really good records. His enlistment is up next year, they are offering land down near Camulodunum. He would be a fool not to take it. This looks to be as civilised a place as I have seen outside of Rome. Aulus and Sextus have another three years."

"They might want to re-enlist. I do."

"I know Flavius and you will be the next Prefect so taking Wolf is just getting ready for the future and whoever is the senior Decurion will need to speak the local language for that is where our next recruits are coming from."

"Right sir, and sir?"

"Yes Flavius?"

"Thanks for explaining!"

"Wolf. Get your horse we are going for a ride."

"How's the eye these days?"

"I don't even notice now sir?"

"Don't lie to me Decurion. I have seen you rubbing it, especially on bright days."

"It won't be a problem sir. The grass around here is so green it must ain the whole time."

"You could be right but why don't you wear the patch?"

"I don't know sir. It's like the patch means I am ashamed of my wound and I'm not."

"And how do you like this army."

"I am glad I joined sir."

"Well so am I and the Decurion Princeps thinks highly of you too."

Ulpius Felix did not take praise well. Praise was for others. He stared at the land around him, the road north was new, he could see it was not word at all and it cut line a burn mark though the green fields. Even the roads at home had been worn. This was the real frontier and yet it looked so peaceful. "Where are we off to then sir?"

"Always impatient eh? We might just be enjoying the scenery."

Wolf laughed, "Sir we never enjoy the scenery. The scenery is just stuff hiding the bastards who want to kill us."

"You may have a point. We are seeking a scout. Just ahead there should be a hut."

"I can see it sir."

"You may only have one eye Decurion but it works. Come on let's see if he is at home."

The hut was little more than willow branches covered with a couple of deer hides. There was no sign of the occupant but there was a pile of smoking ash. They dismounted and walked around calling. "Ho, the camp."

No-one answered. Marius wandered over to the ashes. He was about to kick them with his foot when Wolf stopped him. "Don't do that sir?"

Curious the Prefect asked, "Why not Decurion?"

"Well first off it will piss off the warrior in the bushes who is aiming his bow at you and secondly it will spoil the food."

"What man? What food?"

The warrior suddenly appeared, the bow by his side. "The young one is right. It would annoy me and it would spoil my food." Wolf grinned at the expression on Proculus' face. "You are new Romans. Are you from the fort?"

"Yes we have just arrived." The man put down his bow and then began scraping the ashes away. "Decurion Spurius Ocella sent us."

The man began to dig at the burnt earth with his dagger. "How is his leg? Is he still as bad tempered?"

Marius was so intrigued that he almost didn't answer. "Er yes he is and he is getting better. We hoped that you might scout for us. What are you doing?"

Wolf answered for the man who shook his head at the stupidity of the Romans who could build fine roads and buildings but could not survive in the wild. "He is digging up the meat he put there to cook slowly. We do the same in Pannonia."

"I knew you were not Brigante." He held out his arm, "I am Osgar."

"And I am Decurion Lupus Ulpius Felix."

The Brigante put his head to one side and said, "That is a Roman name. You are a wolf."

Both Wolf and the Prefect stepped back. "How did..."

"Tell me Osgar, he was called Wolf, but how did you know?"

"He has the lean and hungry look of an animal which takes what it wants and I saw the charm around his neck."

Somewhat relieved they relaxed. "Well will you scout for us?"

"We will eat first and then I will decide." As he unwrapped the rabbit from the bark he nodded at Wolf. "Him I like, you I am not sure yet. You smell too clean."

Bemused the Prefect sat down and they shared the rabbit which literally fell from the bone. "At home we put dried plums in with it."

"If I had had them I would have put them in too. It is still good though."

"Oh yes still good."Wolf gave him a sly grin, "It just could be better."

"I will not bathe Roman and I sleep out of the fort."

"That is not a problem. And pay?"

"If I need something I will ask."

"Right well, I suppose I will get back to the fort. We will be riding tomorrow."

"I'll be there." He looked at Wolf. "I will talk more with you then Wolf."

As they rode back to the fort the Prefect shook his head. He was not certain who had offered who a job there. "One thing is obvious Decurion. He will be attached to your turma!"

They had a whole six days to make the camp comfortable and to begin to build wooden barracks. Their time in Germania Inferior had shown them the benefits of a roof which kept out rain. Osgar took Wolf and the other officers on a tour of the surrounding land. Even Aulus Murgus was impressed at the speed with which he could run. He took them to within twenty miles of the hills which rose in the west. The others found it amusing that, even when Flavius was with them Osgar would insist upon speaking to Wolf as though the others were unnecessary. "Those hills run the length of the country. To the north I have never seen their end and to the south," he shrugged as though it was not important for it was not the land of the Brigante/

"Who lived around here? The Brigante?" They had all noticed that there were fewer farms.

"No, it was the Corieltavi. They live no longer."

"Who killed them? Did our people, the Romans do it?"

"Some yes but the Brigante killed them when they tried to attack our people. They thought that, because we had a Queen we were weak." He grinned. "They found that we were not. Out Queen is a warrior queen. She can fight as men do. She can drive a four-horse chariot. Were it not for her tits she would be a man."

114

They all laughed and Osgar affected a hurt expression. "They mean no offence Osgar. I look forward to meeting the Queen."

"That you will not do. She lives far to the north. If we had to go to her then it would mean that she was in great danger. No, she is safe. The snake Venutius sits in the land of the Carvetii and licks his wounds but you and your men will have to kill him one day. Until he is dead there will be no peace in my land."

The Legate arrived with the Tribune and his turma of cavalry. Marius was supervising the deepening of the ditches and he looked up. "That is strange Flavius. I had heard that he had taken a cohort of infantry with him. I wonder where they are?"

His question was answered when he was summoned to the fort for a meeting. The Tribune Gnaeus greeted him at the gate. "Good to see you Marius. Spurius has been telling me all that you have done." The Prefect gave him a puzzled look, "His old comrades have been singing your praises and the other men you have promoted. You have an interesting collection of warriors there."

"And you Gnaeus how is life treating you?"

"This is good cavalry country. I have long been asking the Legates for your ala and luckily our new man is a cavalryman and he sent for you immediately."

"I thought he had a cohort with him."

He lowered his voice conspiratorially, "He will tell you of course, but he left them in the north. Venutius is flexing his muscles again. His defeat by the Legate's brother was some time ago and he has forgotten the lesson. We are going to campaign in the north while the weather is good and then we will winter in camps. They are harsh winters here."

Legate Cerialis was a cavalryman at heart but his family connections meant that he was too high status to command an ala of auxiliaries and a turma of regular cavalry did not give him the numbers he wished to command. He longed for the time of Caesar when Caesar's cavalry commanders had controlled thousands of warriors. At least he now had an ala to command. It was a start. His elder brother had begun the defeat of the rebels such as Venutius and he would finish it. He looked again at the map. Venutius had brought his army to the south of the Queen's hill fort at Stanwyck. He knew that he had placed it on

115

the high moors so that he could strike in any direction. To the south west lay Deva and the Silures tribe. There the Twentieth Valeria was hard pushed to control them. If Venutius joined the Silures then the Twentieth would cease to exist. Equally they could also attack Lindum. His Legion was the only force between the Brigante and the soft hinterland of the Province. The Catuvellauni and the Iceni were pacified but they had not turned their swords into plough shares. They were becoming Roman, far quicker than the Emperor would have hoped but they were no yet converted. The only bright spot was the veterans who were retiring just north of Londinium. They would provide a stable core of hard working men who would resist change.

There was a knock on the door. "Come."

The Tribune entered, "This is Prefect Marius Ulpius Proculus."

The Legate beamed, "Delighted. You cannot believe how long I have waited for some cavalry. The Tribune here does his best but one hundred and twenty men are hardly an army." Marius felt his friend bristle next to him. "How many men do you have then Prefect?"

"We have thirty Turmae and most have thirty two men including Decurion and aquilifer. We have no ancillary staff such as blacksmith and cooks. But we normally do not need them as we share the facilities of whichever legion we are near. By the same token we have no clerical staff. My officers double up on most of the duties normally performed by civilians."

"That won't do. You will not be stationed close to the Ninth. When we have dealt with Venutius you will divide you ala into two halves and each one will have their own fort. I intend to control this province by the use of small forts. The Ninth has already done so. There will be just one cohort here at Lindum. However, that is for the future. I will get my aide to deal with that whilst we are on campaign. Make sure you have all the equipment you need. We will not be able to be supplied on the road." He laughed, "For a start where we are going there is no road. And you and your men will have to range far and wide to find this elusive Venutius."

Chapter 9

As they rode at the head of the column heading for the Tungrian Cohort and the three cohorts of the Ninth, the Prefect discussed how best to organise the ala into two halves. "My thoughts, Flavius, are to give one to you and I will take the other. Wed divide the other five troopers from the Ninth so that I have three and you have two and then divide the new officers and turmae up."

"That would work sir but why divide us at all. We are the only cavalry; it would have made sense to use us as one large group. We could split up as and when we were needed. If we had met the Chauci in the woods with half the men we would have lost."

"I know Flavius but the Legate's aide gave me the written orders before we left." Marius had not liked the pompous young man. Perhaps it was something to do with aides. Gaius Cresens was different from Decimus Bucco but he had the same effect on the Prefect. He had a pudgy soft face and looked as though he might be inclined to fat. As with all aides he seemed to exude an undeserved superiority. The Tribune had told him that Cresens fani8ly had been friends of the Legate's and they had fallen on hard times. As much as Marius sympathised with his family's plight it did not make his conversations with the young man any more palatable. He dismissed the odious man from his mind. As long as he did his job and found a smith, a clerk and a couple of cooks he would be happy.

They were heading for the hills which rose steeply towards the west. They were hardly mountains although Marius could see the steep and rocky sections which would be impassable to all but mountain goats. The smoke from the fires of the legion and the auxiliaries marked their destination. At least there were no mighty rivers like the Rhenus. It looked like his men would be able to cross all the rivers they had seen by swimming for they were less than fifty paces wide. At least their experience against the Chauci would stand them in good stead.

Cerialis gestured him forwards, "You get your men to build a camp over there, close to the river. You will need an early night for I want your two wings to spread out and find me the Brigante."

Marius would have to rely on Osgar and his knowledge of the land which meant that it would be Decurion Lupus Ulpius Felix who would have to take the point and, despite the Legate's intentions, they would have to stay within close proximity.

Wolf and Gerjen were staring to the west. "It looks different from anything I have ever seen before."

"I know Gerjen. The Allfather has made all the lands different. The Prefect told me that there are lands to the south of the Roman sea which are made up of nothing but sand, no grass, no water, just sand."

"What do horses eat?"

"I know not but he told me they have a beast there called a camel which is bigger than a horse and carries its water inside it on its back and they have another beast which is taller than the gatehouse at the fort and it has two mighty teeth and a long snake coming from its head and it can crush men."

Had it been anyone but Wolf telling him this then Gerjen would have doubted the words but the Prefect and Wolf did not lie. The world they lived in was strange indeed. "I hope there are none of those beasts here."

Wolf nodded his agreement. He pointed to the tendril of smoke coming from beyond the fort, close by the river. "If there are any then Osgar will smell them out."

"He is a strange one but I like him. He reminds me of the shaman from the village."

Wolf suddenly remembered the old shaman. "You are right I had forgotten him. Yes and he seems to have the same ability to see into the mind." He told him about the Wolf and Gerjen looked up proudly at the Wolf standard which he had made and carried still.

It was dark when they dismantled the camp. Marius and Flavius stood with Wolf and Horse. "You need to sweep the land before us and spot the enemy before they spot you. Wolf will have Osgar and that may give us an advantage. If you see the enemy then send a man here and trail them."

118

Cava looked troubled. "I am sorry sir but if these Brigantes are dressed like Wolf's scout they will see us with all this red, a long time before we see them."

"I know Decurion but this is not the forests of Germania and I do not think that we are in as much danger of ambush."

"Yes sir." As they left to join their men Horse rolled his eyes heavenward. "That is the trouble with this army, not flexible enough."

"Don't worry old friend. My Osgar will sniff them out believe me."

Osgar trotted ahead of Wolf like a dog. He would pause and look at the ground and then shake his head. He took them, not up the faintest of trails but across the rough moor land. Behind him Wolf hear Gaius cursing. "Don't worry Gaius we will find them."

"I am more worried about my horse breaking a leg."

"You know that won't happen."

By mid morning they had ascended one side of the hills. Osgar had kept them below the sky line. He came over to Wolf. "Leave your horse and come with me." He grinned, "That is, if a wolf can walk on two legs."

"Gaius, take over. I won't be long."

Osgar pushed him to the ground when they were thirty paces from the top and they slithered forwards on their bellies. Osgar tapped the Decurion's helmet and Wolf took it off. It annoyed him for the straps were tight but he also recognised that it made sense. They moved forwards in minute movements until just their eyes peered over. At first Wolf saw nothing then Osgar directed his head to the north and west and he detected movement. He kept watching and, what Wolf had taken to be the shadow of a cloud moving across the moor tops became clearer and he could see it was men. They had found the enemy. He was about to slither back down when Osgar grabbed his hand. He pointed and there a mile away and just riding up to the ridge top he could see flashes of red. It was Cava. His first thought was to shout a warning for, once he rode to the top of the ridge he would be seen and the enemy army was less than six hundred yards from him.

As they slid down Osgar said, "They will get him. Your friend is dead."

Racing back to his horse Wolf shouted, "You don't know my friend. Tiberius, ride back to the column and warn the Legate, the Brigantes are over the rise. "Tiberius needed no urging and galloped off. "Titus, you stay with Osgar and watch the army, let me know it they change direction." He leapt on his horse and fastened his helmet.

"What are we doing then sir?"

"We are going to save the Decurion from being slaughtered by the Brigantes he is there." Wolf pointed towards the hidden ridge and he galloped off his turma trailing in his wake.

Osgar looked up at Titus. "Take your helmet off!"

"Decurion Paterculus!"

"Yes Lucius?"

"Barbarians, fucking hundreds of them over the other side of the ridge." The terrified young trooper had been on point and even as he reported Cava saw the Brigante horsemen screaming over the ridge.

"Retreat, back to the column. Drusus you take the lead." The Chosen Man galloped off head held low over his horse's neck. Cava slid his shield around to cover most of his back. He did not know if they had bows or if they were any good with them but he would take no chances. He too rode low to his horse and when something pinged from his shield he knew that they did have arrows. He risked a glance over his shoulder and saw that there were almost a hundred of them on fast little ponies and they were now gaining on them. To his horror he saw Sextus, one of the older warriors suddenly pitch over his horse's head as it caught a rabbit hole. The sharp crack told the Decurion that one of his men had gone to the Allfather. Now the arrows were striking closer and a glance told the Pannonian that they would be caught before they could reach the column. He stared ahead, desperate for some refuge. He saw a cleft of rocks. It would give them somewhere to make a stand. "Drusus! Head for the rocks." He saw Drusus peer ahead and then wave his acknowledgment. "Get ready lads when we reach the rocks turn and throw a javelin. They might not expect that." He wondered if they did have a chance, if every javelin struck home they would win but that assumed that the

Brigante would just be taking casualties and not inflicting them. The trooper next to him fell from the saddle with an arrow in his leg. Cava turned and saw a tattooed and blue painted grinning warrior raising his bow to loose an arrow at him. He took his javelin and hurled it, more in desperation and hope than expectation but he was so close that the javelin plucked him from his saddle and there was daylight once more. He saw that the others had turned and had formed a mounted shield wall. He reined back hard and his horse almost pirouetted to join the right of the line. He saw a line of warriors hurtling down towards them. They were so close that the Romans would only get one javelin off each and then it would be close quarters.

"Ready! Loose!"

Twenty five saddles emptied. "Draw spatha!" The long swords came out and the two lines of horses collided. The rocks behind prevented the Romans from being bowled over but it was close in work. As Cava took the head from a warrior he reflected that their only advantage was the fact that these warriors did not use armour or shields. Any wound would be deadly. As two more men fell he wondered how long they would last and then he saw to his surprise the man before him fall with a javelin in his back and then he realised that there were Romans attacking the rear of the line. They were brave men but they stood little chance and the final twenty raced back up the hill.

Cava saw Wolf grinning at him. "Thought you needed a hand."

"Where did you come from?

"We saw them from below the ridge but they didn't see us. Titus and Osgar are watching them. I think we had better follow the Legate's orders then and watch them."

"What about them?" Cava pointed to the departing Brigante.

"We can head parallel with the ridge and then head up. My man should have made the column. The Prefect will reach us soon."

As they reached Osgar and Titus they could see that the enemy warband had turned to climb the ridge. The two officers could see that they did it fast quicker than a Roman army could have done so. It arrived disordered but the general, they presumed it was Venutius, arrayed his forces along the ridge.

"Look! Chariots!"

They could see a handful of chariots on the flanks with a milling mass of horsemen. The general was not willing to give up the high ground. Both Wolf and Cava knew that the impetus gained by charging downhill was immeasurable, and the chariots would travel even faster. "What do we do when they see us?"

"Good question Decurion Felix. If we follow our orders then we continue to watch them."

Wolf looked to their left where the ground. It looked to be rocky and difficult for cavalry. "If we go down there then they can outflank us with the cavalry and their infantry pick us off. If we cross the ridge, well we are cut off and if we go down there then they will be between us and the ala."

"We are literally between a rock and a hard place. Are there any ideas to get us out of here flitting around that young mind of yours?"

Wolf grinned and suddenly looked like the young boy who had joined up years before. "If we go back the way we came then they will charge after us and try to cut us off."

"So far this plan is not filling me with optimism."

"Bear with me. If we are going down the slope then we will have the same advantage that their horsemen do and we know that the Prefect will be bringing the ala and the army. We can lead them into a trap."

"There are a lot of ifs and maybes in that plan. Suppose the Legate brings the ala at the same speed as the foot."

"Then we are screwed." Wolf waved along the ridgeline. "This is not Germania with forests and river barriers. If anything it is a greener version of home. We have nowhere to hide and we are outnumbered."

"You are right and what about Osgar?"

"Osgar can answer for himself." Sniffed the Brigante scout. "You go back to your army and I will join you there."

"He will be there Cava."

"Right Pannonians, column of twos. Decurion Felix, bring up the rear. You have the best horse."

Wolf grinned. "Don't worry about me. Remember my name! I am lucky!"

The line set off at a steady trot down the slope at an oblique angle to the Brigante. As they had both expected the cavalry and the chariots set off to cut them off. At the rear Wolf could see how quickly they moved the small wheels bouncing off the ground. The men in the chariots were skilled drivers, he could see that. They began to move ahead of the horses and Wolf could see no blades on the wheels; it had been a thought which had terrified him. He felt as strongly about Blackie, his horse as he did about his men and he did not want her legs ripped to shreds. He hoped that Marius and Flavius had left the column as soon as they had received the message for the main army was at least two miles behind them. Suddenly arrows began to fly, somewhat erratically, from the chariots. He saw one of Cava's men fall from his horse as his horse was struck. The rocky slope was littered with death traps for anyone who fell and the trooper died. The same rocks which killed the cavalryman saved Wolf and those at the back as the chariots had to veer to their left to avoid them. It bought them time and that was their most precious defence.

At the head of the column Cava was trying to pick the quickest and safest route down the hillside. He saw that it bottomed out into a natural bowl and he headed for it. The line meant he had to travel a little close to the front of the Brigante riders but as they were coming from the left it gave them the best protection for they carried their shields on their left arms. The chariots at the front began to loose their arrows and soon there was a regular crack and ping as they struck helmets and shields. An occasional cry told Cava that a leg or arm had been struck but, glancing over his shoulder he saw that there was still just one casualty. As soon as he reached the bowl he veered left and he hoped that the chariot drivers would be slower to react. As he flicked a glance over his shoulder he saw that he was wrong; they skilfully tugged on the reins and the bowman leaned to one side to facilitate the turn. The Decurion's horse was tiring and he wondered if they ought to turn and fight as they had done before, but all there was before him was a slight slope at the other side of the natural bowl. Perhaps the slight slope would slow up the chariots. He would have to see what the land was like on the other side of the rise. Suddenly he saw a flicker of red which appeared and then disappeared. He wondered if his eyes were deceiving him and then the red became an uneven line and the ala appeared in a long line over the ridge. He glanced behind and saw that the Brigantes had slowed up. They, too, were forming a line.

"Ride through the ala and reform behind." He saw Flavius and Marius at the front and they had left a gap wide enough for the column to pass through. As he approached he grinned and shouted, "Couldn't wait for you sir. Thought we would bring them to you!"

He saw Flavius grinning although the Prefect was checking their line. As he slowed to rejoin the line he saw the main army about a mile away lumbering along. At the same time he hear, "Javelins!"

Marius and the ala outnumbered the horse and the chariots, but not by much and the speed the Brigante had built up meant that they would hit the Pannonians at some speed. "Make gaps to let the chariots go through. Aim for the horses!" Suddenly they met with a mighty class of metal on wood as javelins were hurled and arrows loosed. The Brigante charioteers aimed their horses at the ala which quickly found that they were fighting for their lives. Wolf and his men had rejoined the line and four chariots emerged through the gaps at them. Tiberius fell with an arrow in his throat and Wolf hurled his javelin at the driver. The archer had slung his bow to aim at Wolf but the driverless chariot hit a rock and the man was catapulted into the air while the chariot crashed into the next one spilling the driver and the archer. Wolf hung low in his saddle and swung the spatha back. The archer was turning with his bow when the blade sliced upwards to split him from the crotch to the throat. He wheeled the horse around just as the charioteer had bravely pulled his dagger out to continue to fight. His defence soon ended. Wolf glanced up at the line of troopers. It was still holding. Just then he heard the thunder of hooves on the turf behind him as the Tribune rode up with his turma. As he rode by Spurius winked at Wolf. "Still lucky eh son?"

Gnaeus Celsus halted his troopers. "Form line!" He kicked his horse to stand next to Marius and Gerjen who were behind the

124

front rank. "Well done Marius. The Legate wants you to split your ala and protect the flanks. He is sending the foot sloggers to attack up the middle."

"Attack uphill?"

"Don't worry the barbarians will break themselves against the Ninth. I have seen it before. I will take the right flank."

"I will send Flavius there. Decurion Princeps, on my command take turmae fifteen to thirty to the right flank." He turned in his saddle. "Felix, Paterculus on my command take command of the left flank with Turmae one to fourteen."

"Sir."

"Ready Serjenus?"

Gerjen grinned, "I was born ready sir."

"The ala will divide, now! Disengage." Gerjen waved the standard and every trooper threw his javelin and then retreated either to the left or the right. There were few cavalry and chariots left and the ones that were retreated themselves as the gap appeared and there, less than a thousand paces away tramped the Ninth legion protected on its flanks by the Gauls.

The Brigante commander, Venutius, marked by a golden looking helmet with a white plume, must have thought that he had the Romans where he wanted them and he raised his sword to launch his wild Brigante down the slope. They hurtled in an uncontrolled mass. The ala barely had time to evade as the barbarians raced to be the first to take a Roman head. The few cavalry who remained charged the ala but their horses were blown and it was a coming together rather than a clash of arms. The longer swords of the ala and their shields soon eliminated the threat of the cavalry but the Brigante outnumbered the five thousand Romans who locked shields to meet them. On the right they heard the Tribune take charge. "Into their flanks!"

On the Roman left Marius repeated the order and the horsemen closed with the barbarians at the sides of the warband. Although unarmoured they hacked at the legs of the horses and when the troopers fell at their feet they were hacked to death. Wolf had trained Blackie to be aggressive and he pulled back on the reins and the powerful steed crashed his hooves into the skulls of the men who were attempting to hit him. The ala was, at best, holding its own but at the cutting edge of the attack the

First Cohort was slashing and stabbing its way uphill. The Brigantes were minced into a pulp by the relentless war machine that was the legion. The Ninth had fought them before and knew they could beat them. When the braver, better warriors at the front fell there was a sea change and some of the warriors from the rear began to retreat. Venutius was busily engaged with the cavalry but he soon saw the retreat begin and they heard him shout something. The warband suddenly disintegrated and ran back across the hill. The ones at the front who were still engaged carried on fighting, buying their comrades time and by the time they were dead, the Brigante army, still with substantial numbers was silhouetted against the skyline. The ala and the Tribune's horse were exhausted and in no condition to continue the pursuit. The ala gathered their wounded while the legion ruthlessly despatched the wounded.

The Legate was beaming. "Well done Prefect your men did well."

Marius gestured at Wolf and Cava who were busy looking for the men of their turmae. "It was Felix and Paterculus. They led them to us."

"And a brilliant move it was. We will soon catch them and defeat them. We will make camp here and you can send troopers to follow them. Osgar appeared beside Marius like a wraith, making the horses of the officers start. He sniffed, "No need." He pointed to the north west. "They'll be going to Carl Wark, it is a hill fort at the end of the ridge. A proper hill fort from the old times. Built out of the natural rock. They will stay there until they think you are bored."

The Legate got over his surprise and, ignoring the Brigante scout said to Marius. "All the same we can send a turma to watch them and let them know we are coming and, "he glared at Osgar who seemed oblivious to the stare, "we will remove them for we will not be bored!"

For Wolf and the other officers, it was a sad time as they had suffered more casualties than in any other battle. It was particularly sad for Wolf and Gerjen; only Panyvadi, Darvas and Kadarcs, all now Decurion survived. The other comrades who had travelled across a continent to fight for Rome lay dead. "They died as warriors Wolf. They died with a sword in their hands."

126

"I know but I will miss them." Wolf had lost more than half his turma for all his old friends from childhood still fought with him. "And it is strange Gerjen, I suddenly feel older than my years. It is like a father losing his children. I thought I would be the one to die first."

"Not you Wolf, you are lucky, you are Ulpius Felix. You will outlive us all. The Allfather has another purpose for you. You will not die here."

They laid their friends in a grave together. Above it they placed a cairn of rocks. Wolf spoke a few words to send them on their way. "You were oath brothers who did not break your oath to me and you kept your oath to Rome. You died with honour and we will remember you when we fight again. Wait for us brothers and watch over us."

The next day they tramped to the hill fort and even the Legate was taken aback at the size and strength of the place. It was built from a natural rock formation and had three sides which were solid rock and unassailable. The front had a wall built and before it was a pool of indeterminate depth. That was the only place from which they could launch their attack and they would have to do so whilst being attacked from above. The gate was its weak point but it lay directly behind the pool. The Legate had relented his opinion of Brigante scouts and seek the opinion and advice of Osgar who seemed to take it as understood.

"The pool is only as deep as a man's leg but beneath its waters there are rocks and stakes."

"Is there any way to attack?"

Osgar looked at him as though he was stupid. "Just wait."

The Legate's mouth dropped open, "Wait? That isn't the Roman way."

Marius said, gently, "Tell me Osgar, why wait?"

"They have no food. They have too many men in the fort and the only water is the water in the pool." He pointed to the rocks to the sides of the pool. "Your men can hide in the rocks and throw your spears at those who come to get water." He looked up at the skies, which were clear. "If there is no rain, then three days."

The Legate dismissed him with a wave of his hand. He turned to First Spear. "We build a camp and tomorrow you attack. We will show this Brigante and those in the fort that Rome does not need to wait for barbarians to surrender."

First Spear gave the back of the Legate a look which left the other prefects under no illusion about his opinion of the Legate's plan but he was a professional soldier and he would obey orders, no matter how ridiculous they were.

The next morning the Gauls were placed on the flanks with their javelins ready to support the Second Cohort which would bear the brunt of the assault. First Spear led the assault and they had a half century frontage as they began to make their way across the pool. Their shields were ready to go into testudo formation as soon as they came under attack but First Spear wanted as much light on the dark pool to identify obstacles. A legionary on the right discovered the first and fell back into the water with a stake embedded in his leg.

"Fucking lillia! Watch for traps. Put your feet down gently!"

No sooner were the words out than the barrage from inside the fort began. They used javelins and arrows but mainly the plentiful rocks from within. The Gauls targeted those who stood to hurl the largest rocks and they fell but there were enough men inside the stronghold to throw from within its walls with impunity.

"Testudo!" As the shields came up and around the casualties from the missiles stopped but suddenly men fell within the testudo and the integrity was broken. It says much for the courage of the men of the Second Cohort that they closed ranks and continued to the gate. Once they began to hack at the wooden gate but the Brigante had expected this and the huge rocks which were either side of the gate were levered down. The eight men at the gate were crushed to death and the sudden gap allowed the defenders to throw their spears and javelins at the men who were suddenly exposed.

"Fall back!" First Spear could see the futility and they braved the trapped filled water.

The Legate stood defiantly at the other side of the pool having seen over a hundred men die needlessly. First Spear, his face bloodied from a head wound, threw an arm to point at the fort. "They have blocked the gate and they are trapped. The only way out now is to climb the walls and they won't do that! We will wait."

128

It was not a request and the Legate could see it. "Very well then we will wait."

In the end they only had to wait one day for any man who tried to reach the water was slain by the Gauls and a voice from inside called out. "We wish to speak with your general."

The Legate looked for Marius. "You, Prefect come with me and bring that scout of yours." With four legionaries guarding him with their shields the Legate approached the edge of the pool.

Venutius appeared at the top of the ruined gate. "Further bloodshed is unnecessary. We will surrender. We will go home."

Osgar translated and the Legate said, "Tell him his men must come out one by one and leave their weapons behind." Osgar threw him a look of disgust but did as he was ordered. Venutius disappeared.

"You can't let them go sir? He will only do it again."

Leave the grander schemes to me Prefect. If I kill these men and their leader then I will risk a full-scale rebellion. This way he goes home with shame. He may well rebel again but it will not be for some time. He will have to walk home to the land of the Carvetii and you and your men will follow him all the way."

It was a much smaller ala which set off to trek through the whole of the land of the Brigantes to the homeland of the Carvetii, Venutius' people in the far north west. They had lost almost eighty men in the encounter, either wounded or dead. Aulus Murgus had been wounded too and would have to return with the infantry to Lindum. The Brigante rebel, Venutius did not like his escort. He had told the Legate that he had given his word but the expression on Cerialis' face had left him in no doubt that an escort would be provided. The legion too had suffered losses. First Spear was all for crucifixion as a message to other rebels but Cerialis was pleased with his relatively bloodless victory.

"We will now surround their land with forts and they will be controlled."

In the days which followed Wolf spent every waking moment with Osgar learning the language and the ways of the people. Flavius had asked him why. "If we can understand them both their words and their actions then we can understand how to defeat them. I have looked into the eyes of their king and he is not finished. It will not be finished until his head is no longer part of his body. I have been listening to them as they speak. I can translate more of their words than they know and he is already planning to attack again when he has sufficient men." Flavius looked at Osgar who nodded. We need to know every uncia of this land so that next time we do not stumble up a ridge and lose men and we need more scouts like Osgar. We need many more in the ala. These men are good trackers. Osgar saved me and my men. Cava lost men not because I am a better Decurion but because I had more help."

And so Wolf became the ala expert on the Brigante. He spent time talking to them and asking about their homes. At first they were reluctant but there was something about the young man which made them forget he was an enemy and open up to him. His scarred eye marked him as a warrior and the respect afforded him by the Brigante Osgar compounded it. When they finally reached the land of the lakes close to the Ituna Est, Decurion Lupus Ulpius Felix knew far more about his enemies and his allies than any other Roman. It would help to save lives in the future.

Chapter 10

Cataractonium 56A.D.

It had been two years since Nero had gained the Imperial throne. Many people had suggested that he had murdered not only his mother and step father but also his half-brother, Britannicus. Of course, no one voiced these views in public; there were too many political appointments for that. Every fresh-faced patrician who joined was a suspect, especially to the Pannonians. The Romans who commanded them had proved that they were warriors over and over again.

Since Venutius had been defeated and finally sent home, over a year ago the frontier had had an uneasy peace and Queen Cartimandua had been so pleased that she had invited the Prefects, Tribunes and Legate to her hall for a celebrations. When Marius came back and they asked her about the Queen he seemed unable to talk coherently, "She is beautiful beyond words and has a power and an energy which I would have expected from a man. She has thrown out her husband and taken with a young warrior, Vellocatus who is younger than Gerjen. The people love her and she even has an old centurion, from the time of the invasion who is her guardian; even he seems totally enraptured by her."

"If you don't mine me saying so sir, so do you."

Proculus smiled at Flavius. "You may be right but wait until you meet her and you will see. We all suggested to her that she ought to build her army up but she seemed quite happy to let the Roman army do that for her."

"We heard she has a magical sword."

"Aye, the Sword of the Brigante. We saw it for she likes to show it off. It is encrusted with jewels but that did not interest us; it was the blade for it was not only sharp but strong. Gerantium, the centurion told us that he had seen it shear an ordinary sword in two. It is a powerful weapon and the Brigante regard it as a symbol not only of the power of the ruler but the life blood of the people. "

A year later and the Prefect had returned from the new fort being constructed at Eboracum for the Third Cohort of the

Ninth. "The good news is that the Ninth are going to be based a little closer to us than Lindum. The new fort at Eboracum is less than a day's ride from here and the Via Nero is being built already to join it to us. The bad news is that the Legate is going to tour the forts and check on our readiness for war."

"War sir? The Brigante as at peace."

"True, but the Silures are not and the Deceangli close to Deva are rattling their swords. It means that the Twentieth can no longer extend their influence north. Venutius is reported, according to the queen, to be building up an army. At the moment it is not large but we know from our last battle that they can move quickly."

Flavius murmured, "First Spear was right we should have crucified the bastard."

Ignoring the comment of the Decurion Princeps the Prefect addressed all of the officers, "And now to more mundane matters. Where is Publius? I need to see our roll and what equipment we require. The Legate will expect everything in order when he comes."

Flavius shook his head with a smile on his lips. "You are getting old sir. Remember when you went for your weeklong meeting we had a farewell party for Publius. You probably passed him on your way north. He is heading for Camulodunum. He is to be a farmer."

"Of course I forgot and you Quintus, when do you retire?"

"Next year sir. I have a little place close to Verulamium all picked out."

"Looks like I am losing my oldest officers eh? So we need a new Decurion."

"We are fully manned at the moment sir. Aulus stood with some difficulty. The wound in his leg had healed but left him with a bad limp. "He pointed out of the window. "We have sixty recruits but they are not fully trained yet." None of the turmae are up to full compliment."

"Thank you Aulus. I was going to ask Quintus to be the new Quartermaster but if he is to retire in a year then we should have someone who will be here longer. I thought of you Aulus."

"Sorry sir, much as I would like the job I think I will be going out the same time as Quintus. I would have signed on for another five years but," he smacked his leg with the vine staff he affected, "this slows me down too much. I am not the soldier I was and for me that isn't good enough. I will do the job until you find someone and then train them up."

"Very well." He shook his head. "Perhaps I ought to retire her too."

The Decurion Princeps became serious. "No sir, please don't do that. That prick Cerialis would dump one of his acolytes on us and we would all have to resign."

"Yes I suppose we will have to suffer the insufferable Cresens again. Very well make a list of your needs and give it to Aulus and then return to your forts. I will be stationed at Isurium Brigantium."

Isurium Brigantium was the fort closest to Stanwyck, Queen Cartimandua's sometime capital, and had been built with the express purpose of protecting her. By contrast Derventio was far to the north east, almost a day's ride from Cataractonium.

"Close to the Queen eh sir?"

"Decurion Princeps are you suggesting that I might just be stationed there to be close to the Queen and the amazing feasts she throws?"

Wolf laughed, "We would all be there in a flash sir. All we hear are your reports. We have never even seen her."

"Decurion Ulpius Felix she would eat you alive in a moment." The laughter was all directed at Wolf who blushed and then took the ribbing in the way it was intended. "By the way how are the new recruits?"

Flavius nodded at Wolf, "They are better thanks to our master of languages here Felix. He can actually speak to them and let them know what we intend. Oh and we now have three more Brigante scouts. I sent one to Derventio, one to Isurium and left two here."

"Why do you need three Decurion Princeps?"

"We train the recruits sir. It gives us more interpreters."

"Very well. Carry on."

Wolf went directly to the gyrus where Gaius, his Chosen Man awaited him. "The new recruits all settled in Gaius?" Although it had been a year since the heavy losses at Carl Wark the Second Turma had had to wait until all the other turmae had been brought up to full strength. As Flavius had pointed out it was easier to replace two or three men rather than sixteen. It meant that Wolf and Gaius had the most recruits of any of them. The rest of the turma lounged against the rails as the sixteen new recruits sat awkwardly on their new horses in their new armour and with their new arms. They had been shorn weeks earlier and had spent the next four weeks working with Sextus and Numerius on simple commands. Wolf and the turma had patrolled as far north as the river which marked the border of the land of the Brigante and the end of the Roman Empire. Now, as he surveyed his new men he thought of them as rough clay. When he had taken over the turma it had been with fellow Pannonians but these were volunteers from Britannia and Gaul. The Gauls came from areas where they had too many volunteers for the cohorts and the surplus were shipped to the alae which needed them, regardless of an ability to ride.

"Welcome to the best turma in the ala." He pointed to Osgar who was busy cleaning a rabbit skin. "We have the best scout." Osgar spat and Wolf smiled as he pointed towards Gaius and the other troopers, "And we have the most decorated troopers in Britannia because we are the toughest and the bravest. You are joining an elite team and if you do not meet its standards then it will be off to the cohorts with you." He smiled, "And the loss of pay." He strolled along the front of the line of horses staring at each man as he passed. "I am Decurion Lupus Ulpius Felix. That was not my name when I joined so I don't want to know the names you had. You are Romans now and I will address you as a Roman. For those who are still unfamiliar with Roman names let me tell you that the Lupus means I am like a Wolf. When you were growing up at home and you listened to the howling of the wolf you were afraid. When I yell then you should be afraid too. Felix means I am lucky." He pointed at his scarred eye. "I was lucky because, when I was stupid enough to think no-one could harm me the Allfather saved me and just took an eye. That is why I am lucky. Some of you came from this province; others from the recruitment camps in Gaul. Your background does not interest me. What does matter is if you can ride or not. We will now discover that." They all glanced nervously at each other. "Just ride one circuit around the gyrus."

They had all basic riding lessons and Wolf did not expect them to fall off. He just wanted to see who looked comfortable. After one circuit he sent them for a trot. He covered his mouth to hide a smile as he saw some of them slip from side to side. He let them rest and smile in that self satisfied way that shows someone thinks they have done a good job; even though some of them had been lucky not to fall off. "Now then, one by one, I want you to gallop around as fast as you can and then stop in front of me." He paused, "Do not hit me!" The troopers smiled in anticipation; this would be their chance to have fun at the recruits' expense.

The first recruit gritted his teeth and galloped around the gyrus. His face was a mixture of terror and exhilaration. As he turned the corner his face turned to horror as he realised the horse was not slowing and Wolf was only ten paces away. In desperation he jerked the reins to the side and pulled back. The horse gamely tried to turn and stop but he couldn't and they crashed in a heap at the Decurion's feet. He looked down at the youth who gave a half smile up at Wolf. "Well at least you didn't hit me."

The others all had similar fates until there was just one left; he was the youngest looking of the recruits and Wolf prepared for another fall. No-one had struck him yet but many had come close. The troopers had fallen about laughing and they eagerly watched the last one. He looked confident as he galloped around he had a calm expression as he raced up to the Decurion. There was a collective intake of breath from both the recruits and the troopers as the horse was but ten paces from the officer when the recruit grabbed the reins and pulled savagely back. The horse's nose snorted into Wolf's face but it was a hand span away. Wolf looked up at the youth who grinned and said, "Like that sir?"

"Well done son. What is your name?"

"Marcus Aurelius Maximunius, sir."

"You ride that with some ease. Are you Roman?"

"No sir, my home is in Hispania and my village was destroyed by the Romans. The one who captured me, the centurion, sold me as a stable boy and gave me my name. I have had it for seven summers."

"Well Marcus you can ride!" He looked at the others. "Take lessons from this one. He is the nearest thing to a Pannonian I have seen. Mount and I will find out who you are."

He walked down the line. "Gaius sir, from Gaul."

"Lentulus from the Atrebate tribe."

"Metellus the Catuvellauni tribe."

"Drusus the Gaul."

And so it went on. He had a disparate team from both Gaul and the province but they all showed keenness. None of them had shown fear after they had fallen and had all tried it again. For Ulpius Felix it was the superb rider who would need no training which had made his day. He would, once again, have the best turma in the ala.

After they had finished their training for the day Wolf joined the others in the office they shared. They used it like an informal club. There was normally an amphora of wine and dried venison strips. Osgar was an excellent hunter but his nephew Gaelwyn was even better and, as the new scout in the ala was keen to win praise, his hunting expeditions did so.

"I hear you have a rider amongst the recruits?"

"Yes Cava. He stopped his horse that far from my nose." He demonstrated. "I nearly shat myself!"

"Makes a change; most of them can't tell the tail from the head."

"But they are keen Aulus."

He leaned over to pour himself a large beaker of wine. "Aye but they are keen for the money. If the infantry paid better salaries they would join them."

Sextus chose a large piece of jerky. "Be fair Aulus it's why we joined the cavalry and not the infantry, the money."

"Speak for yourself I just didn't fancy being one of Marius' Mules and carrying my life on my back."

"Yeah I prefer life from a horse and speaking of pay. You are the new paymaster. When is the next payday?"

"Same as always the end of the nundinal cycle."

"Now don't confuse me you know I am an old man. The old nundinal or the new one?"

"Don't give me that Sextus you are not old you are just crafty and you know that if it is the new one, which it is, then it is tomorrow and you have gained a day!"

Sextus shrugged. "I am just saving for my retirement and I want to make sure it is safely in my box."

"Are we letting the lads into the vicus then?"

"Not certain Lupus. It depends on the Decurion Princeps. The last thing we need is a bunch of lads pissed up around the vicus."

"You mean like we were in Germania."

"I mean exactly that."

"Well I think they deserve it; they have worked hard. How about if a couple of us had a wander around to make sure they are behaving themselves?" Wolf cared about his young recruits, especially as he had felt so guilty about the young ones who had died at the battle of Carl Wark.

"Count me out I have a bad leg."

"Now you are getting old Aulus. There was a time when you would have been the first to go and keep an eye on them."

"Well I have changed and what good will a one eyed man be to keep an eye on them!"

They all laughed and Wolf affected outrage. "I can't believe you are mocking the afflicted. Luckily I am in a good mood and I will turn a blind eye to that comment."

Cava laughed, "Your jokes do not get any better but I will join you. Might be interesting to see them off duty."

Eventually the Pannonian officers with their friend Gerjen decided to take a stroll after payday to ensure that their charges behaved themselves. The vicus had grown because of the fort. The Brigante who lived there could be sure of safety from bandits and raiders; the new road as they called it, the Via Nero passed through and ensured visitors and businesses flourished. There was an inn which put up merchants and visitors for the natives had learned they could make money out of Pax Romana and there was an alehouse marked by the sheaf of barley hung outside. The woman who ran it, Maeve, was a widow whose husband and sons had been killed in a raid by the Caledonii. She wanted her daughter safe and saw the chance to be safe and to make money. She was a powerfully built woman and had fists

137

like a man. There was little trouble in her alehouse. The rest of the dwellings contained those who made money from the soldiers; tanners, leather workers, smiths and weapons makers. There were also a couple of girls who were prostitutes. Some of the troopers took a turn at them but, after a while, their lack of expertise and the fact that they just lay there made them less enticing and most men went back to the tried and trusted solo method. The two girls would make their money when the new recruits visited them for the first time. The virgins were the ones they liked the best; they had no means of comparing.

Wolf and Cava made sure that they were in the vicus before the troopers and they warned the businesses that the troopers would be coming but they did not want the recruits robbed. Cava had huge fists and was particularly persuasive. Maeve just grinned. "Do you want I should water it down Decurion?"

"What, are you going to make it all water or just going to piss in it?"

She laughed, "I just do that for the officers."

"And we can tell."

When they visited Eide and Sare, the two whores, they used Wolf's persuasion rather than Cava's intimidation. For some reason his injury made him attractive to women and the two young girls were always trying to bed him, normally together. Wolf called them girls but he thought they were his age. It was hard to tell for they put a red substance made from beetles on their lips and the dye from flowers on their eyes. To the recruits it would appear exotic. "Oh Decurion we'll do you for free!"

"A tempting offer but I am on duty. Now if we hear you have charged these recruits more than the going rate we will stop them coming here altogether. Do you understand?"

Eide pouted, "But they are virgins and we are doing them a favour really teaching them how to be lovers."

"If you are doing a favour then it should be free eh?"

"You are so persuasive Decurion. Just a quickie?"

"Sorry Sare. We have more businesses to see."

Gaius Cresens had tired of his function as Legate's aid. It meant he had to run around after the Legate. He had hoped for promotion before now but that seemed unlikely. He had seen enough in the time her had been in Britannia to know that he did not wish to be an infantryman. Although the officers sometimes rode, they frequently joined their men marching and fighting in a shield wall. He had watched the cavalry fight and saw that there were opportunities to hang back and avoid the fighting; especially in the auxiliary. He had decided to ingratiate himself into the good graces of Prefect Marius Ulpius Proculus. He was, therefore, really annoyed to find that the Prefect was not at Cataractonium but had chosen to visit Derventio which was just a little too close to the blue painted savages who inhabited the land north of the Dunum. It was too late to return to Eboracum which was nothing more than a building site and quite basic and the officers of the ala, most of them barely beyond barbarians themselves shunned him. He eyed the vicus; he would spend the night there and perhaps, away from prying eyes indulge himself in those pleasures he enjoyed the most.

Trooper Marcus Aurelius Maximunius was more popular with the other recruits since he had demonstrated his skill as a rider. Even more importantly he had a natural ability with horses. It was almost as though he could talk to them and the more nervous of the riders had reason to thank the young Spaniard for he had helped them control their horses. He was the youngest of the troopers and he and the next youngest, Lucius, had formed a close friendship. The barracks was a noisy and intimidating place and Lucius, in particular, was a shy youth with a face which made him look little more than a child. He was lucky to be in Wolf's turma for they were protective as well as proud to be serving what they took to be the best turma in the ala.

As they headed towards the vicus they were all excited. They had their first pay and it was burning a hole in their purses. They couldn't wait to get into the vicus and spend the money. "They have whores there!"

Lucius' eyes widened, "Women who sell their bodies for money?"

Drusus laughed, "Well I hope so or I will have to spend more on the ale they sell in the tavern."

Metellus put a bear like arm around the two young troopers. "Tonight boys, is the night we become men and we find out what a woman feels like."

139

The two young troopers looked at each other in terror. They were still close to being children and to them women meant mothers. Marcus shook his head. "Perhaps next time. Lucius and I haven't had ale before, well not men's ale. We just had small beer. We are looking forward to that."

Drusus laughed, "Well I can manage both. My dick is so big the women will be begging me to drink more ale and make it smaller."

"I never knew a Gaul yet who wasn't hung like his horse! "

"I am from Gaul Lentulus and I do not boast."

They all laughed as Drusus said, "We all saw the way you fell from your horse and we aren't sure you have anything left down there at all." He turned to the two young troopers. "You are probably right lads. Pick another night because after they have had Drusus then I have ruined them for other men!"

Once they reached the vicus they split into two groups; Marcus and Livius headed for the tavern while the others headed for the queue outside the whore's hut. Drusus shouted. "The rest will join you lads quickly but I may be some time. Don't drink all the ale."

Metellus shouted over his shoulder, "He'll probably take one look at them and spill his seed there and then!"

Marcus was glad that he and Lucius were not going to the whore house; he had barely known his mother, having been taken from the corpses of his tribe at the age of seven but, to him, she was always smiling, pretty and loving. It would take some time before he would think about a woman as Drusus and the others did. They saw Wolf and Cava outside the tavern. They both stood to attention and saluted. "Sir!" They chorused.

Wolf smiled. The two lads were about his age when he had joined and he wondered had he ever looked that young, with baby faces that did not need shaving and the terrified look of frightened deer when officers appeared. "Relax lads. You are off duty. Are you going in for an ale?"

"Yes sir, I have never tried one before."

"Well, take it slowly Lucius. Strong ale can make a man behave differently and Maeve serves strong ale."

"It's not a problem sir. I will look after him."

Wolf looked at the young rider with a raised eyebrow, it made his good eye seem absurdly huge, "Oh and you are the experienced drinker eh?"

Shyly he said, "Well not really sir but when I worked in the Thracian stables in Gaul I watched the troopers drinking. Two is my limit besides I don't want to waste my pay in one night do I sir. I think I will save up and have a nice little pugeo made."

Wolf turned to Cava. "See Decurion, they are not all like Drusus and the others. Some of my lads can not only ride but have sense. Enjoy yourselves lads." The two officers headed over to the queue at the whorehouse where there was a little pushing and shoving taking place.

When the boys walked in the place was relatively quiet as most of the men had chosen to use Sare and Eide before they drank themselves into oblivion. Gaius Cresens was seated in the corner, by the fire; he had booked a room in the inn and was awaiting his food. When he saw the two young boys walk in his eyes lit up. The queue for the whores had meant his first choice was off the menu as he did not fancy following a bunch of hairy arsed barbarians after they had finished with the girls. He would visit them another time but the two boys, well one of them was definitely pretty enough and who knows, they could both be virgins.

Maeve eyed them up as they came in. She had learned to assess potential for danger as soon as a trooper walked in and these two were her perfect customers; young and quiet. She knew that when the rest came in , later on, they would be noisy and boating of their sexual exploits which, she knew from Sare and Eide were all a fiction. The fact that these two had come here first told her of their mettle. "Right lads, two beakers of ale?"

"Yes please."

Her heart warmed to them. They were polite. Had her sons lived she hoped that they would have turned out the same. The troopers thought she was a hard woman, and she could be, but he could still soften and seeing these two, who would have been of an age with her son, made her eye moisten a little. "Right sit in the corner, where it's quiet and I'll bring them over."

Marcus was pleased that the others had visited the girls first. He had dreaded them all having a drinking contest. He only intended to have a couple and this way they could. They would tell them that they had had five beakers when they came in and then they could return to the barracks. Marcus had seen the Thracian troopers returning to their barracks and spending the night vomiting after a heavy drinking session and the next day he had seen them fall from their horses. That would not happen to him. He suspected Lucius felt the same. "You are from this land then Lucius?"

"Yes, like Drusus I am Iceni."

"The flat country close to the sea?"

"Yes. Our king Prasutagus, is an ally of Rome and likes all things Roman. He encouraged all the warriors our age to join the Roman army."

"What about the older ones? Why not them?"

He lowered his voice, "They do not like the Romans and they hate the way our king panders to them. It is said that his wife Boudicca is a priestess of the Mother cult."

"The Mother cult? I did not hear of that in Gaul."

"The centre is on Mona, where the legions are fighting the druids and they are a fierce enemy of Rome. They worship Mother Earth and make sacrifices. It is rumoured that the Queen and her daughters are all priestesses."

Maeve brought their ale and smiled maternally, "Now you take it steady. That will be a denarii and I will give you one more for that price." Then she leaned over, "And after that go home eh? This will be no place for you when your mates get here. It will be a bit rough."

"Thank you gammer." Maeve ruffled Lucius' head and went back to the back room dabbing her eye.

"What does that word mean, gammer?"

"It is a word of this land it is a term of respect for someone older, a woman, it sort of means, mother. We use the word uncle for a man who is an older man worthy of respect."

"Ah well to us all older men are gaffers."

Lucius nodded. "We too are taught to respect our elders." He sipped his ale. "Tell me Marcus, what happened to the Decurion, his eye I mean?"

"I was told that he was the standard bearer when he was a young man and had no shield. An enemy stone took out his eye."

"His other one works well enough. He misses nothing."

Marcus laughed, "He is not called Wolf for nothing but I am glad we serve him. Ulpius Felix is the best officer in the ala, believe me."

"How do you know?"

"I worked with the Thracians for eight years and I saw many officers. You learn to see who the good ones are and who are the nasty ones. He is a good one; although most of the others seem like good officers."

"What even Decurion Murgus?"

Marcus laughed, "He is all show. You can tell he has a good heart; he is just strict."

By the time the second ale had come they knew all there was to know about each other. "I think if we go back now we will avoid their stories about how big their dicks are."

"Good idea Marcus. Thank you gammer."

Maeve came out to see them off, "Come again boys. You are more than welcome."

As they reached the door Gaius Cresens pounced. He moistened his pudgy red lips in anticipation of his evening of pleasure. He had watched them from across the room and knew which one was his prey, the diffident shy one. "Ah boys. You serve with the ala?"

They both saw he bore the uniform of the Legate's staff and they stood stiffly to attention. "Sir, yes sir."

Cresens put a flabby hand on Lucius' shoulder, "I have my horse in the stable and as you are cavalrymen I wondered if you might look at him. I am not sure he is walking right."

Lucius tried to disengage himself. "Marcus is the trooper for that sir."

Cresens had an edge to his voice and his hand gripped the Iceni's shoulder. "No trooper. I am ordering you to come with me and look at my horse."

His eyes pleaded with Marcus for help as he said, "Yes sir."

Cresens led him off to the stable and Marcus shouted, "I'll come with you too."

Cresens face was dark and angry as he hissed. "You go back to the barracks! That is an order."

Marcus did not like the look of the staff officer but he did not know what to do. He thought of returning to the bar but what could Maeve do and then he saw, at the end of the vicus the Decurion. He was watching the rapidly diminishing queue outside the whores. Marcus ran up to him. "Yes, Marcus what is it? Off back to the barracks?" He looked behind Marcus. "Don't tell me young Lucius has gone to the whores?"

Marcus' face showed real concern as he blurted out, "Sir a staff officer insisted that Lucius looked at his horse. We tried to tell him I was the horse warrior but he insisted and... well I..." He tailed off, not knowing how to tell the Decurion what he feared. He had seen men do things to each other in the stables and the staff officer had that sort of look on his face.

"This officer was a little podgy looking?"

"Yes sir!"

"Cresens. Come with me."

They raced down the vicus and the men in the queue stared and wondered why. The tavern and stable was at the end of the vicus on the road north. When they entered the stables they saw that Lucius was lying unconscious on the floor and his buttocks were bare, Cresens stood above him and his intention was obvious. Wolf did not hesitate, he ran up to him and, swinging his leg as far back as he could he kicked him as hard as he could. The heavy caligae connected and the fat officer fell as though struck with a poleaxe. "Get Lucius outside."

As Marcus poured water on the boy's face Ulpius Felix took out his dagger and placed it next to Cresens' ear. "Listen you fat pervert. If you ever touch one of my boys again I will castrate you and then feed you your own balls. You are only alive now because you did not have your way. Do you understand me?"

The staff officer tried to struggle to his feet. "How dare you! I am on the Legate's staff!"

"Listen to me, you sickeningly depraved piece of shit, I don't give a fuck if you are the Emperor's cousin. No-one touches my boys. This will be a reminder of what can happen if you ignore me." In one swift motion he sliced off the lower lobe of his right ear. The blood flowed and he screamed.

144

Wolf felt an arm on his shoulder; he looked up to see Cava above him. "Marcus told me." He leaned over to speak in the officer's whole ear. "Whatever my friend threatened it goes double for me and I would not visit this vicus again or you will not leave whole. And we will make it quite clear to everyone just what you were trying to do if you mention to anyone. I am sure that your promising career would end here in Britannia if it came to be known that, not only were you a bum boy but a rapist too." He then pulled his arm back and smashed it into the face of Gaius Cresens. They left the unconscious officer face down in a pool of his own blood.

Chapter 11

The Legate's party was visible for many miles as it rode up the Via Nero. He was escorted by the Tribune and his turma of cavalry. It had been some weeks since the incident with his aide and Wolf and Cava had wondered when he would make return visit. They had told the other officers, but not the troopers, of the attempted rape and their treatment of Gaius Cresens was seen as mild by all of them. Flavius told Marius who was not surprised. "It may be against the law but that does not mean that half the senators do not engage in it on a regular basis but Wolf and Cava did the right thing."

"What if he makes a complaint?"

"Then I will deal with it. Of course, he had no reason to be in the vicus. The troopers had permission; he did not."

The turma rotated in pairs and on the day that the Legate returned to Cataractonium it happened to be Wolf and his friend Kadarcs on patrol. Marius was at the Porta Praetorium to greet the Legate and he noticed that Cresens was present and his face and ear still showed signs of his beating..

The Tribune and the Legate entered the office and the Legate dismissed the clerk so that they could talk privately. "Is your Decurion Princeps still at Derventio Prefect."

"Yes we alternate the duty. It stops us getting stale. Variety you know sir."

"Quite. Well the new fortress at Eboracum is coming on well. The First Cohort will be based there and I want the second one based here while they extend the Via Nero as far as the Dunum."

"There is no bridge there sir."

"There will be when the Ninth build it. Oh not a stone structure you understand, just a wooden affair so that we can extend our influence."

"It risks the barbarians using it as a way in to the Province."

"From what I understand the river is not wide and if they chose they could get across easily enough."

Marius nodded, "You are probably right sir. You want my ala to be based at Derventio then?"

"No I want you based here, all of you. Derventio is not as important now that we have the fort at Eboracum and I want the Ninth protected from any raids by Venutius. He may just resent this new road across his land."

"It will be a little crowded sir."

"Oh the Ninth can throw up their own camp I daresay. But, and this is the reason I made this visit myself, when my aide was up here he was attacked in the vicus."

"He didn't say anything to my men."

"Oh I didn't know that. Probably embarrassed. What I need to know is how safe is the vicus? Are there troublemakers here? Do we need to make an example of them?"

"No they are loyal. Their livelihood depends on us being here." He paused and noticed the lightest of smiles on Gnaeus' lips. "If you don't mind me saying so Legate, your aide has the ability to annoy people. His manner you know? He could have upset some of the locals with a throwaway comment. They still see themselves as independent of Rome."

"Which of course they aren't whether they like it or not. I suppose you are right." He leaned forwards, "Between us three I am doing a favour for an old friend. However I want you Prefect to ensure that the vicus is safe. I don't want to put the men building the new road at risk eh?"

"I will initiate patrols sir."

"How is the rest of the Province then sir?"

"The Silures and Deceangli are being stirred up again by the druids so that the Governor is having to organise a campaign. It means that we have to patrol as far south as the land of the Iceni now. When you have finished on the road we will have to move some of the ala further south."

"But I thought the Iceni were allies?"

"Oh they are but Prasutagus is not well and his wife, she is a real bitch let me tell you, is not so enamoured of Rome, in fact the rumour is she wishes we were back in Gaul. Of course she doesn't say that to our face. The annoying part is that the Province to the east and south is peaceful and even here, in the north, there is little trouble. Anyway I will be leaving with the Tribune to inspect the land to the Dunum. Could you supply us with a couple of turmae as scouts?"

"Of course sir. I'll go and sort one out."

"Good. Tribune go with him and meet our liaison and then if you could send in your clerk and my aide with some wine?"

"Of course sir."

As he sent the two men in Marius glanced at Wolf's handiwork. He had carved well and, until you saw the other ear you could not tell that half of it was missing."

As they walked to the barracks the Tribune said quietly, "That ear looks like a pugeo did some serious damage." Marius quickly looked at Gnaeus. "Do not worry Marius your secret is safe with me. Half of my men have wanted to gut that creepy little fat man. What was it? A young boy or a girl?"

"One of my troopers. He does this often then?"

"Whenever he can. Fortunately never with any of the Legion. He would have his balls around his ears if he tried that but they have seen him with the civilians and they don't like it. Ah well Spurius has made some money then."

"How do you mean made some money?"

"We had a book on who did it. He took one of your officers." He looked questioningly at Marius who nodded, "And if I am any guess I would say either young Wolf or Cava?"

"You know my men well and yet you have barely fought with them."

"I know Pannonia and I saw in the battle at Carl Wark, the mettle of your men. Any of them could join the regulars and not be out of place."

No-one was unhappy that Derventio was to be abandoned. It was peaceful over in the east but the troopers stationed there missed the comradeship of their fellows. The vicus and Maeve in particular were delighted at the arrival of even more men with money to spend on ale. Flavius, in particular preferred being back with the others and he enjoyed the new activity for they had to escort the carts from Eboracum containing the cement and then patrol along the periphery of the construction site. It kept the whole ala busy. What impressed Wolf was the speed with which they built the road. He and his turma were selected to perform the close watch which meant they could see the legionaries actually building the road. The spears, shields and armour were neatly stacked in tent groups which, as the Centurion told them , was only possible because of the turma. Otherwise they had to keep half the men armed in case of attack. The ditch was dug and the section to be built levelled. Then they added a layer of small stones which the legionaries tamped down. This was followed by bigger pieces of rock. They were fortunate that there were many rocks close by which the Ninth collected whilst the ala watched. Next they mixed fine concrete with small rocks and overlaid that with larger blocks of cut stone, Finally they put a raised footway and edge stone. The whole turma was impressed by the skills of the legionaries and each day the road crept further north.

One of the legionaries saw their keen attention. "Hey optio how about asking these horse shaggers if they want to have a go at working for a change and not sitting on their arses like they normally do."

The young optio picked up a piece of concrete and threw it to catch the noisy soldier on the back of the head. "Shut up and get on with it, you horrible little man."

"Could have hurt me that could. Besides, why don't the cavalry ever get to build the roads. Their horses cover them in shit anyway?"

"You are a stupid man Donkey don't you know that? The cavalry are the ones we stick out in front of us in a battle so that the hairy arsed barbarians whip their bollocks off and not ours. Mind you we could put you out in front and there would be no harm done." The grumbling Donkey set back to work grumbling.

Wolf rode up to the grinning optio. "Donkey?"

"Yeah, got the brains of a mule and once he is sat on his arse you can't get him moving."

Osgar mooched up having run a circuit around the building work. "There is no-one nearby Decurion."

Just then they heard the creak of carts as the fifth turma arrived with more concrete. The soldiers all groaned and there were murmured complaints. The Centurion who had been busy at the front of the road strode into sight. "Come on you moaning bastards I am going to show you how good I am to you. Instead of making you tamp down the stones I am going to let you off for a while." A small cheer went up. "Instead you can unload

149

those carts! Get a move on." He winked at Wolf as he came by. "What's life without a little joke?"

Panyvadi joined Wolf. "I have been ordered to relieve you. You are to take Osgar and head for Stanwyck. The Queen is visiting Eboracum and she reported strangers north of the stronghold." He turned back and shouted, "Gaelwyn, join the Decurion."

The newest scout, Gaelwyn who was Osgar's nephew, jogged forwards. "Don't you need him?"

"I think I can find my way back down this road to the camp besides Flavius asked if he could hunt some pig, Aulus was moaning on about porridge for every meal."

Wolf waved his arm in a flourish. "They are all yours old friend. Osgar, take your nephew and lead us to Stanwyck."

They left the partially built road and followed the small stream north west of them. The land rose and fell in undulations which could hide any number of enemies. Although they were close to the Queen's capital they were also just a river away from the land of the Carvetii and Venutius. It did not pay to take chances. "Gaius, take Drusus and Lentulus and trail us by eight hundred paces. We might as well give them some practice. We can't keep giving all the hard jobs to the more experienced troopers and send Marcus and Lucius up here. I'll give them some training too."

The two young troopers rode just behind him. "Come up here, one on each side. There is no road and the land will serve." He glanced at them and contrasted their riding styles. Lucius was a competent rider but he gripped his reins with both hands. Marcus was far more natural and kept one hand on the pommel of his sword. "Lucius, look at Marcus' hands. He has one on his sword and I would bet a beaker of Maeve's ale that if I asked him to he could ride without using his hands. Isn't that right Marcus?"

Marcus grinned, "Yes sir."

"Well go on then, show him." Marcus dropped his left hand and his horse continued walking in a straight line. "And I bet he could trot too." Marcus looked at the Decurion and Wolf nodded impatiently, "Go on, stop being shy." Marcus kicked his heels and the horse trotted forwards." Right then trooper back here in the same position." To Lucius' amazement Marcus leaned slightly to one side and the horse came around in a loop and was back next to Wolf in no time. "Well done so now stop being a smart arse and get hold of your reins." Marcus grinned and did so.

"How does he do it sir?"

"He uses his knees and his body weight. You have learned much Lucius but you haven't fought yet from the back of a horse. You have thrown your javelins at targets and engaged in mock combats but you have never had a warrior coming at your blind side, "he grinned, "which in my case is something of a problem. Sometimes, in fact, most times you have to fight with two hands and not fall off your horse. When you can then practise those skills."

Marcus looked across at Wolf, trying to pluck up the courage to ask the question which was in his head. "Come on son. If you have a question then ask it. The worst I can do is shout at you and I may even answer it."

"Decurion Felix how do you avoid hitting your horse with your sword when you are fighting."

"Worst thing you can do that, kill your own horse. It is simple." He took out his own sword, "This is a slashing weapon." He swung the sword on a horizontal plane at his own head height. "This blow will make another cavalryman duck. If he ducks he can't see where he is going so you smash him in the head with your shield. Now if it is a foot soldier then the best movement is this." He swung the sword vertically down the side of his horse's head. "Those are the two blows you use."

"And why do you have a gladius in your belt as well as your spatha?"

"The spatha is good from a horse, it outreaches the weapons of most barbarians but on the ground if is too clumsy. You need a stabbing weapon. When I was aquilifer I learned to fight with two swords at once. I was fairly shite with my left hand but it was better than nothing."

"Decurion!"

Gaelwyn the scout appeared from the bushes to their left. "Yes scout what is it?"

"Uncle, er Osgar has found tracks. Carvetii."

"Close up. You two behind. "Trot." The Decurion trotted after the lithe Brigante boy who seemed to float across the grass.

They found Osgar in a clearing. "Twelve Carvetii camped here last night. They were heading for Stanwyck."

"Then these can't be the ones the Queen mentioned can they? There are two bands." He turned to the turma. Tighten belts, check your shields and prepare your javelins. There could be two small warbands up ahead and I want them surprised not us. Listen to what Osgar says. If he warns you of Carvetii then trust me they are there." He nodded at Osgar who waved Gaelwyn to his left. Marcus noticed that both scouts now carried bows with arrows already notched and he made sure that his two spare javelins were in his shield hand, with his reins whilst he held the javelin loosely across his horse's mane.

They went forward and the two scouts disappeared into the scrubby bushes which lined the shallow valley. It was more intimidating now, especially for the young recruits. They were now closer to the barbarians than they had ever been and their first action could soon follow. The soft grass hid any noise their horses might have made and the slight bridge favoured them as it was below in their faces. Lucius tried to hold the javelin the way he saw Marcus do but it felt clumsy. Marcus saw him struggle and was desperate to tell him how to do it but he did not wish to risk the wrath of Ulpius Felix. After what seemed an age and, with a wooded glade coming up, Osgar suddenly appeared. He pointed to the trail which went into the wood. He held up both hands twice and pointed to his left and then both hands once and pointed to his right.

Wolf waved his acknowledgement. He turned and said, "There is an ambush ahead. We will sweep around to our right and take the twenty warriors on that side. Do not stop to finish any off but keep going and we will then take the ten on the left. Marcus on my right, Lucius on my left." Marcus looked over his shoulder at the rest of the turma. "Don't worry son they know what to do and Gaius will look after the other new lads."

Decurion Lupus Ulpius Felix kicked Blackie's flanks and held his javelin above his shoulder; he hoped the new troopers would try to copy his action. This was a harsh and dangerous place to learn. Marcus noticed that as soon as they began to ride the rest of the turma spread out on either side with Drusus riding next to Gaius, the chosen man, alongside Lentulus whilst Tiberius, the aquilifer, was with the other new ones. They rode around the wood and then swung in so that Gaius on the right had to kick his horse and gallop to maintain the line. Wolf smiled as he saw the new troopers struggling to keep up. Suddenly they were in the woods and the sudden darkness took moments for their eyes to adjust. The dead leaves slightly muffled their approach but the Carvetii must have been aware of their approach if not the actual direction. Wolf saw them and kicked hard on Blackie's flanks. Speed was now of the essence. He saw two men fall to the arrows of the scouts and then he threw his javelin at the warrior with the torc, who looked like a chief. He wriggled like an insect as he was pinned to the elm tree. The Decurion drew his spatha, aware of other Carvetii falling to javelins and then there was daylight as they crossed the path. The rest of the warband had realised that their ruse had been rumbled and were fleeing south, towards the stream. Rather than wasting time sheathing his sword and taking another javelin Wolf galloped after the nearest barbarian. He saw the white face turn as Blackie's breath and hooves seemed to be directly behind him. He began to turn his head but Wolf sliced down and split his skull. Out of nowhere a Carvetii leapt at him with a war axe. Ulpius Felix desperately tried to bring his sword around but he knew that he would not make it. Suddenly the warrior was thrown to the ground by a javelin and Wolf waved his thanks to Marcus.

And then there were no more Carvetii before him. He reined Blackie and patted his neck. He turned and saw his men despatching the wounded. "Get their weapons. They are not as easy to get hold of and check for any bracelets and coins." Marcus looked at him in surprise. "Better in our pockets son rather than being eaten with the bodies." He looked to see if there were any empty saddles. There were none. "Gaius, any injuries?"

The voice called back from the darkness of the woods. "A couple of cuts, nothing too bad." There was a pause. "The new lads have all had a valuable lesson."

Wolf smiled. A light wound was a lesson well learned as the alternative was death. He glanced up at Marcus and Lucius who were still close by. "You did well. Good throw Marcus. How many did you kill?"

"Two sir."

Lucius?"

His face fell in shame, "Just one I think."

"One, even a possible one is better than a none and a dead trooper. Remember you are all worth ten dead barbarians at least."

The troopers were rubbing down their horses when Wolf entered the Prefect's office. "They knew we were coming. It was an ambush."

"But the Queen herself told us that there were Carvetii there."

"Sir, with due respect I don't think the Queen saw them with her own eyes. Someone told her and I would like to ask them some questions."

"You are suspicious Felix."

"Sir I had a turma mainly made of recruits. If it were not for Gaelwyn and Osgar they could be dead and I hate wasting time training recruits for them to die on me the first timeout."

"Point taken. I will visit Stanwyck myself and find out the truth."

"Thank you sir. I hate being tricked."

Prefect Proculus took Gerjen, Kadarcs and the Fifth Turma to visit the Queen when she had returned to her hill fort. Stanwyck was less a place of refuge and more a defensible settlement. The ditches and mounds had been built in antiquity but, as a busy stream ran through the middle of it the place could be used as a home as well. The Queen's guards acted as sentries on the main gates although half a cohort could have taken it easily had they chosen to do so. The Romans were waved through by serious looking Brigantes who wore torcs and battle amulets. They did not scowl at the Romans but Marius could see they wished they could have tested their courage against the Roman war machine. The residence of the Queen was obvious. It was the only building which had any stone in its construction. The round huts of the Brigante were as their ancestors had lived but the Queen wished to live as a Roman and it was obvious that Imperial Engineers had designed the building.

"You lads water the horses and wait outside. I will not belong."

154

Kadarcs and Gerjen looked longingly at the door. "Can we not join you sir. We have heard of the Queen but never seen her."

"No Gerjen. This is an official visit. I don't want the pair of you slobbering like horny ferrets in heat."

"Sir!" They both returned to their horses in disgust.

Marius knew he was aggravating the situation for the mystery of the Queen grew each day. In truth she was a creature of mystery and myth. What other woman would take on her enemies and defeat them with a combination of guile and cunning. The Brigante had suffered fewer losses than any other tribe; mainly because Cartimandua had not fought the Romans and only the rebels who had sided with her husband had left her. It meant there was a huge untapped force of warriors. Should Rome want them they could be a great asset.

There was an antechamber and he waited there until the old centurion who had been left by Claudius as her adviser strode out. He still affected the grizzled hair cut of a centurion and a gladius hung at his waist. He nodded to Marius' sword and Marius sighed as put the sword on the table placed there for that purpose. She was a careful Queen and even her allies had to meet her unarmed.

She lounged on her throne and the young warrior Vellocatus stood behind her, demonstrating his position in the court. He stroked her hair and she played with his hand, like a pair of young lovers although the Queen had to be in her thirties, at least. "Ah Prefect. I hear you caught those Carvetii. Give my thanks to the troopers who killed them."

"Thank you, your majesty. That is why I am here. Those Carvetii planned to ambush my men. Luckily our scouts spotted them."

Suddenly she flicked Vellocatus' hand away in irritation. "I see and what is the purpose of your visit?"

"We would like to know who told you that there were Carvetii seen."

Her eyes narrowed and pierced Marius as though she was trying to see inside his head. "And what do you suspect? That I wished your men to be ambushed?"

"Of course not but it may be that someone deliberately planted that information with you which you, in good faith passed on."

She waved an imperious finger at Gerantium who bowed and wandered forwards. "Where did the news come from?"

"It was your cousin, Brennus. He was travelling from his estates in the land of the lakes when he said he saw them." He spread his arms in apology. "As he was your uncle we did not think that his word was to be doubted."

"And where is he now?"

"He returned home the next day when your majesty left for Eboracum."

"Apologies Prefect but as you suffered no losses we were lucky. However I will verify all information I pass on in future and I will have a word with my uncle soon." There was an icy chill to her words and Marius reflected as he left the hall that she would be the wrong women to offend.

The work continued on the road and the Pannonian officers and men who had never seen the Romans building roads were impressed. By the time winter was drawing on they had build the road and were constructing the bridge. Tribune Celsus and his turma arrived and met with Flavius at the bridge works. "Your ala's work here is finished Decurion Princeps. We will watch the construction but I am afraid we have extended your patrol area."

Flavius gestured towards the wooden structure. "I think this is a mistake tribune. It just makes it easier for the barbarians to raid over the frontier and I know the Legate says they could swim over but they couldn't do that with slaves or cattle could they?"

"I know Flavius but it is progress. The Empire must expand. The Emperor is thinking of cutting his losses and pulling back from the whole province. Think of all the sacrifices which have been made. They would all have been in vain. The veterans who have settled in this land would be slaughtered. No the Governor and the Legate have to make the Province profitable gain and this bridge will open up that trade."

When Flavius returned he was just in time for the meeting Marius held, each week, with his officers. The mundane matters such as sentry duties and patrol areas had been assigned when Flavius walked in. "Sorry I am late sir but the Tribune was speaking with me. They are building the bridge."

"I know Flavius and I know the reason he spoke with me. What you may not know is that the Emperor, for some reason loaned a large amount of money to the tribes for self improvement." He grinned, "I saw how the Queen used it when I visited her home. And now, for another unknown reason, he wants it back. We now have to enforce the tax collection for some of the tribes. There will be unrest. I am keeping four turmae here and the rest of you will be assigned an area and a tax collector who will be responsible for collecting the Emperor's loan."

"That will cause problems sir."

"I know Cava. I will send the turmae who have those volunteers from Britannia to police their own tribal areas. It may help to have someone with local knowledge." He looked around at the depressed faces. He wished he had some good news to give. "Oh and Decurion Felix. You were right. There was a traitor who gave false information to lead you into an ambush. It was the Queen's uncle Brennus." He paused. "He is dead and his family and the relatives of Venutius are now hostages to the good behaviour of the others." He sat down with a tired look. "She is a ruthless woman. Make no mistake. I would not wish to get on the wrong side of that lady."

The turmae left for their new patrol areas the following day. Decurion Ulpius Felix and Cava had the furthest to travel for they were based south of Lindum. The Second Turma would have to visit the land of the Iceni. As they rode south Cava was philosophical about the whole matter." At least we get to spend some time in barracks and we won't have to build camps."

"I know Cava but I have spoken with Drusus and Lucius, both are Iceni and they have said that their people resent the Romans already. The Queen and the King do not agree on their policies. He is an old man. What happens when he dies?"

"I know not but remember when we were recruited; the Tribune was collecting taxes then in our land and our people paid."

"Yes but we had been conquered for a whole generation. We are collecting taxes from the warriors we defeated, not their sons and grandsons."

Chapter 12

They separated at Lindum each with an official, a body guard and driver and a cart. The Second Turma was heading for Venta Icenorum, the capital of the Iceni. Cava and his turma were set for Derventio, close to Carl Wark and the tribes who lived there. Wolf had never seen such flat land and they had a long time to appreciate it for, despite the excellent road, travelling at cart speed was slower than protecting the legions. The wind whistled from the east bringing the tang of the sea. It was strange to think that Germania Inferior was but a hundred miles, or so he had been told, due east of where he was. He had chosen not to lead, while on the road, but to ride at the rear and watch his turma. It would do Gaius good to be at the front as a leader. He would be the next Decurion, Wolf was in no doubt about that and then he would need another Chosen Man. The one he would choose would be Marcus but he could not due to his youth but he had every quality you wanted in a leader. He was clever, thoughtful, a superb horseman and an excellent warrior and he had something that you cannot create in a leader, personality; the men liked him. It would probably be Tiberius who would follow Gaius. There were plenty of candidates for aquilifer. The cocky Drusus would be the one to have that honour. It would teach him a little more humility.

The Iceni capital was deep in the heart of the land of the Iceni and their journey seemed to last forever. Eventually they saw the settlement which showed clear evidence of the Roman influence. Brick built buildings stood cheek by jowl with round houses. Wolf trotted next to Drusus and Lucius. "Right lads what can you tell me?"

As he expected it was cocky Drusus who spoke first. "I didn't come from this part of the land sir but I can tell you that the warriors here are the fiercest of the Iceni. They all believe they were never defeated and our, sorry sir, their king gave in too easily." He shrugged. "He likes all things Roman sir, what can I say?"

"Lucius?"

"I did live here sir. The Queen and her daughters choose not to live in the King's home. They prefer the hut they used before the times of the Romans." He hesitated.

"Come on Lucius out with it. I would rather I know the truth before I get there rather than find out the hard way."

"Well sir Drusus is right. The Queen is the power in this land and some say she is a witch."

"Drusus?"

"There are rumours that she journeys to Mona but…"

"Thank you for that intelligence. When we are there you two keep your ears open as well as your eyes. They may not know you are Iceni and say things they shouldn't when you are near to them."

The guards at the gates were contemptuous as they saw the Romans approach but their position as allies meant they had to allow the cart and cavalry in. They said something and Wolf was pleased that neither Iceni trooper reacted. It was a good sign. The tax collector looked nervous and gestured for Wolf to approach. "I have been here before Decurion. Please keep your men close to the cart and I would appreciate a close escort."

Looking at the cold stares they were getting Wolf could understand it. "I will come with you and three of my men. How is that?"

The official nodded gratefully. He had hoped that the tough looking Decurion would come with him. He had been afraid of him and he hoped that the Iceni would too. "I do appreciate that Decurion."

The driver skilfully negotiated the crowds who jostled the busy streets. The big cavalry horses flanking the cart help to carve a path to the stone building ahead. As they dismounted Wolf turned to Gaius. "Watch the cart. I will leave Lucius with you, he may hear things. I will take Drusus, Marcus and Metellus with me."

"Sir they are all young recruits."

The Decurion grinned, "How touching Gaius. You are worried about me. Never fret. I have the easier task for the king apparently likes us." He waved with his hand. "Every one of these bastards wants to slit your throat."

Leaving a bemused Gaius, he strode up the stairs with the tax collector and bodyguard. "Drusus, Marcus, Metellus, with me." The three recruits raced after him and the diminutive tax collector gave a weak grateful smile as the four warriors surrounded him.

When they reached the door two Iceni warriors stood there with their spears crossed. "Leave your weapons before you go in."

Wolf strode up to them. "I am Decurion Lupus Ulpius Felix of the Second Turma, First Pannonian Ala and the only man who tells me to take off my sword is my Prefect so step aside before I knock you down."

Marcus had a sharp intake of breath and then he noticed that the Decurion was wearing his gladius and not his spatha. He was ready for trouble. One of the guards began to lower his hand to his sword and Wolf said quietly, "You will lose your fucking hand as well as your life if you draw that."

Suddenly the tension was broken as an official came to the door and said something in Iceni. The two red faced warriors stepped back but the one Wolf had threatened said, "This is not finished Roman."

"Don't flatter yourself. If it was finished you would be dead."

"Come with me officers and apologies for the guards," he shrugged. "Men with swords eh?" Realising who he was talking to, he stammered, "Sorry Decurion, obviously I do not mean you and your men."

"It does not matter. How is the King?"

"He is still unwell but he was insistent that I bring you to him."

King Prasutagus was dressed like a Roman equestrian. Unlike his warriors he had short hair and his clothes were white expensive linen. He waved them forwards. "Welcome allies. How is the Emperor, the Divine Nero?"

Wolf looked at the tax collector who shrugged. "He is in good health your majesty. I am Decurion Lupus Ulpius Felix of the First Pannonian Ala and this is Quaestor Appius Sulpinus."

"You are both welcome and what is the purpose of your visit?"

Appius gave an apologetic shrug, "We are here to collect the Emperor's taxes."

Wolf was as relieved as the Quaestor when the king gave a bored shrug. He turned to the official who had brought them in.

160

"Arrange it." Turning back to his guests as the official scurried out he said, "While we wait would you care to share an amphora of wine with me. This one comes all the way from Sicily. I think it travels particularly well."

Grinning at his men Wolf took the proffered beaker. "The Quaestor and I will join you majesty but these boys are too young for such fine wine. It will be wasted on them." He gave an imperceptible nod to Drusus and touched his ear. Drusus acknowledged it and he moved away from the king to stand closer to the guards who were talking furtively to each other. The wine was fine but their enjoyment was curtailed when the whirlwind called Boudicca burst into the room.

She was a wild looking woman and if the King looked like a Roman then Boudicca looked like an Amazon. Her red hair hung down her shoulders and her green eyes flared like her nostrils. She was armed with a pair of wicked looking daggers and she wore warrior amulets and a torc. This was a formidable woman. "What is this I hear? Not only do the Romans impose their will on us they ask us to pay for the privilege."

"It is taxes. Perfectly normal." The king seemed uninterested in the Queen and her views. Behind her were her three daughters all of them looking equally as wild and untamed as their mother.

"It is not enough that you have left our land in your will to this Nero and me jointly. You are now giving away the money the people will need."

Prasutagus stood and Wolf saw that he would have been a powerful warrior in his time. "I am king here and my word is law. Not the cult of the mother!"

She pointed a long-nailed finger at him accusingly. "You blaspheme. It was the Mother who protected you. That protection is now no longer there. Beware my husband." She turned to leave and then glowered at Appius and Wolf. Appius cowered behind the Decurion who met the glare of the Queen without flinching. "And you, Romans, your time is coming to an end." She grinned evilly. "Go back home now while it is still safe."

Wolf stepped forwards. "Until my Emperor tells me otherwise Queen Boudicca then my home is Britannia."

She nodded a grudging acknowledgement. "Well at least one man in the room has balls!"

She strode out leaving all but Wolf reeling in her wake. "Apologies for my wife. She can be difficult."

Appius nodded his agreement and Wolf added, "Which is why I have never married King Prasutagus."

"Then you are a wiser man than I Roman." He resumed his reclined position and Appius began to count the coins as they came in.

While he was doing so Wolf spoke quietly with Drusus. "What did you hear?"

"The guards were the ones who summoned the Queen. All of these," he waved a surreptitious arm around the room, "are loyal to her and not our king." He looked dismayed. "I never knew."

"It matters not so long as we can leave with the taxes safely."

Appius stood, a relieved look upon his face. "They are correct your majesty."

"Good will you stay for food?"

Appius gave a nervous glance in Wolf's direction. "No majesty. We have far to travel."

"Thank you again and give the Governor my good wishes. It is some time since he has visited and I miss good company."

As they left Wolf felt sorry for the king who seemed lonely and isolated. Money and power were not the most important things in life as he had come to appreciate. Your friends were the rock upon which your troubles would crash. Once outside, Wolf sensed the hostility of the crowd. He saw Boudicca, her daughters and a band of men standing close to a hut festooned with mistletoe rosemary and ears of corn. He did not like the look she was giving him. "Gaius , Lucius." The two men approached.

"Sir?"

"Well Lucius?"

"I heard the Queen talking to one of her men and they were talking of getting back the tax."

Gaius jerked his head around to look at the Queen. "When? I heard nothing."

Lucius smiled. "She spoke in Iceni."

"Any idea where?"

"They didn't say."

"I am guessing it will be away from the town. Even though they are all on her side they will not want to do it this close to the king." He gave Blackie two handfuls of grain as they talked and kept the empty bags in his hand.

"I would go further sir. I would think that they will wait until we are well on the road to Lindum and then it could be just bandits."

"You are probably right Gaius. Quaestor." The boxes had been stored and he sat on the cart awaiting the move. "They are going to rob us, on the road." He looked around in panic. "Keep calm. I have a plan. Those boxes you just stored. Could their contents be placed in bags?"

"Yes but how does that help?"

Wolf ignored the questions. He looked at the cart which was pulled by two horses. It had a canvas cloth protecting it. "As soon as we leave the settlement and are out of sight I want you to get under the cover and begin to put the taxes in bags."

"Where will I get the bags?"

In answer Wolf gave him his bags the ones they used to carry the grain for the horses. "In these and then my men will carry them."

Appius shook his head. "Most irregular. How do I know your men won't simply ride off?"

"Because, you miserable little bean counter I say they won't and the alternative is that we get caught and you die. So..."

"Very well."

"Turma, ride." As he rode through the troopers he said, "Have your grain bags ready. If you have any food in them then feed your horses when we stop." If they were surprised by his command they did not show it. Decurion Ulpius Felix rarely did anything without a good reason. "Gaius, take four men and trail us by a mile. I don't want us followed. If there is trouble then let me know early."

"Sir!"

Passing the gate, they saw the evil smirks on the faces of the guards. One of them looked down at Marcus and pulled a finger across his throat. Drusus saw it. "Well that confirms it then. They want us dead!"

163

Wolf turned in his saddle until he was certain that they were out of sight. He yelled over his shoulder, "Quaestor!" If it had not been such a serious matter Wolf would have laughed at the sight of the official burrowing into the cart with just his skinny legs showing. Wolf rode down the line, "Keep moving. When I tell you take your bag to the cart, the Quaestor will fill it with the taxes and you will keep them on your saddle. Titus, take that fucking grin off your face. If there is one coin missing, I will be having roast troopers balls for breakfast." By the time he reached the Quaestor the two bags were filled and Wolf draped them over his saddle so that they balanced on each side. "Titus, Tiberius, bags!"

They were five miles from the settlement by the time it had been completed. Six of the troopers had not needed to use their bags. "Right Quaestor. I don't know if you can ride but you and the carter here are going to have to learn bloody quickly. We are going to leave the cart and get to Lindum as fast as possible."

"Impossible! That cart has been signed for by me."

Wolf nodded reasonably. "Then you stay with it Quaestor for as soon as we can we are going to gallop as hard as we can."

The carter said, "Don't worry sir. I can ride and I would like to hang on to my balls." He glared at the Quaestor meaningfully.

The official shrugged, "I can ride, sort of."

"Good man!"

They heard the drumming of hooves and every trooper's hand went to his sword. They were relieved to see it was Gaius. "Iceni sir, chariots and horses. They are about a mile and a half back."

"Right you two. Time for a ride." As the carter unhitched the horses Wolf shouted to the bodyguard. "Right sunshine, you start to do your job now. No matter what happens to us get your boss to Lindum. We will do the fighting. You guard the body. Right?"

"Right sir."

The two men were on the carthorses using the blankets as saddles; the carter had cut down the traces to make reins. "You three ride. Don't gallop, just keep a steady speed. We will follow." As they trotted off he said to the Turma. Get this cart under cover. I hope they wait a little further before they try anything." As the men did so he gestured for Tiberius. "Take the standard and Lucius. Guard the Quaestor. Lucius can speak the language if you get into trouble."

"But sir the standard should stay with the men."

The Decurion glared at him. "Just follow the orders eh?"

"Sir."

The two men rode off. Wolf nodded his approval, he could see no sign of the cart and the hoof prints obscured any tracks there might have been. "Turma, trot." The Chosen man and Decurion rode together. "Now we need a little luck on our side Gaius. They will come after us steadily and expect to catch us on the road when we camp. If they are any good then they will send fast scouts ahead to find us and if not... well we shall escape."

The flat featureless land seemed to take forever to traverse. The rider at the rear, Lentius, shouted, "Riders sir, about a mile back."

"They aren't good then Gaius, no scouts." All the time the Decurion was scanning the sides of the road for any sign of ambush. The legions who had built the road had done a good job and the undergrowth had been cleared for twenty paces on either side. The farmers had planted hawthorn, beech and blackthorn bushes to protect their fields and that was the only cover. The sun was beginning to dip when Lucius galloped up. "This is trouble Gaius.!

A breathless Lucius blurted out, "Sir the aquilifer sent me. One of the horses has gone lame. the carter and the tax man are riding double."

"Well there goes our luck. Here is what we will do. We will gallop ahead to the place where the road rises. Marcus and I will wait on the road as though one of our mounts has gone lame. Split the turma on either side of the road behind the bushes. If they attack us then throw your javelins and then get to the Quaestor."

"And if they don't attack?"

"Then we will talk to them and ask for help. But I suspect that they will come hunting bear. And Gaius, get the chariots and the horses first. It will block the road. Now ride and may the Allfather be with us this day."

They galloped quickly and, once they had crested the rise the turma split into two groups. "Right Marcus, dismount and let us examine our horses' hooves. Slip your shield around to your back."

As they did so Marcus asked, more to relieve the tension than anything, "Why choose me sir?"

"You are the best horsemen in the ala, apart from me of course, and you are clever. You don't panic. Now stop looking for compliments and watch over my shoulder."

"They are coming sir, and riding hard."

"Let me know if they are slowing."

"No sir. And the chariots have blades."

Wolf turned and saw them forty paces away with weapons raised. They intended harm. "Mount and let's ride!"

The first arrow whistled over their heads as they mounted whilst their horses were running. They both lay low over the horses' neck to maintain a low profile. Wolf felt a crack as something struck his shield and he looked under his arm. The Iceni were almost at the ambush point. "Ready to turn Marcus! Turn. Draw your sword."

The Iceni were still forty paces behind them and their faces showed that they anticipated an easy victory. Suddenly the three chariots which led the chase disappeared in a mass of broken wheels, terrified horses and screaming warriors. Marcus and Wolf charged and threw their javelins at the two horsemen who were trying to continue the chase. "Fall back!"

The turma raced along the hedgerow and Marcus and Wolf wheeled their horses to gallop down the road. "Well done Marcus. Good to see your nerves match your riding skills."

Gaius and the turma joined them at the next gap in the hedgerow. "I think we slowed them a little sir. I counted ten men down and eleven horses injured. The chariots are useless now."

"Good," he pointed ahead, "because if my eye doesn't deceive me there is our tax man."

The three horses ahead were being led by the carter who had given the horse to the Quaestor. They pulled up and Wolf ordered the carter to get behind Lucius. "He is the lightest and we have only slowed those bastards down not stopped them."

Riding along Gaius asked, "Where are we going to camp tonight?" He pointed to the civilian horses. "Our mounts could go further but they are all in and we can't afford another lame horse."

"I was hoping to make it to Durobrivae but I think that is too far. We need to look for somewhere we can defend, just in case they are persistent."

By the time they saw somewhere suitable the horses were almost at the point of collapse and it was close to dark. The found a deserted group of round houses. They had obviously been eliminated by the Roman road builders for there was half a round house twenty paces from the road and then the other three deserted one. There was still the semblance of a ditch which would afford some protection. "Get the civilians and their horses in the house the furthest from the road. Marcus, Drusus, Lucius, hobble the horses, let them feed in the field and then put them in the second round house. The rest of you, deepen the ditch and extend it to the road. Cut down some of the bushes and we will cover the ditch with them when we are done."

One tired voice in the dark moaned, "Dig with what?"

"With your hands if you have to, just dig. Gaius, come with me." The two of them went across the road to the blackthorn tree. Its wickedly sharp thorns were perfect for lillia. "Cut down about twenty of these branches and stick them in the bottom of the ditch."

He strode down the road.

"Where are you off to sir?"

"It's dark, they can't see me but I can hear them."

He walked two hundred paces down the road and looked back at the huts. In the dark it was hard to see them and he could only make out vague movements. That was good. Once they were settled down for the night they would be invisible and it was possible that the Iceni would miss them in the dark. He listened and, at first, he could hear nothing. He took off his helmet and put his ear to the stones of the road. He felt a faint vibration. They were coming.

As he hurried into the improvised fort he said as quietly as possible. "Cover the ditches, get the horses under cover and arm yourselves. We have visitors." He ducked into the hut with the three civilians in. "Arm yourselves we may have visitors. We will try to hold them off. If I think they are going to break in I will yell Quaestor run. You go into the next hut, cut the hobbles on the horses and take the horses with you. The taxes are still on the saddles and you should be able to escape in the dark. There is a fort fifteen miles ahead. You should be able to make it."

The bodyguard and the carter nodded, grateful for the sacrifice but the Quaestor looked puzzled. "But what of you?"

"We are soldiers of Rome. We will do our duty." With that he left. The men were waiting for him close to the ditch. "Get rid of your cloaks they will only trip you up. Use your swords we don't want you hitting each other and wait for my command."

The newer troopers found that they all needed to pee and that it was suddenly cold. Gaius felt Lucius shivering and murmured. "Don't worry son. It will go away when we start fighting."

The Iceni were good horsemen but one of their beasts let them down. The whinny told them that the pursuers had caught them. Wolf drew out his gladius and the others slid their blades silently from their scabbards. Although they were outnumbered Wolf was confident that they would win. They had shields and armour and a ditch. The Iceni assumed that they would be in the huts and that gave the troopers the edge. There was a rustle as the invisible warriors approached the ditch. Then there was a scream as one of the warriors stepped onto a blackthorn stake quickly followed by a second and a third. "Wait!" hissed Wolf.

There was a collective roar as the Iceni hurled themselves at the huts. The ditch tripped and trapped some of them and the first few through the barrier found themselves hacked and stabbed by the waiting turma. Soon, however, the numbers were more even as more of the Iceni clambered through the trap. "Go for their legs, they have no armour." Although not honourable and not part of the warrior code, the long spatha could outreach most of the shorter weapons wiled by the enemy. Their swords held high to protect against the expected sword they fell to the ground as the long blades sliced into their thighs. Those who did manage to strike a blow found they hit a shield or a helmet and did no damage. Their leader, whoever he was, knew they could not win and a call in Iceni sounded above the combat. "He is telling them to retreat," yelled Lucius.

"Let them go!" They heard the scramble through the brush and the galloping of horses down the road. "Gaius, check for casualties!"

He looked down at the Iceni who lay at his feet, his life blood draining through his leg which was cur through to the bone. He spat at Wolf's feet. "You have no honour you Roman dog. You could not fight me as a man!"

"A man with honour does not sneak up to his enemies at night." He kicked the man's sword out of reach. "And you will die without a sword in your hand."

The man suddenly laughed. "That is your belief, not mine. I will go now to the Mother and I will return stronger from the Earth. This is why you will never defeat us Roman." Wolf watched as the man slowly died, the last sigh of live whispering from his dead lips. "Arminius is dead and three others have slight wounds."

"We will bury him in the morning. Half sleep and half watch." He saw Gaius' pained expression. "They may come back. Better to be safe than sorry. Wake me at moonrise."

They found two horses wandering in the fields nearby as dawn broke and they slung two of the dead Iceni on to their backs. The travelled wearily to the Roman fort, handed over the Quaestor and taxes and the dead Iceni to the Prefect. "They could be bandits Decurion."

"They could be but both you and I know they are not."

The Prefect took Wolf by the arm and lowered his voice. "There will come a time when we exact revenge for this but that time is not yet. You have done well Decurion and it was a clever ruse to carry the taxes on the horses. I will say so in my report."

"That will not bring back my dead trooper but I understand that politics sometimes makes for unpleasant decisions. We will, sir, with your permission, head back to Lindum. Our work here is done."

As he left the Praetorium the Quaestor grabbed his arm. "Thank you, Decurion and my apologies, for doubting you. It is thanks to you that I am alive and I know that."

"Thank you, Quaestor, but I was just doing my duty."

"But you would have given your life for me and those of your men."

He nodded, "It is what we are paid for."

Chapter 13

Marius and the ala had been summoned from their forts to the embryo fortress of Eboracum. Although still a wooden structure there were now docks and the Classis Britannica was able to bring men and supplies directly into the erstwhile capital of the Roman north. The Legate was happier to have direct access to support now that his forces were so stretched.

Centurion Maro, First Spear of the Ninth was there as was Prefect Spurius of the Gallic Cohort. "Things are moving in the Province. Gaius Suetonius Paulinus is leading the Twentieth on an attack on Mona. We will finally be rid of those vipers and King Prasutagus of the Iceni has died. It means the Emperor Nero now rules jointly with Boudicca the Queen."

First Spear snorted, "And with due respect sir, how in the God's name will that work. We know from Decurion Felix's report that she hates the Romans and has just been waiting to take power. She is no Cartimandua, she is the opposite."

"Yes well that is as may be but we have been asked to move a cohort to Durobrivae with half of the ala as a contingency plan in case they rise up."

"One cohort and five hundred horsemen will not stop the Iceni."

"We are sending the Gallic cohort as well First Spear."

"That is still just two and a half thousand men Legate."

"I will be commanding them." He said it as though his presence was worth another thousand men but the centurion just rolled his eyes heavenward. "We will leave at the end of the week. Prefect Proculus stay behind for a moment."

The others nodded to Marius as they left. The Legate sat with fingers together looking at the map. "Sir?"

"Oh sorry Prefect. Now when you leave half of the ala at Cataractonium I assume that you will leave the Decurion Princeps in charge of the half ala."

"I had not thought that far ahead."

"Well I would like you with me so let us leave him there. And how about your older officers?"

"Decurion Murgus retired last year and moved to Verulamium. Decurion Sextus has retired but stayed on as Quartermaster."

"So you have enough stability there."

"Yes sir."

"I think we need a second Decurion Princeps."

"Well there are two obvious candidates; Decurion Felix and Decurion Paterculus."

The Legate shook his head. "Both good men and worthy of their position but they are Pannonian and we need Romans."

"In that case Decurion Buteo, he is the last of the original Troopers."

"I think he is a little too old."

Marius wondered where the Legate was going with this; he obviously had a candidate in mind. "Who would you recommend then sir?"

"Gaius Cresens."

"No sir!"

The Legate's eyes narrowed and he suddenly sat upright. "What exactly do you mean Prefect?"

"I mean that I do not want that pervert in my ala at all and I certainly do not want him as Decurion Princeps."

"You forget yourself Prefect. I am Legate and, in the Governor's absence, I make all appointments and Gaius Cresens will be the Decurion Princeps in your ala. Need I remind you Prefect that your family name does not give you security in your post?"

"That sounds like a threat to me Legate."

He shrugged nonchalantly, "To be honest I do not care what you take to be a threat or an order. But it will happen."

Marius wanted to reach over and punch the pompous Legate in the face but he knew he had no power at all. "Very well sir but I will not be responsible for his treatment in the ala."

The Legate stood and spoke with a pause between each word to emphasis its meaning. "You are the Prefect of the ala and if anything untoward happens to Gaius Cresens then there will be a new Prefect in command of the ala."

"Sir!"

The ala was camped close to the river and, as he walked back, Marius wondered how he could break the news to his officers.

There would be no easy way and he owed his officers, and the men, honesty. He felt himself colouring already before he even met them. This was embarrassing and a mark of his family's fall from favour. He just hoped they would understand. He walked slowly into the tent. There was a good atmosphere and he could tell that they had been drinking. It was not often that they had the chance to relax and let down their guard; here at Eboracum they were safe.

"Hello sir! And where are we off to now?"

Kadarcs had never changed and, even as a Decurion he was still irrepressible. "Just down south Decurion. We are going to be close to the Iceni."

Wolf gave Cava a sharp look. He had told his friend about the threat and warned that they would have to move further south. "Prasutagus?"

"Yes Wolf, he has died."

"Then we are in for a shit load of trouble."

The mood had instantly changed and Marius knew he had to be honest. "The ala is splitting in two. The Decurion Princeps will remain in Cataractonium with half of the turmae and we will go south to Durobrivae with the rest and the new Decurion Princeps." Flavius shrugged.

They all looked in anticipation at Wolf and Cava. There was much nudging and murmuring. Flavius knew the Prefect well and this did not look like good news. "Who is it to be then sir?"

Marius took a deep breath and looked assiduously at Wolf. "It is Gaius Cresens."

The one Decurion that Marius had expected to react the most strongly just sat there; a cold hard expression on his face. The rest all began talking at once. Marius held up a tired hand. "It is done; it is the Legate's decision." The noise subsided. "If he is hurt then there will be a new Prefect. He will meet us at Durobrivae."

The euphoria and excitement of the moment dissipated like fog on a summer's morning. Wolf stood and, putting his hand on the Prefect's shoulder, said, "It is not your fault Prefect. We will not let you down and we will deal with it." The threat in Wolf's voice sent shivers down the prefect's spine.

The Selgovae did not normally raid in winter and certainly not into Roman territory but they had seen the new bridge being built in the autumn. They had waited for the fort to be built but, inexplicably, the men of iron who built the road had disappeared and, gradually, the dreaded horse warriors had stopped their patrols. To Tad, chief of the Selgovae warband who lived close to the thick forest in the north, this was too good an opportunity to miss. They were hard men and a journey through the cold land in the shortest days did not worry them. It was as though the gods were aiding them by providing the cover of dark. The Brigante had women who could be slaves and many animals to feed the Selgovae through the winter. The soft Brigante had become too used to the protection of the Romans and now, as Tad led his men across the wooden bridge in the cold dawn of winter, he thanked the Romans for making their lives so much easier. They were not mounted for they were a forest people but they moved swiftly through the frosty land.

The first settlement, ten huts in all, was still asleep when the wolves of the north fell upon them. Their men were slaughtered and the women and children bound. Tad sent them and their animals north with an escort of ten men. He still had thirty warriors, which was more than enough to deal with the second settlement, a little further west and close to the river. This collection of eight huts had neither ditch nor fence to keep out intruders but they did have an old man with a weak bladder. He saw the raiders and yelled a warning, "He died with an arrow in his chest but he had died honourably, helping his people. The few men and boys grabbed whatever they had and hurled themselves at the enemy in an attempt to defend their families. The headman, Cynbel wished his son Gaelwyn and his brother Osgar were with him for then they might have had a chance. As he slew a Selgovae with his axe he saw that they would die and he yelled to the women and children, "Flee to the woods! Find the Romans!" The handful of defenders paid with their lives for the chance to escape but sadly but one boy managed to escape. The Selgovae slaughtered the defenders and then set off after the women and children. One small boy, Adair, made himself as small as possible and hid under a bramble bush. He heard the Selgovae hunting but he lay undiscovered. When he was sure that they had gone he emerged and, despite Cynbel's instructions he returned to the village, hoping to find some who still lived. There were none. Remembering the last orders, he set off to the south, heading for the Roman road which would bring him to the Roman fort and the horse warriors.

Flavius was still brooding about the appointment of Gaius Cresens when the sentry reported the boy's arrival. "Bring him in." Gaius Cresens was not a threat to Flavius but he would upset the morale of the ala and Flavius could not see why the Legate had ignored the advice of the Prefect. All thoughts of Cresens left his mind as soon as the weeping and bloody boy was brought before him. "Send for the Capsarius and Gaelwyn the scout." He went to the outer office, "Julius bring some food and water. This boy is about to collapse." The ala clerk was an efficient man and he brought the boy some warmed watered-down wine. Flavius nodded his thanks. As the boy wolfed down the bread and gratefully drank the warming wine. His fingers and lips were blue. Flavius knew he would get no sense from him until he was warmer.

The capsarius quickly dressed the wounds and Gaelwyn came in as the medical orderly was finishing. "You sent for me...Adair!" As soon as the boy saw Gaelwyn he burst into tears and threw his arms around the youth.

"You know him?"

"He is from my village."

"Find out what happened."

Between sobs the boy called Adair blurted out the story. Grim faced, Gaelwyn held the young boy in the crook of his arm. "The Selgovae raided my village sir and they killed all the men, including my father, and they took our families."

Flavius knew he had no time to lose. He went to the sentry. "Sound to arms. The ala rides within the hour." Turning to the capsarius he said, "Look after the boy. Come Gaelwyn we shall need your skills this day."

Gaelwyn needed no urging as he led them unerringly to the village. The devastation was clear. "Gaelwyn, we have no time to honour the dead now, let us follow."

"Sir!" The youth scanned the ground and then set off around the edge of the village. His voice came from the bushes. "This way sir. They are heading for the bridge."

The passed the first raided settlement saw they neared the bridge. Once they reached it they could see that they had been too late. On the northern bank lay the bodies of two of the villagers who had been too slow to continue the journey. Their lack of clothes and the way they lay left the pursuers in no doubt that they had been raped before they had died.

Flavius had the bodies brought back and Gaelwyn waited on the northern bank. "Come on sir. We will lose them."

Flavius shook his head. "These girls were killed many hours ago." He pointed to the sun which was setting. "We will not find them this night and I cannot follow north, we are the only soldiers in this part of the world. No Gaelwyn, when the ala returns then we will rescue them."

Gaelwyn's face filled with tears. "But sir my mother, my sister Duana, my cousin Ailis?"

"I know Gaelwyn but you have my word that they will be recovered but we will stop any more incursions. Destroy the bridge."

Decurion Buteo rode next to his friend. "Is that wise? Have you the authority?"

"The bridge was built when we had a legion here and a full ala. Until they return this is the frontier once more. It is my decision Numerius and I will take any blame."

"We all stand with you." He nodded to the youth. "He and his uncle Osgar will take this badly you know?"

"I know but we cannot do aught else."

As the ala, the Gauls and the First Cohort marched into Durobrivae a messenger was already travelling from Dubris with a message for the Governor. He did not know its contents but it was like the tiny flame which would engulf the whole province. As he rode north, first to Londinium and then to Durobrivae the Legate himself was receiving news from Mona that the Governor had almost defeated the druids but at a great cost.

Gaius Cresens had stayed close to his sponsor, the Legate whenever he could. He had not been assigned a turma and the

Prefect had assiduously omitted to give him any duties. In the first weeks at the fort the Legate was too busy to notice but as the days began to lengthen slightly he summoned the Prefect. Gaius Cresens sulkily sat in the corner. "Prefect, my orders were for this officer to become Decurion Princeps. Why has this not been put into action?"

"It has sir. This officer is now my deputy."

"Don't try to be funny with me Prefect. He has not been given any duties nor has he been given men to command. Do so now!"

"I cannot create a turma sir. We are not at full strength yet."

"Very well. There are thirty recruits here and they will be given to the Decurion Princeps as his turma. He can command and train them and you will ensure that the rest of the ala understand and respect his position."

"Very well sir!"

The recruits had not been trained yet as Marius did not like the look of them. These were no the young warriors of Britannia, like Lucius and Marcus, these were the ones rejected in Gaul and Batavia by Prefects who knew trouble when they saw it. In a way Marius was perversely pleased that they had been given to Cresens but at the same time he was proud of the ala and did not want its reputation tarnished. He was pragmatic enough to realise that he could not win in this situation.

Their camp was adjacent to the fortress and his officers had been training the men in readiness for a spring campaign. They all knew that the Iceni were in a state of unrest and it was only the winter which prevented them from showing their displeasure. Wolf had a smaller turma than most but they were well trained. The Prefect used his turma to patrol the northern borders of the land of the Iceni. Osgar did not know the land and he did not like it. "Flat and boggy! The Iceni can keep it."

Wolf smiled at his scout. "Good farmland though Osgar."

"Farmland! Give me a forest for hunting a river for fishing. I have looked in these piddly little rivers. There're only a few eels in them. Not real fish, salmon."

"Concentrate on getting the lay of the land. When we are needed then we will have to ride quickly and I remember when we were here in the autumn. I want to be better prepared."

They were on their way back and approaching the Via Claudia when Drusus who was at the rear shouted, "Sir, rider. He looks to be Roman."

Wolf halted the patrol and the Imperial messenger galloped up to meet them. "Ah good, Romans; I was worried you might be bandits."

Wolf shook his head. "I take it this is your first time in Britannia?"

"Yes Decurion. It is the wild frontier is it not?"

"This is the civilised part. Who is the message for?"

He hesitated, wondering if this scarred Decurion was to be trusted and then he continued. "It is from the Emperor himself and is for the Governor or whoever is in command in this region."

"The Governor is in the west and, believe me, you do not want to go there. They really are savages there but the Legate Cerialis is in Durobrivae. Then your job is done."

The young messenger grinned. "That is a relief. It is my first important message and it has weighed heavily upon me."

As they rode into the camp Wolf gestured at the fort. "The Legate is in there. He likes his comfort." The messenger rode off and Wolf led his patrol into the stables. As they dismounted he noticed the new recruits leaving the stables. He liked neither their looks nor their attitude. Since Gaius Cresens had taken them over they seemed imbued with a sense of ill-deserved superiority. They slouched past him and, as he stood in the stable entrance he shouted. "You troopers, halt." They slowly turned around. "When you see an officer, you salute." They stared at him. "Do it!" The bark worked and they all saluted. Wolf would not normally have made a fuss but he resented Cresens and his influence.

As he entered the stable he heard the Decurion Princeps as he shouted, "Those are my men and I order them not you Decurion." The pudgy officer came out of a stall.

Wolf turned to Gaius, "Watch the door." Gaius threw him a warning look. "Just watch my back." As Gaius turned Wolf leapt forward and pinned Gaius Cresens against the stall. "Let us get one thing clear you are only here because the Legate ordered the Prefect to accept you but there is not a single officer or trooper who will obey you." He whipped his pugeo out and held it close to Cresens eye. "You remember this don't you? Well here is a

178

warning. You order your little bunch of bandits around but no-one else. Now I know what you are thinking. You will go to the Legate and you will tell him of my actions. I can see it in your piggy little eyes. Now if you do I dare say I will be reprimanded, perhaps even flogged." He shrugged. "I can live with that. Maybe even demoted. I don't care for if you do tell the Legate then you will be killed. This is no idle threat. I should have killed you for what you did to Lucius but that is my mistake and I will live with it but you, you fat, evil fucker will keep away from the rest of us. Do you understand?" The point of the pugeo was incredibly close to Cresens eye. Cresens remained silent. "I understand about eyes you know? I lost mine in a battle. They are very fragile things. If I was to push this forwards it would enter your eye. If I pushed a little further and twisted it would pop out like a cork from an amphora. Let me ask you again, do you understand?"

The terrified officer croaked, "Yes."

Wolf released him. "And remember. There is not just me who wishes you harm, there are five hundred troopers here and another five hundred at Cataractonium who would do as I promised and when we go into battle... watch your back! For no-one else will."

The white-faced officer stormed past Gaius. "You want to watch him sir. He's a sly bastard."

Decurion Lupus Ulpius Felix grinned and it was a grin without humour. "I have not yet finished with the fat one."

As the Legate was reading the Imperial missive a trooper rode in to the camp from the north. It was one of the troopers from the tenth turma. He reported directly to the Prefect. Wolf was walking to his tent when Marius waved him over. "Where is Osgar?"

"He is probably hunting himself some supper sir why?"

"News from the north; his village was attacked, the men slain and the women and children taken as slaves."

"His brother then?"

"Aye and Gaelwyn's family too. It will go hard with him."

Wolf shook his head. "He will not show it but he will remember, it is the Brigante way. I have learned much about them since working with him. We will see no tears but the

Selgovae had best watch out for he is a wicked enemy. Would you like me to tell him sir?"

"If you would and speaking of wicked enemies, who upset our new Decurion Princeps?"

Wolf gave the prefect his most innocent face. Not easy with a scar running down it." Couldn't say sir."

"Lupus, be careful he is a dangerous man."

"No sir, I am a dangerous man he is a pervert with a nasty streak. That is the difference and do not worry sir. I will be careful."

Wolf sought Osgar and told him of the disaster. As he had expected Osgar just nodded. "Sir," he smiled, "Wolf. I do not know the country around here and the young Iceni troopers you have know as much as I do. I think Gaelwyn will need me."

"Of course, Osgar. You have my permission." He smiled, "Take a horse. You will get there quicker."

"Very well, but just the once and if I get piles again I am blaming you, sir"

The Legate summoned the senior officers to a meeting. It irked Marius somewhat to see Gaius Cresens present but he could not say anything about it. "We have our orders from the Emperor Nero himself." Cerialis said it as though the word had come from Nero's lips directly into his ear. "We are to enforce the terms of the will of King Prasutagus. The Emperor and the King's daughters are to inherit the land of the Iceni. Of course the girls are too young to inherit and so we will invest their capital and take the treasury."

"But sir what if they resist?"

"Your Decurion, er Decurion Felix reported that there were but three hundred warriors in their capital. We will take the Ninth legion and a cohort of your ala to enforce the decision. I will take the Decurion Princeps and his new turma. The rest of your ala and the Gallic Cohort will ensure that no aid comes from the outside. Once I have enforced the Emperor's wishes," he tapped the letter, "and they are precise, then we will have no more trouble from the Iceni and, now that the druids are subjugated we can have peace in this province at last."

As they were leaving First Spear walked out with Marius. "Did I hear a rumour about your new Decurion Princeps?" Marius flashed him a sharp look. The veteran centurion held up his hands. "If you tell me it is false then I will believe you."

His shoulders sagged with resignation. "Sadly, they are true but if I say that he is sponsored by the Legate then you will understand why my hands are tied."

"From the rumours that is one of Gaius Cresens specialities."

"Don't it is not funny."

"I know. I will get the Tribune to keep an eye on him. From what I know it should not be a problem. The Iceni have not fought since the first invasion and their warriors are spread over a large area."

Prefect Spurius joined them. "What?"

"I was telling the Prefect that the Iceni are, apparently spread over a large area."

Decius Spurius shook his head. "The Queen was close to Caractacus and she is close to the Druids on Mona; if she decides to rebel it will be more than the Iceni. I think all we are doing here is making sure that our Legate enforces the Emperor's orders."

They walked on in silence. As they came to the gate where they would part First Spear drew them aside, out of the hearing of the sentries. "Tribune Celsus told me that he thinks that the Emperor's solution will be a final solution."

"You mean execution?"

"It would tie up loose ends."

"But the girls are too young, they are virgins."

First Spear suddenly looked very old. He shook his head sadly, "At the moment they are…"

Marius suddenly understood First Spear's probing questions. "I wondered why he chose Gaius Cresens and his rabble to be the only cavalry presence."

Prefect Spurius looked confused, "Gaius Cresens, the fat man who was the Legate's aide… oh I see." He put his arm around Marius' shoulders. "I did worry that he would try to palm that piece of shit off on to me. Sorry."

"You never know he may end up with an Iceni blade in his back."

"No, his kind survives and the good die young. It is the way of the world."

First Spear laughed, "Well as the oldest bastard around here I guess that makes me the baddest bugger too!" Clapping them both around the shoulders he led them back into the fort. "Come on I have a particularly fine amphora of wine, well not the finest but let us finish it, if only to take the bad taste in my mouth away."

In the Praetorium Gaius Cresens and the Legate were holding a private meeting. "This is where you repay all the favours I have done you. The Emperor wants the bitches dead but we must be seen to do things right. I secured your appointment as Decurion Princeps for just this occasion. Serve me well and I will let the Emperor know."

"You know I am not cut out as a regular officer. You know of my needs."

The Legate shivered and closed his eyes. "It is why I chose you for this task. Now your turma, have you men in there who would do your bidding? Regardless of the act?"

"Almost all of them. The Prefect thought he was hurting me by giving me all the disreputable characters he had left. We will not be fighting but we will be doing your bidding Legate. "

"Good then when we reach Venta Icenorum I will inform the Queen and her daughters of the Emperor's decision. She will have bodyguards with her. Your men will ensure that they do not cause any trouble. I will endeavour, and I do not think it will be hard from what I hear, to rile and annoy the Queen. She and her daughters can then be punished. You and whichever of your men you decide can rape the girls. When that is done they will be executed and the lands and coffers of the Iceni will be Rome's."

"Rome's alone?" The greedy eyes of the Decurion Princeps lit up in anticipation.

"After we have taken remuneration as a reward for our service of course."

"Of course."

Chapter 14

With spring approaching the Iceni were busy in their fields and the capital was almost empty. Boudicca did not mourn Prasutagus. He had not been a true king who felt for his people. He had been a supporter of Rome. At least her daughters would now rule and already the Queen was making plans to raise the land against the Roman invaders. The treasury was in a healthy state and she had secretly ordered and paid for many weapons with which to arm not only her people but those supporters of Caractacus who had remained hidden, waiting for this day. She and the priests on Mona had carefully ensured that the army of the Iceni was spread out and did not attract the attention of the Roman Governor. Sadly, this had meant that the Romans had focussed all their strength and all their attention on the West and Mona had been captured but that suited Boudicca. With the legions away, there was no-one to stand in her way.

Tuathal, the leader of her bodyguard burst into her hut, "Apologies your majesty for the interruption but the town is surrounded by Romans and they are outside."

"How dare they!"

"They outnumber us majesty."

"Prepare horses for my daughters and myself. We will escape this night. See to it."

"Majesty."

"And send my daughters to me."

The two teenage girls had barely made their mother's side when Legate Cerialis strode in flanked by Gaius Cresens and ten of his men. "How dare you enter my home unannounced!"

"I am Quintus Petillius Cerialis, Legate of Britannia and I have an instruction here to take over the treasure and lands of the Iceni as stipulated in the will of King Prasutagus. You and your daughters will be taken to Camulodunum for your own protection."

"Protection from whom?"

Ignoring her words he said, "Decurion, take her and her daughters, bind them."

Inflamed by the assault on her person the Queen pulled out a knife and tried to stab one of the guards. "How dare you! Take her outside and tie her to the entrance of the door." Two men took her and Cerialis said quietly, "When I return I want there to be no virgins left in this hut!"

Cresens licked his fat lips in anticipation. "There won't be. Hold them down a lift up their tunics!"

Once outside Cerialis noticed that a large crowd had gather. "First Spear! A protective line and prepare to witness punishment."

First Spear did not want to obey but he was a twenty year veteran; it was not in his blood to disobey a general. "Face the crowds and lock shields." At least his men would not have to witness the abomination which was about to take place.

Boudicca was now tied to the door posts and the trooper before her ripped her top off revealing her bare back to the crowd and her breasts to the troopers who leered before her. "Trooper, twenty lashes."

The sound of the whip cracked across the settlement and the Queen's moans, which she fought against, masked the screams from inside the hut as her daughters were raped, first by the Decurion and then other troopers. The Queen's tears were not tears of pain but tears of rage and anger that she was impotent and could do nothing. When it was finished and she sagged against the ropes, her bloody back testimony to the savage beating Legate Cerialis spoke. "The Emperor Nero has, by the terms of the King's will, inherited the land and treasury of the Iceni. You will all now enjoy the benefits of Pax Roman and you are now all liable to the punishments for misdemeanours. Tomorrow the Queen and her daughters will be taken to Camulodunum to be tried for crimes of insurrection against the state. First Spear, disperse the crowd and then disarm the warriors."

The reluctant legionaries pushed the crowd back. They outnumbered the unarmed inhabitants but the Iceni were a proud people and only retreated reluctantly. Cresens had emerged from the hut. "Decurion, secure the Queen in the hut with her daughters and mount a guard on the entrance."

That evening, as the Treasury was being escorted north by Tribune Celsus' cavalry and four centuries from the First Cohort, the Legate and the Decurion enjoyed a meal and the knowledge that they had done the Emperor's bidding. Both of them would benefit from such loyalty. "These barbarians are no match for Rome and its power Gaius. They had no order and no systems in place to rule effectively. There is nothing to stop us."

Cresens waved a hand around the King's hall in which they sat. "And even when they try to emulate us this is the best that they can do."

"And the Queen prefers a wattle hut!" They both laughed. "Your men are guarding her?"

"There are three shifts of ten men on each shift. They will be safe."

Tuathal knew nothing of the flogging. He had been too busy gathering the men he needed and as a result had managed to keep thirty warriors who were armed and he had not had to witness the humiliation of his Queen. Although the legionaries guarded the gates this was no Roman fort with four secure entrances and exits, this was an Iceni settlement; there were other ways to leave if you knew the right places. Ten of the warriors who had been disarmed waited beyond the gates with the forty horses which had been grazing in the nearby fields. Had there been Roman cavalry they would have secured the beasts but the legion was not concerned with such things and that oversight was to cost the province dear. The ten troopers who guarded the hut were lazy, they were sloppy and they were drunk. They complimented each other on their success and toasted the Decurion and Legate who allowed them to rape young girls and give them the plum jobs. They laughed at the thought of the other troopers spending the cold spring night out in the open while they toasted themselves by their fires drinking captured ale and food. This was a good life.

Tuathal contemptuously threw the dead trooper aside as did his fellow warriors. This had been ridiculously easy and if this was the measure of the Roman army then they would soon destroy the much-vaunted war machine. When he saw his Queen, he wished he had made the troopers suffer a more painful death. Boudicca's green eyes flamed with cold anger. "We will have our revenge but first we must escape. If they take

185

us to Camulodunum then the three of us will die. Are there horses?"

"Waiting outside."

"And the messengers have been sent to raise the army?"

"Yes majesty."

"Good. Have two of your men carry my daughters. They have been grievously hurt." When the bluff warrior saw the bloodstained tunics, he knew what it meant and he just wanted to kill and maim Romans. The Queen saw his look and restrained his arm. "There will come a time for vengeance and it will soon be here."

They left by a hole her warriors cut in the rear wall. The dead troopers were propped by the door as though still on guard. It would not fool a close inspection but Tuathal hoped that they would have escaped long before their deaths were noticed. The guards on the walls were doing what they always did, they were watching for those coming in and not those trying to escape. The Queen and her party disappeared south long before the alarm was raised. The rebellion had begun.

Legate Quintus Petillius Cerialis was incandescent with rage when he discovered that the Queen had escaped and Gaius Cresens bore the brunt of his ire. First Spear took some satisfaction from that but he was annoyed. His men would have prevented the Queen's escape. "Destroy the village! And then we will head back to Durobrivae. I want this bitch and her spawn caught and crucified!"

Wolf and his turma were close to the road. Their orders were to stay there and make sure that the Iceni were not reinforced from outside. They had made a small camp made of brush and bushes cut to form a perimeter with the horses within. It would merely give early warning but the Decurion did not trust the Iceni. "Tell me Lucius why did you not stay and fight as a warrior. You are a good man with a sword."

"The Queen is a devoted worshipper of the Mother. It is said that she is a priestess of the cult and has studied with the druids on Mona."

"And that is bad?"

"One of my mother's sisters was sacrificed to the Mother as a child. My mother never got over that. She died three years ago still grieving for her little sister. I could not fight for a Queen who not only allowed such things but encouraged them and the king, well had he been stronger, I might have stayed but he was weak." He looked to the east and his homeland, hidden by night's cloak. "The land seemed blighted by a cult which should have been a joyous one but Boudicca changed it for her own ends. There were rumours she and Caractacus were lovers which is why the Queen of the Brigantes, Cartimandua handed him over to the Emperor; for spite."

"You seem to know a lot about the royal family Lucius."

"My mother was the Queen's cousin."

"Which makes you almost royalty."

"Minor royalty but as my father died too when I was young, we had neither power nor influence. No, I am happy to serve as a warrior of Rome."

Wolf and four troopers took the first watch, not that Wolf expected anything to happen. The night felt too quiet but it gave him the opportunity to think about his men and what he knew of them. When he had first joined the men, he had fought alongside had been his friends and he had known them since birth. Now they were not only strangers but they came from a different land, with different religions. He would need to work to get to know them for these were the men who would protect his back. These were the oath takers he fought with now, not his childhood comrades. He was about to wake Gaius when he heard the thunder of hooves and he saw a column of riders heading south. That they were not Roman was obvious from their garb, but as the moon flashed from behind a cloud for an instant, he caught a glimpse of flowing hair. It was the Queen. It was Boudicca.

"To arms. Mount!"

His turma might be young but they were well trained and within a few heartbeats they were mounted and riding south. He did not gallop for he knew they might have a long ride ahead of them and who knew what dangers. The fickle moon kept appearing and disappearing but he saw, in the occasional flashes of white light that they were a mile ahead. He slowed the chase down to match the speed of the Queen and her riders. He did not have enough men to tackle them but he could, hopefully ambush them when they rested.

As dawn broke they saw that the Queen and her entourage had halted. "Gaius, take half the turma. We'll…" Before he could put his improvised ambush into action the Queen's party left the road and began to head south east. "Forget it. Where is she going?"

Riding just a little close now that they were off the road the troopers headed through fields lined with hedges and occasional woods. Every time they disappeared into a wood Wolf slowed, worrying about an ambush. As they emerged from a particularly thick wood, to his horror he saw that he could no longer see them and there was a low hill and ridge before him. "Come on let's see if we can see them from the top of the ridge." Remembering Osgar's advice they halted before the top of the hill and Gaius and Wolf crawled to the top, desperate to see the Queen still within sight. As they peeped over the top they saw, not only the Queen and her party but the whole Iceni and rebel army.

"Shit sir! There must be over fifty thousand warriors there."

Wolf shook his head, "Too many for us to ambush that is for sure."

They slid back down the hill. "Well sir what now?"

"We return to the fort and tell the Legate. We aren't going to miss this army and even I could follow their trail. It looks like the rebellion has started. The question is where they will attack first!"

"Camulodunum! That is where we will strike. It is their most important town and it is filled with the Romans who have retired to this land. We will slaughter every man woman and child and then we will move to Verulamium and Londinium. All of their precious cities of stone will fall and the land will return to the Mother!" The roar from her men was as much for her as a leader and a symbol as for the action they were going to take. The warriors had waited a long time for this chance to show the Romans that there were still free men in Britannia who would throw off their shackles and return the land to the people.

By the time they made it back to the fort they were exhausted having ridden hard since they had left the Iceni army. The Legate and the rest of the forces had just returned and were equally weary. Wolf's news was greeted with dismay. "Are you certain Decurion of the numbers? You were tired after all."

"With respect sir when an army stretches as far as the eye can see from one side of a valley to another and when you cannot see the end of it then it is safe to assume that it is a big army. I have fought in battles with two legions and three cohorts. Those numbers were dwarfed by the army of Boudicca."

"You saw the Queen?"

"I saw the Queen. I had already met her when I visited Venta Icenorum with the Quaestor."

"How far away are they?" The Legate was already ensilaging how he could get his paltry forces down to the vulnerable heartland of the Province before the barbarian hordes were unleashed.

"Using the milestones as a guide I would say forty or fifty miles. The barbarians were moving quickly."

He sighed. Very well we will empty the garrison and march south. We will head for Camulodunum. I want a messenger sending to the Governor. We will need the legions and Tribune, send a rider to bring the other cohorts."

Prefect Spurius blurted out. "Surely you are not going to take on that army with two and a half thousand soldiers?"

"May I remind you Prefect that they are barbarians and we are taking with us professional Roman soldiers? We will defeat them." The three professional soldiers exchanged looks of dismay. The policy of keeping pockets of troops in different parts of the province was going to cause unnecessary deaths. A full legion and a full ala might have been sufficient to, at least, slow down Boudicca but the three men knew this was too small an army to do anything other than die.

When they headed south the Legate placed himself close to the Ninth's regular cavalry and Cresens bandits, as the ala called them. The other troopers were spread out ahead in a long column ready to investigate any sign of the enemy. Travelling with the infantry meant that they could only manage twenty-five miles a day and at the end of it the legionaries were just fir to sleep and nothing else. They found the place where the party head left the road. Cava was sent with his turma to investigate while the behemoth that was the Roman vexillation trudged wearily south.

Cava was glad to be away from the slow-moving column. He was a horse man and he needed to ride. "Wolf was right. A blind man could follow this trail."

His Chosen Man laughed, "Are you having a go at the Decurion then sir?" Cava looked puzzled and Chosen Man pointed to his own eye.

"No son, he is just half blind but he sees better than any man I know."

"It looks like they are heading for Camulodunum."

"Well I hope Decurions Tulla and Murgus have kept their swords sharp. They will need them."

"They should be all right there sir. Wasn't it a legionary fortress?"

"Aye. It was the first one they built but I don't think it is stone. Still they have as good a chance of surviving there as anywhere."

Soon the course of the barbarian army became obvious. They saw burnt out villas and, after having inspected two of them realised the futility when they found the inhabitants spread-eagled on fires. Boudicca was making them pay for her humiliation. "Graccus, ride to the column and tell the Legate I think they are heading for Camulodunum. If you head west you should meet the road. Tell them to hurry. The bitch is set on revenge."

The Iceni were busily venting their spleen on the outlying farms and settlements. The burning of those villas and the slaughter of the inhabitants gave the people of the finest city in Britannia time to organise their defences. The procurator, Catus Decianus, sent riders to nearest forts and then ordered the garrison of two hundred Thracian auxiliaries to march and meet the Iceni and halt them. Fortunately, there were many veterans in the city and they began erecting defences. Publius Tullus had thought his fighting days were done but he did what he had done for twenty five years; he organised the defence. The women and children were sent to the most secure building they had the Temple of Claudius. Made of stone and the largest building in the province the non-combatants would be safe there. The five hundred vigiles and veterans armed themselves and gave each other the knowing look of warriors who are about to die and know it. As they clasped arms they looked into the eyes of other men who were too old to fight. The procurator was like a rabbit before a snake; he was terrified. He was a man for peace and a stable city. He was not a man to resolutely fight against a vengeful Boudicca.

The auxiliaries who marched north had no scouts out. They saw burning buildings and the centurion who led them assumed that it was a larger than usual bandit raid. He headed for the nearest flames. The smoke from villas further afield suggested he would be too late and he was a pragmatic man. If they could catch the raiders while they were attacking a villa then surprise would be on his side. "Over to that small hill. We'll be able to see better. Optio, run over there and take a look. You have younger legs."

Grinning the young optio jogged up the hill. As he crested the rise his jaw dropped. This was no bandit raid; every Iceni in the Province had to be there. He saw chariots and cavalry and thousands of screaming warriors. He started down the hill. This was too many for the two hundred auxiliaries. He began yelling, "There are thousands sir. Too many…"

That was as far as he got for a huge warband had seen him on the hill and raced to reach him. The spear plunged into his back and the centurion watched with horror as the Iceni flooded down the hill. "Lock shields!" It was too late for any other formation and the Thracians locked shields and presented a wall of spears to meet the charging warriors. It was a futile gesture; the sheer weight of numbers overran the Romans. Even through the front ranks of Iceni perished there were so many that they simple surrounded and slaughtered the Romans. The centurion braced himself for death, determined to take as many of them as he could. He parried with his shield and stabbed with his gladius. He was, quite simply, too good for the Iceni but, as the men around him fell he was surrounded and, even as he stabbed the next warrior in the throat and axe sliced into his spine and a spear was rammed into his neck. Within moments his head and those of the auxiliaries who had fallen with him adorned their own spears.

The Legate received the message from the procurator at the same time as Cava's messenger reached him. "Prefect, take your cavalry by the shortest route to Camulodunum. Tribune, accompany him. Leave your Decurion Princeps and his turma as my escort. We will use the road. Slow them up."

Gnaeus and Marius rode at the head of the column. The land was flat which made life slightly easier but there were many obstacles to be negotiated. Soon they had a better idea of their destination as the saw the pall of smoke rising into the sky. "Well we know where they are at least." Gnaeus looked over his shoulder. "What we can do with less than six hundred men is beyond me."

"I think that the Legate expects us to die."

"We all have to die some time Marius."

"This would be a pointless death. The Iceni can easily destroy the entire south and there is nothing that we can do. This needs Paulinus and the Legions from the west."

"Even if they get the message tomorrow they could not be here for at least fourteen days."

"I didn't say it wouldn't be a disaster Gnaeus but throwing away half an ala, a cohort of the Ninth and a cohort of Gauls strikes me as foolish."

"Welcome to the Imperial Roman Army."

Decurion Paterculus saw the flash of red and the armour to his right. He had been watching the destruction of the auxiliaries helplessly; desperate for the chance to fight them but aware that it would be suicide to do so. "Looks like the Prefect is here." Leading his men to meet the column he reined in and saluted. "Decurion Felix was correct sir. There are at least sixty thousand of them." He gave a wry smile, ""e had time to count. They seem intent on burning everything they see." He pointed to a pile of bodies and the spiked heads. "Someone in the city sent a handful of men against them. They did not last long."

"And the city will not last long unless we can distract them."

"You have an idea Marius?"

"It is like when you hunt a boar. You make it charge someone who can escape it and lead it to the other hunters. If we spread our line out and attack them then they will assume we are the whole army and attack us. We can lead them away from Camulodunum and towards the Legate."

"Still intent on dying then?"

"No Gnaeus, intent on doing what we can to save the civilians in the city."

"It is as good a plan as any. Ninth, form line!"

"First Pannonians, form line!"

Wolf was on the right of the line with his turma. He could see where the Prefect was from the Wolf standard still carried proudly by Gerjen. The line had the illusion of power but, although it stretched for almost a thousand paces it was thin. They began to trot towards the enemy who were still destroying anything which looked Roman. Buildings were being torn down by bare hands and any Roman they found was thrown into the buildings which had been set on fire. Their preoccupation with destruction meant that they did not see the Roman line approaching until it was too late. The line hit the Iceni at the gallop and the javelins of the troopers caused great destruction amongst the Iceni but there were simply too many. They did not run away they just turned and charged the cavalry. The Tribune had a buccina with his standard and Wolf, busily defending against the encircling Iceni, heard the call for retreat. "Right lads, fall back!"

They began to disengage. The field was already covered in bodies and Lucius' horse stumbled and fell as its hooves became entangled with a pair of dead Iceni. The young trooper crashed to the ground. The pursuing Iceni saw him and eagerly leapt forwards. Marcus and Wolf saw the youth's dilemma at the same time. Wolf hurled his javelin at the nearest warrior and kicked Blackie hard to make him surge back to the wall of swords and spears. Marcus put his sword in his left hand and lay low over the saddle with his right hand out. "Lucius, grab my arm!" Lucius grabbed the arm and began to swing up behind Marcus. Two Iceni tried to stab him. Marcus' left arm came over to cleave the unprotected skull of one of them in two while Wolf reared Blackie to crush the other's back.

"Come on let's go now!"

The three troopers were the last to leave the line and yet the Iceni raced after them. Gaius and the rest of the turma had slowed to see where their Decurion was and, against all orders they turned back to throw another shower of javelins which took out their nearest pursuers. They kept running for another mile and then the buccina sounded for recall. Their horses blown and lathered they looked around to see who remained. Their numbers had been badly thinned. Lucius gratefully slid off Marcus' horse. "I owe you my life Marcus."

"You would do the same for me."

Drusus had found a spare horse which had lost its rider and followed the rest. "Here brother, try not to lose this one. I hear the loss of a horse is a flogging offence."

Lucius shook his head, "If I thought I was going to survive this and be flogged I would take it."

Marius' voice rang out, "Decurion! Casualties!"

Lupus counted his men. There were but fifteen left. He had only started with twenty-five but he had lost ten. He rode up to the Prefect. "Fifteen men sir!"

Gerjen grinned at him and gestured at the standard. "The Wolf still rides old friend." Wolf grinned back and then his face fell as he realised that there were three of the officers represented by their chosen men. Panyvadi, Darvas and Kadarcs were not there. Gerjen saw his look and nodded. "They fell for they were close to the wolf and the Iceni made for it. They fulfilled their oath and they died protecting the standard. We will meet them ere long."

There were now just two of the original wolf warriors left; Gerjen and himself. He quickly looked up to check for other losses and breathed a sigh of relief when he saw Cava.

Tribune Celsus rode up. "We had better head towards the Legate." He pointed across the fields. A wave of Iceni was lurching towards them. It looked as though the sea had broken across the land and the water was the sharpened iron of Iceni warriors.

"I agree and I am down to three hundred and thirty men."

"I have but sixty. But at least they follow us and Camulodunum is safe… for the moment."

The horsemen continued to keep ahead of the pursuing Iceni. The Legate had pushed his men as hard as he could and the two halves of the rescue met close to the road which led north to safety. "Were the numbers exaggerated then Tribune?"

Marius shook his head. The Legate was still doubting the word of the Decurion. "No Legate. If anything, they were an under estimation. There are more than sixty thousand just behind us. We need to deploy now."

Paling he looked around for anything which could be defended. There was nothing save a few hedgerows and small streams. "Prefect Spurius put your cohort to the left. Prefect Proculus put your ala on the right. First spear we will occupy the centre and Tribune you and Decurion Princeps Cresens can be the reserve."

Marius almost burst out laughing if it had not been so serious. A reserve was the last thing that they needed. "Right lads. Three lines. Decurion Cava, take the left. Decurion Felix, take the right." He rode to their front to address them. "First Pannonians today we fight for the first time in a battle. The Iceni before us are fierce and they include women in their ranks. Do not be misled; they will gut you as soon as look at you. We can afford no mistakes today. If we are to emerge from this intact then we will need to fight as we have never fought before. You will do your duty and I know that I will be proud of you." The roar from the ranks made the Prefect smile. They had come a long way from the fields of Pannonia. He glanced to the rear and Gnaeus raised his sword in salute. First Spear and Prefect Spurius did the same. It reminded Marius of the arena when the gladiators said,' We who are about to die, salute you'. Except that this day there would be no spectator. At the end of this would be the victors and the dead."

Boudicca, or whoever was leading the Iceni, had seen the Roman formation and halted her army. To his dismay Wolf saw the lines extending across the horizon. They would not attack merely the Ninth; they would surround the Romans and use weight of numbers to achieve their ends. He could see chariots with wicked blades attached to their wheels and a horde of horsemen facing his ala, or the remains of the ala. There was a blaring of horns and suddenly the whole Iceni line lurched forwards. Wolf looked across at Marius; their only hope was a counter charge and he saw the Prefect's dilemma. After a moment he saw Gerjen dip the wolf standard. "Charge!"

Wolf turned to Gaius. "Kill the chariot horses and then we can fight their cavalry!" He saw the nods of the other troopers. His only advantage was that he had fought chariots before and they did not frighten him. He had two javelins left and he surged ahead of his men, Blackie was like a greyhound off the leash, and he hurled his javelin. The chariot driver ducked but the weapon struck the left hand horse and, as it fell to its death it pulled the chariot over, the two men flying through the air to be crushed by the hooves of the turma. The second chariot struck the wreck age of the first and Marcus struck the horse of the third chariot. The chariot charge ended in a wreck of broken wheels and horses. Wolf and his men had no time for satisfaction; they had to take advantage of the gap. Wolf wheeled to the left and threw his last spear at the chief with the torc who was trying to rally the Iceni. As he fell to the ground Wolf drew his spatha and led his small wedge into the side of the Iceni horse. He knew there were warriors behind him but he had to create a gap. The troopers had shields and armour and the Iceni did not. The powerful horses bowled over the Iceni and the long swords ended their lives. Decurion Felix reined Blackie to enable him to assess their situation. To his horror he could see neither the Prefect nor Gerjen, but worse than that the Iceni had rolled over the Ninth and the Gauls. The remains of the ala were now trapped and surrounded.

Suddenly they heard the sound of the buccina, signalling retreat. "Retreat!"

Titus laughed nervously, "Where to sir?"

"Just follow me!" Spinning Blackie around he headed for the remains of the Ninth who had formed a shield wall and First Spear was desperately trying to retreat in some kind of order. Wolf could see that the only chance his men had of surviving was to attack those who were attacking the Ninth; their backs were to them. His men and those who remained from the charge followed the man they all knew was lucky and the thin line struck the Iceni. In their moment of victory the warriors found themselves attacked on two sides. Wolf saw First Spear raise his gladius in thanks and then, as the last of the Gauls was massacred around their standard the whole of the right wing of the Iceni screamed and charged the remains if the Ninth. He heard Cava's voice, "We can do no more Wolf! We have to save our men."

Wolf nodded, unable to take his eyes off the Ninth as they defended their leader and their standard. They took many Iceni with them but eventually, stabbed and hacked on all sides Centurion Marcus Sextus Maro died along with the rest of the First Cohort. In their eagerness to despoil the bodies, the remains of the ala managed to flee the field and follow the Legate and Tribune Celsus. By the time they stopped, there was no more pursuit and the survivors could finally look around and see who still lived.

The Legate looked in shock and the Tribune smiled grateful when Wolf and Cava rode in. "I am glad that you survived. Your charge helped some men to escape. We will have to build a camp. In case they come."

Cava laughed. "If they choose to come then a poxy ditch and a bit of fence won't stop them."

Tribune Celsus shrugged, "It is the way we work. Besides we need to wait here for survivors."

Wolf looked around. "There are but two hundred of us left." He spun to take in all the survivors. "The Prefect?"

Gnaeus shook his head, "He and the ones in the centre fell. They did not have as much success against the chariots as you did. The last I saw was the wolf standard as it fell beneath the Iceni charge."

Wolf sank to his knees. "Then I have failed. I did not protect my own standard and I am the last of the boys from my village."

Cava put a protective arm around his friend's shoulder. "They died as warriors."

"There was a time when I thought that was the best end for a warrior. Now I would have my friends with me."

Marcus and the others had been standing nearby and they came closer. Marcus looked at the Decurion, "Sir you have." He waved his arm at the turma. "We are here."

By the time the next day dawned, another three hundred troopers, auxiliaries and three legionaries stumbled into the camp. There were less than five hundred survivors and Boudicca had no one left to fight save the civilians and veterans of Camulodunum.

Chapter 15

Publius Tullus, one-time Decurion and Quartermaster had done all that he could to prepare Camulodunum for the onslaught which he knew was heading their way. He could not understand why there had been a respite, for the Iceni had waited a whole day before they advanced once more on the beleaguered colonia. He was grateful to the gods for the opportunity to bolster the defences and organise the veterans. The procurator had been well out of his depth and Publius had assigned him the task of calming the civilians in the Temple of Claudius. The Procurator was not a brave man and he decided to leave for Dubris. There he would take ship for Gaul. As he rode away he justified he escape and desertion by persuading himself that he was bringing help. He was not missed by the ones he deserted but they were left leaderless.

It seemed eerily quiet as he and the veterans of four legions calmly waited for the Iceni to descend. Publius could see them massing before the walls. He laughed at the situation in which they found themselves. There was neither a bow nor an arrow to be found and the mighty ballistae and other heavy weapons were with the legions on Mona. They were less prepared than the Britons had been when they had invaded almost twenty years earlier. They would die, Publius knew that and the saddest part was that he would die without his comrades from the Ninth and the ala he had come to love. He wondered if he should have taken up the offer of the Prefect to be Quartermaster. He would have lived a little longer, that was for sure, but he wondered if this marked the end of Roman rule in Britannia. Certainly the Temple of Claudius was the largest monument in the land and if that fell...

"They're coming!"

Hearing the cry, the cavalrymen hefted the large scutum and gripped the unfamiliar gladius in his hand. "Make them pay dear for this land. It has been an honour to fight and die at your side!" The roar from the veterans made him feel better. He was not alone. He would die amongst brave men.

The Iceni threw themselves at the small wall which leapt them from their prey. The first six who tried to take down the grey haired warrior who smiled as he killed them were taken by surprise. They had seen the greybeards and thought they would pour over them; they were the Iceni and they had slaughtered the legions. They had thought the old men would run when they charged. None fled; they stood and they died for they had nowhere to run and in that knowledge came courage for, if you were to die then why not die as you had lived, as a warrior of Rome. Publius was vaguely aware that he could not feel his left leg as he plunged his sword into the throat of the screaming Iceni. And his left arm felt heavy, the scutum seeming to drag it down. Still he stabbed with the wickedly sharp Spanish sword and twisted it as he sliced open the young warrior's guts. Finally he had the relief of darkness as the axe took his head and he fell with the other defenders; the bodies of the Iceni a testament to their courage.

Boudicca screamed a terrifying war cry and her warriors rushed forward to the huge Temple of Claudius. As they looked around for something with which to batter down its door her women began to despoil and disfigure the veterans who were beyond caring. The huge army she had had been swollen by the women who followed the Priestess of the Mother and they were the ones who took pleasure in making the last moments of the wounded excruciating and in tearing the bodies of the dead to make them unrecognisable. When they found nothing with which to destroy the doors Boudicca screamed, "Bring wood! Burn it!"

As the flames began to rise and the smoke filled the temple they heard the screams from within. One or two tried to flee but when they died at the door the rest remained within and the air was filled with the smell of burning flesh as every inhabitant in the colonia who did not die defending the walls was burnt to death. Their thirst for revenge was not assuaged and the horde continued their orgy of death in Verulamium where Aulus Murgus took thirty enemies with him and finally Londinium where every living creature was slaughtered. After killing eighty thousand people Boudicca and the Iceni felt that they had won and the days of Rome were numbered.

When Decurion Princeps Flavius Bellatoris brought the rest of the ala into the fort at Durobrivae it was like coming into a world of the living dead. The other nine cohorts had been rushed to bolster the defence of that part of the world. Gaius Suetonius Paulinus had marched with the Twentieth Valeria down the main road from Mona but, when he had approached Londinium and seen the fires he knew that it was fruitless to waste men trying to save it. He was already bringing his battle and road weary troops to the last remnants of Roman rule in Britannia. All that remained outside of this tiny enclave was the Second August at Caerleon which for some inexplicable reason had not joined the Governor. Every auxiliary force which could be found was heading for Durobrivae.

When the last soldier marched through the gates the Governor held a meeting with his surviving senior officers. As the most senior officer in the ala Flavius attended along with a shocked Legate and Tribune Celsus. The governor himself looked exhausted and the only officer who looked as though he had stepped from a relaxing session in the baths was Tribune Julius Agricola who had been seconded from the Second Augusta.

"We find ourselves outnumber I am afraid. Julius here has checked the numbers and the most numbers we have available to fight this Boudicca is ten thousand. If the Second Augusta reaches us in time," he threw a weary glance at Julius Agricola, then we might have fifteen thousand. A turma of Acting Prefect Bellatoris' Pannonians has reported that the horde is now at Verulamium. They are busy destroying all evidence of Roman occupation and the enemy has grown to almost a hundred thousand." There was a sharp intake from all of them and the Governor gave a wan smile and held up his hand, "Fortunately the officer who conducted the patrol," he looked at Flavius who nodded, "Decurion Felix, did say that almost a third were women and families but even so we are outnumbered by seven to one."

He stood and went to the map on the wall. "I intend to send our scouts out again and find a suitable field on which to fight these barbarians."

Quintus Cerialis stood, "We must send to Rome. We cannot fight so many."

"I am afraid that the Emperor is not enamoured with this Province and is thinking of withdrawing the forces that are here. He believes it is not worth losing Roman lives for and we will have to fight with what we have. Julius here has some ideas about the terrain and I will send him with your troopers Acting Prefect. I think that the Decurion who went out the first time would be a suitable leader. He appears to be level headed. "He threw an irritated glance in Cerialis' direction, "And we need that in our leaders now."

Gaius Cresens had kept a low profile since returning from the battlefield. He had been glad that he had been with the Legate. The Iceni had terrified him. He and his turma had remained at the back of the Ninth's cavalry, a fact which had not gone unnoticed by Tribune Celsus. Now he was trying to avoid joining what he knew would be the last stand of the Romans in Britannia. He hoped that someone would need a turma to ride to the Second Augusta to summon them but despite all his efforts no one had taken him up on the offer. The one bright spot was that Decurion Felix was being sent to scout the battle lines. With the God's help he would not return. He truly terrified Gaius Cresens and he knew that the man's threats were not idle ones.

Flavius had bolstered the Second turma with troopers from others even more depleted than Wolf's and he left with the young Tribune leading a full turma. His young recruits had grown up during the battle and now looked like veterans, despite the lack of beards.

"Why do they call you Wolf?" The Decurion sighed and told the story. "I hear that the men all regard you as lucky, is that just because of your name?"

He shrugged. "I am lucky. There have been many times when I should have been killed but I have survived. I am lucky in that my men are intensely loyal and protect me."

"That is not luck; that is good leadership. I shall watch you Decurion for I would be as good a leader as you are."

"I would not look to me tribune. All of the men I led from Pannonia now lie dead."

Agricola gestured behind him, and yet all of these still follow you."

Wolf shrugged and they headed on the road which went from the fort directly to Camulodunum. They had been travelling for some time when Julius asked the question which had been playing on his mind. "Why stay on the road? Is it not dangerous?"

"No Tribune. It is the quickest way and the Queen, Boudicca, hates all things Roman." He pointed to the stones, some of which had been pried loose. "See she even has her warriors destroying the very road. Even though it aids them it is Roman. Those Druids you destroyed on Mona, they are of the same religion as she. They believe that we should work with the land, Mother they call it and not change it. They will not build from stone and they worship trees and plants. As you probably know."

"How do you know all of this? You are Pannonian."

"Some of my troopers are Iceni and they told me."

The smoke from the destroyed buildings and fields had gone but they still passed the bodies of those caught and killed by the rebels. The land was a haven for those animals which lived from the dead. Wolf gestured at the bodies. "The Queen would probably approve of this. Humans feeding the animals which feed the earth." As the land became more desolate he asked, "What are we looking for exactly?"

"Somewhere easy to defend where we cannot be outflanked easily."

"That makes sense. They like the frontal attack. We will follow a river then. Drusus, Lucius." The two Iceni troopers galloped up. "We need a river; preferably one with some hills and woods."

"Not many hills here sir." Drusus looked off to the east. "Does it have to be a river sir?"

"No, just somewhere narrow where the enemy can't flank us." He looked at Lucius, "The valley of the rocks?"

"It might do."

"Right then lads, you lead us."

Wolf became warier the closer they came to the site the two Iceni had identified. Firstly they were well away from the road and, they were close to Verulanium and that was where Boudicca and her army were indulging their passion for death and destruction. The good news, as far as Wolf was concerned, was that they were close to the main road to Mona and that meant that the Governor would have a clear line of retreat if he needed it. Wolf placed a screen of scouts between them and the Iceni to give advance warning.

Lucius was almost apologetic when they came upon the site. "That plain looks a little big sir. We thought the rocks and the gorge were perfect but we had forgotten about the plain."

Agricola leaned over and patted the Iceni's arm. "Let us investigate it all before we decide it is no good. I have not seen anything better yet." As they rode across the plain the two officers noticed that the plain narrowed to a rocky gorge with two small spurs guarding the sides. Behind it there was a forest.

"This looks perfect to me Decurion."

"But we have nowhere to retreat."

"No and they have no way of outflanking us. All we need is some way to make the Queen come headlong at us."

"That is easy sir."

Agricola looked at him in amazement. "How?"

"Gaius Cresens, he is the officer who always hangs around with the Legate."

Intrigued the Tribune said, Go on. I am fascinated to see how one officer can make the Iceni attack."

"His men flogged the Queen and then he and his men raped her daughters. As soon as she sees him she will charge."

"If you can get the fat bastard to do it!" Gaius' voice showed the contempt he felt for the man.

"Not popular then? Well no matter. The Governor will order him."

"Excellent, now it we can only get her to kill him as well then we will all be happy." When Julius gave him a strange look Wolf explained, without naming Lucius, what the Decurion Princeps had done.

Agricola had shrugged, "There are many men like that in Rome Decurion."

"So the Prefect told me. Just another reason not to go to Rome."

The Governor, the Legate and Julius Agricola were closeted together at Durocobrivis where the Governor had moved the whole army when the patrol returned. "Quintus, this man Cresens is one of your aides I believe? What can you tell me of him?"

204

Quintus found his friendship with Cresens embarrassing; he had hoped that, by promoting him in the ala he could forget him but now, thanks to the one they called, the Wolf, that would not happen. "I was a friend of his father, I did him a favour."

"That is not what I need to know!" Paulinus' voice had an edge to it. The future of the province hung in the balance. "Did his men flog the Queen and did he rape her daughters?"

In a quiet voice he said, "Yes, he did."

"Good, then the Decurion spoke true and the plan might work." He walked over to the map. "The horde is here. We will send the ala, or a large part of it to be within sight of the Queen. This fellow, Cresens will be at the fore. Hopefully the ala will draw them on." He turned to Tribune Julius Agricola. "You will go with them?"

"Of course, but I think only three turmae. The rest should be as we discussed on the wings to enable us to chase them down when we turn them." Quintus Cerialis looked in amazement at these two men who thought they could defeat this barbarian horde! "Leave Flavius Bellatoris with the ala and I will take this Decurion Felix, Wolf as he is called."

"Colourful name."

"And a colourful character." He looked meaningfully at Cerialis. "I believe he can make Cresens do as we wish."

Quintus Cerialis, for once, was in agreement, although he did not know it with Decurion Lupus Ulpius Felix; he also hoped that Cresens would not return.

The next the day the whole army left for the site chosen by Julius Agricola and Wolf. The Governor relied on Agricola quite heavily. He had seen in the young man a general in the making. Cresens had been given his instructions and now rode between Agricola and Wolf; both of whom enjoyed his obvious discomfort and desire to be anywhere else.

"I expect you will be glad to get back to Rome sir?"

"No Wolf I like Britannia and I like the people. I believe I could conquer this whole island with nothing but auxiliaries."

Cresens looked as though Agricola had grown two heads. "I think I agree sir. The legions are fine soldiers but this land has parts which do not suit the rigid organisation of the legions. If you visit the land of the Brigante you will see what I mean;

many small valleys and steep slopes. It suits the auxiliary but not the legionary."

When they reached the gorge the Governor was delighted. "This is perfect. Well done you two. Now we will make it defensible and then Decurion Princeps Gaius Cresens you shall have your moment of glory and draw Boudicca into the range of my legions. She will not leave!"

Decurion Princeps Gaius Cresens was not a happy man. Far from being hidden behind the rest of the army, he was to be the bait in a trap for the Queen. The Legate had played him false; he had been used. The irony, of course, was that he had thought he was using the Legate. Now he found himself in the worst of all worlds, not only was he in a fighting ala but his means of escape, the Legate, had abandoned him. As they rode towards the barbarian army, which was somewhere ahead, he was already planning how to extricate himself from this mess. Glancing over his shoulder he saw Cava, the man they called Horse, watching his every move. He suspected that Decurion Felix had arranged that placement. He could not understand how these warriors could ride into danger so fearlessly and so frequently. From his standpoint at the last battle it seemed a ridiculous notion. The only reward for winning was to fight again and the result of losing appeared to be death. He had watched two thousand Romans die in the blink of an eye. He shuddered.

"Cold, Decurion Princeps? Don't worry when the Queen chases after you and your bollocks you will warm up."

The brute behind him had voiced the other concern in Cresens' mind. What if he fell into Boudicca's hands? He was under no illusions there. His death would be both slow and painful.

Drusus galloped back to the main column. "Sir. The Iceni camp is a mile ahead. They have wagons which they have placed in a circle and they are within it. "His normally cheerful expression had been replaced by a grey and haunted look. "They have some Romans sir. They appeared to be torturing them."

"Very well Drusus. Well done. Decurion Princeps. Would you care to join us?" Wolf took pleasure in summoning the man he hated. This would not repay Lucius for what he had tried to do to him but it would, at least, be a part payment.

The reluctant hero nudged his horse next to the Tribune and away from Wolf. "Sir?"

"You and Wolf need to ride at the fore. We will be but a hundred paces behind you. When they have taken the bait Decurion Felix will escort you back to safety."

The Decurion Princeps wished it was any but Wolf who was with him but the Tribune had obviously been sent so that he had to obey. "Yes sir."

As they rode forwards Gaius Cresens felt vulnerable and exposed. He could see, some way ahead, the shapes which he knew to be the wagons of the Iceni and every step put him closer to danger. "No escape here. You can't hide behind the Legate this time. You are going to learn what it is like to serve in the Pannonians this day." Even though he was talking to the Decurion princeps, Wolf was scanning the sides of the road for signs of an ambush or scouts. The Iceni were so confident that they had destroyed all the Romans that they had become lax. He wondered how close they would have to get for Cresens to be recognised? It didn't have to be the Queen, of course, for the whole of Venta Icenorum had witnessed the flogging. All it took was one person to see him and the Queen would know. With a grim smile Wolf acknowledged that they would know if they had been successful if they had to flee for their lives. The wagons drew ever closer and still no-one saw them. He was able to see the huge wooden wagons which carried the women and children of the Iceni to witness their warriors when they fought. It seemed bizarre to Wolf and it swelled the numbers of the enemy. Suddenly there was a shout and twelve eager warriors galloped from the enclosure. "Well, they have recognised you, now let's ride. Come on Blackie!"

Wolf did not care if Cresens fell now; he had served his purpose but a desperate desire for life made the portly officer lash his horse. Cava had seen their return and the three turmae were trotting back to the Roman trap. They allowed the two men to ride between them and then they closed ranks and galloped after them. Horse kept glancing over his shoulder. The Iceni were slowly falling behind. "Slow up. We are losing them." It was important that they report the Roman army and its, apparent, foolish deployment. Soon the exultant Iceni had closed to within sixty paces of the turmae. As they turned off the road towards the gorge the Decurion noticed just how wide the plain was. When the scouts reported back to Boudicca she would seize the chance to defeat the last Roman army in Britannia.

As soon as the warriors saw the Roman army they returned to the Iceni camp. "Majesty not only have we found the man who violated you and your daughters we have found the Roman army. They are just a couple of miles up the road."

Screaming like a primeval creature she grabbed the warrior. "Well done. Break the camp and we shall have them before they escape."

The Iceni moved quickly and the plain filled with the warriors. The wagons were placed behind in a semi-circle enabling the camp followers to observe the battle, much as a Roman crowd would enjoy the arena. The Queen and her daughters mounted her chariot and paraded before them. *"But now,"* she said, *"it is not as a woman descended from noble ancestry, but as one of the people that I am avenging lost freedom, my scourged body, the outraged chastity of my daughters. Roman lust has gone so far that not our very persons, nor even age or virginity, are left unpolluted. But heaven is on the side of a righteous vengeance; a legion which dared to fight has perished; the rest are hiding themselves in their camp, or are thinking anxiously of flight. They will not sustain even the din and the shout of so many thousands, much less our charge and our blows. If you weigh well the strength of the armies, and the causes of the war, you will see that in this battle you must conquer or die. This is a woman's resolve; as for men, they may live and be slaves."* There was a huge roar and the warriors began banging their shields and their swords.

At the Roman lines the Governor was checking the deployment when he heard the roar. The two legions were in the centre and on their flanks the auxiliary foot. The few cavalry available to him, both regular and auxiliary were on the two wings to deter a flanking movement. Paulinus knew that the Ninth had lost their best troops and would be less confident and the noise of the enemy appeared to enhance their numbers. He saw some nervous looks. His Twentieth were still enjoying the euphoria of having defeated the druids but the legate needed to make his men fight and he turned to address them. *"Ignore the racket made by these savages. There are more women than men in their ranks. They are not soldiers - they're not even properly equipped. We've beaten them before and when they see our weapons and feel our spirit, they'll crack. Stick together. Throw the javelins, then push forward: knock them down with your shields and finish them off with your swords. Forget about plunder. Just win and you'll have everything."*

Wolf was with Flavius on the right of the battlefield. They would be observers at first for the Iceni would have to narrow their front the closer they came to the legions. Every legionary had his two pila; they had a shorter range than the javelins used by the ala but they were heavier. When they struck a shield or a man they broke and could not be thrown back and, more importantly, they made shields impossible to wield. Each cohort was in a three deep line and the skill and training of the legions meant that they could rotate easily to place the freshest men at the front. It was a tried and tested method. The whole line looked like small wedges upon which the Iceni would be spiked.

Although the noise continued unabated the whole Iceni line, led by the Queen in her chariot raced forwards. Every one of the fifty thousand warriors desperate to be the first to claim first blood. The Twentieth stood calmly to receive the charge. Wolf clearly heard First Spear above the cacophony of noise. "Loose!" A thousand pila flew into the air followed a heartbeat later by another thousand. Wolf watched in awe as the second line moved to the front and threw their two pila and finally the third rotated and their spears did their damage. The whole of the front line of the Iceni lay like a macabre dying sculpture of broken men, horses and chariots. The Iceni in the other ranks roared forwards to get at the Romans. First Spear calmly brought up the next cohorts and they too hurled their spears into the packed ranks. The Iceni were very obliging and they ran over the bodies of the dead and the dying to try to kill the pathetically small Roman army which faced them. If they thought that the legions had thrown their mightiest weapon they were in for a shock as the cohorts used the gladii to stab and hack at the bare bodies which seemed to want to die. At the rear the women were screaming for their men to kill the Romans and the brave warriors tried to do as their women wished. Boudicca, now unhorsed, looked in horror at the bodies of her dead daughters. One lay awkwardly her neck and back broken by the crashing chariot while the other lay with a pilum in her young chest, the red stain spreading over her white tunic. Boudicca drew her sword and exhorted her men to greater deeds of valour. "Iceni! This is our time! One last push and we will have them!"

Paulinus was mounted a little way up the gorge and was pleased with what he could see. The Iceni had lost thousands already and the warriors at the front were being chopped to pieces by the relentless lines of gladii. He noted, with satisfaction the rotating of the lines so that the exhausted Iceni kept meeting fresh legionaries and even their greatest Iceni, Atrebate and Catuvellauni warriors could not defeat them. He judged that the time was right and said to the buccinator next to him. "Sound the advance!"

Slowly at first the lines moved and the warriors at the front found themselves pushed back into the warriors behind. Whereas the legions could punch with their shields and stab with their gladii, the longer weapons of the barbarians were useless and they could not bring them to bear. There was nowhere for them to retreat and they were slaughtered where they stood. As they moved back into the plain there was less pressure but the Roman lines spread out to extend their front and bring even fresher warriors into action.

"Sound the cavalry charge!"

Wolf and the ala had been waiting for just such an order. The Iceni and their allies were being pushed back and their escape route was blocked by the wagons filled with women and children. "Form line!" With such a small battlefield Flavius just used a one turma line. The twenty turmae could carve a line through the flanks of the Iceni and, hopefully, meet with the regular cavalry turmae in the middle. Cava was behind the Decurion Princeps and Wolf behind him. They had no javelins and would have to use their long swords but they would avenge their dead comrades. They struck the lines like a hammer striking an anvil. They sliced a huge chunk out of the side of the army but then the warriors on the side milled around the horses hacking at the animals and the

210

legs of the troopers. Flavius just kept on going. If he could cut through the heart of the army then the cohorts could destroy them. Cava saw the warriors trying to get at their leader and he urged his horse on, slicing through the arm which wielded the axe aimed at Flavius' mount. A tattooed warrior punched his shield at Cava's horse which tumbled to the ground and he fell he relaxed and rolled but the warrior had followed up and before Cava could react the warrior's sword took off the Decurion's arm at the elbow. Before he could finish off the Pannonian Wolf rode his horse directly at the man. Blackie's hooves thundered through his skull and he died with his brains oozing out.

"Titus, take the Decurion back to the capsarius. The rest of you, reform on me. Wedge!"

Riding at the front the three turmae began to cut and hack their way through the Iceni lines. Behind him Wolf heard Marcus, Drusus and the others desperately trying to keep up with him and protect him. He felt as he had done all those years ago when he had first led his friends. They were not individuals; they were one weapon and a mighty weapon it was.

The tide changed quickly in the battle and the warriors of Boudicca's army now knew that they had lost. The braver ones remembered the words of the Queen and fought on but some of the less brave souls began to retreat and a retreat is infectious. Soon the bulk of the army was trying to escape but their families and their wagons prevented that. The cavalry found unprotected backs rather than swords and the slaughter began in earnest. None showed mercy. They had seen the bodies of the women with the breasts removed, the babies spiked on spears. They remembered their dead comrades and they killed.

Boudicca could not believe what she was witnessing. Her bodyguard threw themselves at the legionaries advancing to capture her. Her lover Caractacus had surrendered and was now an object of scorn in Rome. Boudicca would not suffer that indignity. She went to the wagons were the once screaming women now stood silent and shocked. She took out the vial of poison. She had intended it for her children and she would have died with a sword in her hand. She now knew that was not meant to be and raising her eyes to the skies and murmuring a prayer for her children the Queen of the Iceni swallowed down the poison. It was painful but it was swift and the red haired Boudicca fell before her people as the cohorts continued to massacre everyone in their way.

The slaughter went on into the dusk. A few escaped but it was only a few and the message they took back to the villages in the south of the land was, do not fight the Romans. It is like trying to hold back the sea, you will lose. It was the end of rebellion and dissension in the south of the province and the end of the warriors who lived there.

The ala scoured the field looking for wounded and dead comrades. There were fewer than they had expected. As they finally went into a camp for the night Flavius Bellatoris was summoned to the tent of the Governor. There were the Tribunes and Prefects of the other forces. "Well done. We have done what I hoped we would do, we have destroyed this threat. I have men counting the bodies of their dead but it seems to be in the thousands." He nodded his satisfaction. "We have suffered less than four hundred dead." He looked darkly towards the west. "Had the Legate of the Second Augusta brought his legion it might have been even less but this is a time for celebration. Flavius Bellatoris. You have led your men well and all speak highly of you as a warrior. I can confirm that you are the new Prefect of the First Pannonian Ala."

Tribune Celsus came and put his arm around him. "Marius would have been pleased. He thought highly of you."

"Make a list of those warriors who deserve phalera and give it to my clerk. Tomorrow we will return to Camulodunum and begin the process of burying and then rebuilding."

Wolf went to the sick bay to seek Cava. He saw his friend, looking paler and with a bandaged and bloody stump.

"I don't think you will be riding again old friend."

"No. Me neither but they saved my life and the capsarius says that the stump should heal well."

"What will you do? Return to Pannonia?"

Horse shook his head vigorously. "What would I do there? No. The capsarius says that I will get a small pension. I have saved a little and I have an idea to open an alehouse in Eboracum. You and the lads will be based up there and the last time we visited there was o tavern. I will clean up."

Wolf nodded. "I think you will."

"Do you have a name for it?"

He gave a wan smile. "My horse died but I still have the saddle. I thought I would hang the saddle outside and call it The Saddle."

"Good name. We will frequent it old friend." Wolf looked sad. "I am the last of the original Decurion now. All my friends I led are dead and now my oldest friend is leaving."

"You will have new friends Wolf, the men you lead."

"No Cava, we both know that you cannot be friends with those you lead. I have learned that now. A leader is lonely. Like a lone wolf it has to rely on its own wits."

"I am still your friend. When you come to Eboracum then you can share your pain with one who knows."

Wolf was delighted when Flavius gave him the news of his promotion. "Well done sir. You deserve it." He suddenly caught a glimpse of a pudgy hand. "That still leaves us with Cresens as Decurion Princeps."

"Don't worry about that Wolf. I am now his master not the Legate. We will watch this one."

"Horse lost his hand sir. He is going to open an alehouse in Eboracum. I thought we might use some of the ala fund to help him. He deserves it."

"Of course. See to it."

Chapter 16

Prefect Bellatoris summoned the officers to his tent soon after dawn. "The Governor has ordered us to secure Camulodunum. There may still be rebels there. Once the army has joined us and the area made safe then we will return north to stop the raids from across the frontier. We will also have to begin recruiting again."

As Wolf led his depleted turma east he suddenly felt old. When he had joined he had been but a young boy now, even though he was not yet twenty eight he felt much older than the young men like Marcus and Lucius whom he now led. He had already told the prefect that he intended to inter and honour his dead comrades when they reached the scene of their deaths. Flavius was in full agreement. It was not their way to forget their dead and they needed to finish the business of the dead and then get on with the duties of the living.

They knew when they were close to the scene of the massacre for there were crows, magpies and ravens squawking screaming and fighting over the remains of the dead Romans. It was even more gruesome than they had anticipated for the bodies had been despoiled. The bodies had been stripped and emasculated. The turmae looked in horror and wondered how they would manage to piece together the dead to give them the dignity of burial. They laid the dead of the ala in one row and the other cohorts and the legion in two others. They would be buried by their own but the Pannonians would bury their own. Eventually they managed to find the bodies of their dead and, while half the ala dug their grave the rest placed them with swords. It was a long grave for there were many dead. They placed the prefect in the middle with Gerjen, Panyvadi, Darvas and Kadarcs. Each had a sword laid on their body and Wolf found the wolf standard. It had been hacked and cut but it was still recognisable as their standard. He placed it reverently next to Gerjen, his oldest friend. Finally, he took the wolf symbol from round his neck and laid it on Gerjen.

"Gerjen, my brother, I owed you a life. I could not give you that life here on earth but I give you the wolf to guard you and my friends in the next life. Today I am Wolf no longer, I am Lupus no longer. Wolf died with Gerjen and the friends of my youth.

From this day I am Decurion Ulpius Felix and Wolf is but a memory."

He stepped back and Prefect Flavius spoke. "Today we honour our dead. We will remember your bravery always. Sleep brothers beneath the soil of Britannia, far from your home." The soil was placed over the bodies which were soon hidden. Then they replaced the turf and the whole ala rode reverently across the grave so that by the time they had crossed there was no sign of the monument to the dead. No grave robbers could spoil it and the ala knew to the uncia where their friends lay.

There was far more destruction at Camulodunum but it was less distressing; these were not their comrades. They began the gruesome task of laying the bodies out. The women and girls that they had caught had been raped and their breasts cut off but there were mercifully few of them. The veterans had had the same treatment and, when they found the head and body of Publius they could see that he had fought valiantly for there were many wounds on his corpse. As with the ala, they buried him apart and left the rest for the legions. The Temple of Claudius had the smell of burnt meat and, when they went inside they saw that the ones inside had all been burned alive. Prefect Flavius Bellatoris ordered his young troopers outside. That was not a task for them. "Build a camp and secure the area. The Governor will have his work cut out here."

When the Governor arrived, he was appalled. "Where is the procurator? Have you found his body?"

"He could be in there sir but they are almost unrecognisable."

"No Prefect. If he had stayed here his body would have been outside defending the walls."

"We laid all of the bodies over there sir. We buried Decurion Publius Tullus for he was one of ours."

Governor Paulinus could see the strain on the face of the Prefect. "I am sorry prefect. I can see that you have done all that you could. Tomorrow take your men north. Use Eboracum as a base. When we have finished here I will send the Ninth north and find you some recruits." He glanced up at the remains of the ala. "You have taken many casualties but at least now you can begin to build your ala with fresh new men and an experienced ala of troopers."

Flavius took the praise as it was intended but he did not see experience he saw pain and distress at the losses they had taken. When he caught sight of Gaius Cresens he became angry. If it were not for Legate Cerialis foisting him upon them the Ulpius Felix would be the Decurion Princeps and he would have someone on whom he could rely. He could not rely on his deputy. At least he still had Sextus back at Cataractonium. He would give them some stability. Tribune Celsus joined him. "There were no survivors then?"

"Not so far but who knows, there may be some. You will have to find them we are to return north tomorrow."

"We shall follow you soon Flavius and I will be glad not to have the smell of burnt flesh in my nostrils."

The task of visiting the other settlements was given to Tribune Celsus. His turma was too small for anything else and he was pleased to be away from the charnel house. Verulamium was the same as Camulodunum had been save that there they had not sought refuge in a temple but they had been slaughtered and mutilated where they fell. Tribune Celsus found the old hard man of his turma Aulus Murgus; decapitated and emasculated he still had the same serious face. "Well Aulus you proved me wrong. You were a fine Decurion and you served the ala well. Be at peace."

Depression was sitting heavily on his shoulders as he headed down Via Claudia. So much death and no survivors. Decurion Spurius Ocella was a born survivor and he lived still; as he said to his Tribune, "I am too stubborn to die." He did, indeed, show a great desire to live and so it was fitting that he should find the only survivors from the great slaughter. As they headed towards Londinium he caught sight of something moving, something which was not an animal. They had seen no one living since the battle and his senses were alerted. He said quietly, "I have just seen something sir; over to the east of the road. I'll take a couple of the boys and investigate." The Tribune did not take offence that the Decurion appeared to be giving commands. He had learned to respect the veteran and his hunches. "First four, follow me at the gallop!" As they left the road Spurius waved first right and then left. The four troopers split up and the Decurion headed for the place he had seen the movement. He drew his sword; the odds were that it was a barbarian and he had not lived this long without learning caution.

Suddenly a youth leapt up to face him with a pugeo held in his hand. The sword in the Decurion's hand sliced down and only stopped when the Roman saw that the youth was standing before five crying girls. "What the... Put the dagger down sonny or you'll be dead."

Relief flooded his face. "You are Roman!" He picked the girls up. "We are saved. He is Roman."

Hooves thundered behind as the Tribune rode up. "So it seems there are survivors. Who are you?"

"I am Gaius Metellus Aurelius and I lived in Londinium with my parents. When the Iceni came they killed my father and my mother. I was not in when they were killed but when I returned and saw they were dead I tried to flee. I found these girls hiding close to the river and I helped them to escape. We headed north for the bridge was burned and I thought to get to Camulodunum."

The Tribune shook his head. "Camulodunum, Verulamium, all are destroyed and you," he waved his arm to include them all, "are the only survivors."

The youth sank to his haunches. "Then Rome is finished?"

"No son it will take more than this little setback to destroy Rome." The Tribune looked down at his Decurion. "Escort them to the Governor; he will know what to do with them."

The boy stood defiantly with his dagger in his hand. "I want to fight! Let me join your men for I can ride."

They all smiled at his courage. "Sorry Gaius, we legionary cavalry and you are too young."

He shook his head, "After what I have seen no one is too young."

Gaius rode double with Spurius while the girls all rode with a trooper. "You are a brave' un I'll give you that. Did you think you could kill me with that dagger?"

"I have killed three warriors in the last few days. I learned to attack first and ask questions later."

Spurius was impressed. The youth might look fragile but he had a courage about him that many legionaries would have admired. "If you want to fight and you want to ride I might be able to help you."

"But the Tribune said…"

"No, he is quite right. You can't join the Ninth but the Pannonians, they lost many men in the rebellion and they are looking for recruits. You seem to me that you might be just the sort they are looking for. I am not promising mind, and they are based in the north. Would you leave your home?"

"What home," he said bitterly, "my home, my family and my world went up in flames. The north sounds good."

Decurion Princeps Gaius Cresens might have been riding alongside Prefect Bellatoris but he felt like a leper as no one spoke to him. He listened to the easy banter of the ala and their officers as they headed up the Via Claudia but he was excluded. It was as though he wasn't there. His turma also felt the same. They had not taken part in the first battle and they, and their leader had been reluctant warriors at Boudicca's end. Flavius too was thinking of the strained atmosphere. When they reached the fort he would have to speak with Cresens, much as it pained him to do so. He had the ala to think about. The road north gave Ulpius Felix the opportunity to think and reflect on the change the few last months had brought. He had gone from being close to good friends to become an isolated leader. The lonely and empty land through they travelled serves as a reminder of his loneliness.

Behind him Marcus rode next to Chosen Man Gaius. "The Decurion says little Gaius. Is he troubled?"

"He is and he has much to think on. His friends, especially Gerjen, have all died and it troubles him. And he is losing me."

"Losing you? Why?"

"I am to be promoted to Decurion. He will be seeking another Chosen Man. Those are many changes in a short time."

"Who will he choose?"

"If he goes on age then it will be Tiberius for he is the most experienced of the men but Chosen man needs to be able to command. Tiberius likes to be popular and that does not always work. No I think our Decurion will wait and choose his deputy carefully." He leaned over to Marcus and lowered his voice. "He is a deep one. The name he gave up, Wolf, suited him for you never knew what he was thinking or what he would do. The turma

218

will need to work hard to read his mind and anticipate his wishes."

It was at that moment that Marcus decided that he would do all he could to become the best warrior possible. Sometime in the future he would become the Chosen Man and he would become Decurion Ulpius' Felix's right hand man.

Eboracum had a deserted look about it when they rode through the gates. A single century of the Ninth had been left as guards and they were eager for news of their comrades. The Camp Prefect summoned Flavius as soon as he arrived. "I have read the reports but they do not tell the whole story for they only give figures. The reports said the whole of the First Cohort died."

"They did."

"Centurion Maro, I thought he was indestructible."

"There were so many Iceni that I am still surprised that five hundred of us survived but the threat is over and they will be returning north soon. We are the garrison until then."

"And you are needed. We have had many raids from across the frontier. Despite the bridge being torn down they seem emboldened. Queen Cartimandua has demanded that we do something about it. Between you and me she fears that her ex-husband will take advantage of the disorder and invade again. Holding his family as hostages is working but I suspect he will attack sooner rather than later."

"I will get my men settled and then have a meeting with my officers. If your clerk could make a list of places that have been raided I will organise some patrols to begin tomorrow. I suspect I will have to station half of the ala at Cataractonium."

"There is just your Quartermaster, the clerk and a tent party. They are the very edge of the Roman Empire. Ten men stand between the barbarians and the rest of the Province."

"So we will need to get straight back to work. I will remain here with the Decurion Princeps." Flavius noticed the relief on the faces of those who would be leaving. He would use their time together to make a few things clear to him. Decurion Felix will take eight turmae to Cataractonium and patrol the Dunum. They are crossing at will. We need to discourage them. As soon as the Ninth arrive and the recruits then we will join you."

"Sir?"

"Yes Wolf, er Ulpius?"

"Don't forget that Decurion Cava is looking for an inn and we did say the ala would help him out."

"I had not forgotten but thank you for reminding me." Decurion Ulpius Felix was a bad enemy, as Cresens had discovered but there was not a more loyal friend and comrade anywhere."

The other officers, including the newly promoted Gaius automatically followed Decurion Felix. All those who were senior to him were now dead or discharged. To all intents and purposes he was Decurion Princeps but he did not receive the pay or the title. He did not care. The campaign against Boudicca had been a wakeup call. Life was too brief and perilous to be squandered. After speaking with Sextus and explaining the deaths he took Turmae two and three immediately on patrol. The Via Nero had had little traffic and he headed for the destroyed bridge. He had heard that Osgar and Gaelwyn had travelled north to find the boy's family and it they returned south they would cross there.

"Marcus let us see how good you are as a scout. Take Lucius and ride to the river. Look for sign of Osgar. We will sweep around the land to the south of the river and look for sign of the raiders. Gaius, take your turma and ride east but keep a mile south of me. We will ride for five miles and then head up to the river."

Gaius looked at his former leader curiously. "Do you know something?"

"Stanwyck is over there. He pointed to the south east. The Queen complained to the Prefect about raiders. It seems politic to make sure there are none hereabouts first eh?" Gaius nodded. "And Decurion Atellus, next time just do it. I hate explaining!" Gaius led his men, grinning. The Decurion never changed.

"Drusus, ride half a mile in front of us. Watch for sign."

The Iceni trotted off eager to impress the Decurion. He rode with his head next to his horse's and was rewarded by finding a piece of cloth caught on a blackberry bush. He rode back to the Decurion. "Found this sir, just ahead."

"You know what this is Drusus?" The trooper shook his head. "Cloth from a Votadini. There are raiders." He turned in his saddle, "Skirmish line, weapons at the ready. There are Votadini ahead."

The Votadini had been to the south of Stanwyck and killed a herder before taking his family and his animals north. They were confident that they were unseen and had avoided detection. Since the Romans had left the Brigante were like sheep deserted by their sheepdog. The ten of them were well armed for they knew that the Brigante were good warriors who defended their land. They had chosen their target well and now, as they drove their booty towards the river they were in a joyous mood. That mood ended as Ulpius Felix appeared from the side of the trail his spatha cutting deeply into the stomach of the lead warrior. Before the others had time to react the troopers of the Second Turma fell upon them; their blades sharply bright. They had learned when fighting the Iceni that you had to make sure a warrior was dead and that he died quickly. They did their job so well that the terrified farmer's family barely had time to catch their breath. Gaius had heard the fighting and raced with his turma. He halted before the Decurion. "Couldn't wait for us eh?"

"There were only ten of them, Decurion. Not enough to bother you. Escort the civilians and their animals home and we will meet Marcus and Lucius."

The Third Turma left and Drusus asked, "What do we do with the bodies sir?"

"Take any weapons, jewellery and torcs. They look piss poor but they may have things of value."

"And then what sir."

He sighed, "Then Drusus we sell it and share out the money. There, enough of an explanation?"

"Yes sir but what I really meant was the bodies?"

"Leave 'em. I can't be bothered to put their heads on spears so let the pigs have them. They will serve some purpose at least. Then we had better ride. The daylight is going and I want to be back at the road before it is too dark."

They found Marcus and Lucius at the destroyed bridge, remnants of which were still visible. "No sing sir. We scouted the banks on both sides. We found tracks in the mud, footsteps heading south."

"Well done son. That was the Votadini we just killed." Marcus beamed. "Right let's head south."

"Found some footsteps but he couldn't see us watching from the bank." Ulpius Felix smiled as Osgar and Gaelwyn stepped out, not ten paces from a shocked Marcus. "It is a good thing you have Brigante scouts or you would find nothing."

The Decurion dismounted and clasped Osgar's arm. "Good to see you old friend."

"And you Decurion." He stepped back. "I see the wolf has gone."

"All of my wolf brothers died and the standard was broken. I gave it to Gerjen to watch over him."

"Good, for you need neither the sign nor the name for you are the Wolf," he tapped the Decurion's chest, "in here."

"Did you find your family?"

"No, we found the ones who took them." He pointed across the river where a grim row of heads peered across the dark water. "But they had sold them on. They are now in the land of the Caledonii. We will find them some day."

"And I will help you."

At Eboracum Prefect Flavius Bellatoris had Decurion Princeps Gaius Cresens in his office. The sentry had been sent away as had the clerk. Flavius wanted none to eavesdrop. "You do not wish to be in the ala; am I right?"

"Yes sir."

"Good for we do not want you. The problem is the Legate. He has made it clear to me that you have to stay here in the north and be a part of the ala. You see my dilemma? You have obviously upset the Legate so, until he is no longer in Britannia you will have to serve. You will be paid as Decurion Princeps but that is it. You have no authority over the other officers, that is my decision. In addition you will make that bunch of criminals you command become soldiers. When we fight I expect you to fight and not hide in the rear. We can have no passengers here." Cresens continued to look sullenly at the ground. "This is no open for negotiation Cresens. Until we are fully staffed again I have to put up with you but I warn you there will be no second chances. Your first mistake will be your last."

An unpleasant silence descended on the office. Gaius Cresens chewed his lip nervously. He was over a barrel. Until he could get some serious money he was stuck here. This was probably the safest place for him for the south had been dangerous and at least the Pannonians knew how to take care of themselves. He would have to make the best of it and toe the line. He was too clever for this dullard of a Prefect and he would find some way to make a profit. "Yes sir I will turn my men around and I will not be a problem sir. You have my word."

Flavius Bellatoris was no fool; he did not believe him for a moment but he had made the consequences clear. The rest was in the lap of the gods.

By the time the Tribune returned it was the winter solstice and the ala's wounds had almost healed. He rode into the fortress at the head of the newly reinforced Ninth. With him were some wagons. There was a burgeoning vicus and one wagon headed in that direction. Decurion Ulpius Felix was at the gate to greet the Tribune and he yelled as he saw the men next to the driver of the wagon. "Horse! You finally made it."

Cava was surprisingly agile for a one-armed man and he put his good arm around Ulpius. "Good to see you. The Prefect told me that the ala had paid for a hut to be built for me so here I am, the new landlord of 'The Saddle'. I just need to get brewing."

"As soon as you are open let me know. I want to be the first one to drink there."

"That is a promise."

The Tribune dismounted. "How are things down south sir?"

"Better Decurion, much better. Once the bodies were buried and the buildings cleaned up settlers drifted back. Many people had fled at the first sign of trouble. Some of the lads from the Ninth and the Twentieth who were pensioned off have settled there." He saw the puzzled expression on Felix's face. "They got prime land and they are a philosophical bunch they don't think lightning will strike twice in the same place. We also got many recruits. A lot of the young men in the south were worried that it might happen again so they joined. We have some here. I am afraid the Tungrians and the Batavians grabbed some of the better ones but Decurion Ocella kept some hidden."

"Where is the Governor now?"

"Heading back to Mona. The Twentieth are going to be based at Deva and Poenius Postumus, the Prefect of the Second Augusta, couldn't stand the shame and fell on his sword."

"Stupid bugger should have obeyed orders."
"You would have made a good legionary Felix. It is just a shame you aren't a Roman citizen eh?"
"Don't worry sir. I am happy just being an auxiliary."
Gnaeus pointed to Decurion Ocella who was heading their way with a column of men. "Here is the Decurion with the recruits he saved for you."
The veteran dismounted and approached Ulpius. "I let the Tungrians and Batavians think they had got the best recruits but they didn't. These ten are the best riders. They are all good lads. Trust me. I can smell a good soldier."
Decurion Ulpius Felix looked at them and then pointed at the one behind Ocella. "He looks to be little more than a boy. "
"You mean like you were when you joined up? This is Gaius Metellus Aurelius and there is more to him than meets the eye. He escaped Boudicca and rescued some children. He killed three Iceni with his dagger. Trust me Decurion, he will do."
Decurion Ulpius Felix also felt that way. He could not explain it but he nodded. "I do, Spurius. Well Gaius welcome to the Second Turma of the First Pannonian Ala. I am Decurion Ulpius Felix and for the next twenty-five years you are mine. We will make this turma and the ala a force that the barbarians will fear. Boudicca and her Iceni have shown us how barbaric they are. Let us show them that we are masters of this island. "
The beaming smile told the Decurion that he had another young trooper. If this went on he would be called the baby minder. He didn't mind. He would build another turma filled with the new Gerjen, Kadarcs. Panyvadi and Darvas and they would live on in these new young troopers. The deaths of his friends had hardened his heart and made him the complete leader. The happy young recruit was gone. He was now Ulpius Felix, a true warrior of Rome.

The End

Historical Background

Carl Wark is an Iron Age hill fort about seven miles south of Sheffield. It is as described and would have been impregnable in the Iron Age before the Romans invaded. However in the age of Rome, as Caesar proved at Alesia and Vespasian at Masada, there was no obstacle too big for the legions.

This period marked a change in the Roman policy of recruiting auxiliaries. In the time of Caesar and Pompey auxiliaries were hired to fight in a campaign. They used their own arms and armour. In the time of Augustus, with the rapid expansion of the Empire this needed to be formalised and although the auxiliaries were recruited in tribal areas they were despatched to fight in other parts of the Empire. When casualties occurred they used local recruiting to fill the gaps in their numbers. Once the auxiliaries took Roman names and attire they began to become Roman. There were still problems such as the Batavi uprising of the mid 60's and the desertion of the Usipi during Agricola's campaign but, generally, the troops were as loyal as the legions and died for Rome in the same numbers.

Quintus Cerialis was the Legate who tried to relieve Camulodunum but, as I say in the novel, he only took 2,500 men and all but 500 of the cavalry, including the First Cohort of the Ninth were massacred. The procurator did behave as suggested in the novel. He sent a mere 200 auxiliaries to face Boudicca and he did flee to Gaul. Boudicca was flogged and her daughters raped by Roman soldiers. In reality Cerialis is not implicated but it suited my novel to make him seem corrupt. Nor was it auxiliaries who raped the queen's daughters, it was legionaries; again it suited my novel. The reasons for the rape are confused but it appears that the Romans were victims of their own sense of order. Virgins could not be executed and therefore the rape would facilitate that sentence. As they were the joint heirs with Nero this would seem a logical precursor to their death. All of which begs the question, why, having committed such an outrageous act did the Romans not execute them? There was a time gap which Boudicca used to ignite the rebellion. I used the escape from the settlement as a means of explaining that.

The lines spoken by the Governor and Boudicca at the Battle of Watling Street are taken from Tacitus. I put them in italics to show what a lazy author I am. They may be fiction (he was writing many years after the event) but if you are going to steal lines then why not from a Roman. In terms of the numbers at the actions they are fairly accurate. It is estimated that Boudicca slaughtered almost 80000 at the three colonia. Paulinus, who emerges as the real hero of the uprising, did only have ten thousand men to face an army estimated to be 100,000 in number. He is reported to have only lost 400 hundred men whilst the rebels were slaughtered. The wagons and their placement, with the families watching on, was an action which had occurred in other conflicts. It cost the rebels their lives as it prevented their escape. The Prefect of the Second Augusta did fail to respond to an order to join Paulinus and, after the Governor's victory, he did kill himself. Apparently his men were a little miffed to have missed a great victory!

Quintus Cerialis did become Governor of Britannia when Vespasian became Emperor after the year of four Emperors in 69 A.D. He was not as good as Paulinus who was, probably, the reason why Britannia remained a colony for another four hundred years. His battle plans suited the Romans but even so the defeat of Boudicca by such a small number of men beggars belief.

The roads were not called Watling Street, Dere Street etc until Saxon times. The roads were named after the Emperor in whose reign they were constructed. As most of them were constructed during the reign of Claudius this must have been confusing although as the action in this book is centred mainly along the A1 it is not such a problem.

Griff Hosker October 2013

People and places in the book.

Fictitious characters and places are in *italics*.

Name-Description

Abad-Pannonian Chief
Aulus Didius Gallus-Governor of Britannia 52-57 AD
Aulus Murgus-Cavalryman 9th Legion
Bucco-A name meaning fool
Capsarius-Medical orderly
Caesius Nasica-Legate who first defeated Venutius
Cava-Pannonian warrior
Cavta-Pannonian village
Colonia Claudia Ara Agrippinensium-Cologne Legionary Fortress
cornicen-The trooper with the cornu.
Durobrivae-Peterborough
Dunum-River Tees
cornu-Roman horn for signalling in battle
Decius Spurius-Prefect 1st Gallic Cohort
Darvas-Pannonian warrior
Decimus Livius Bucco-Corbulo's aide
Decurion Spurius Ocella-Cavalryman 9th Legion
Durocobrivis-Luton
Flavius Bellatoris-Cavalryman 9th Legion
Fossa Lindum-Ermine Street (A1)
Gerjen-Pannonian warrior and aquilifer
Gnaeus Domitius Corbulo-Legate- Germania Inferior
Ituna Est-River Solway, Cumbria
Gnaeus Marcius Celsus-Tribune 9th Hispana
Herrmann-Chauci chief
Julius Salvius Labeo-Legate 5th Alaude
Kadarcs-Pannonian warrior
Marcomanni-German tribe
Marcus Bulbus-Legate Ninth Hispana
Marcus Sextus Maro-First Spear of the Ninth
Marius Ulpius Proculus-Prefect of 1st Pannonian Ala
Navarchus-In charge of ten ships
Numerius Buteo-Cavalryman 9th Legion
oppidum-Hill fort
Nundinal cycle-A Roman week; it changed from 8 days to 7 in the 1st Century

Panyvadi-Pannonian warrior
Publius Tullus-Cavalryman 9th Legion
Quintus Atinus-Cavalryman 9th Legion
Quintus Petillius Cerialis-Legate of the Ninth and later Governor
Quaestor-Roman official or tax collector
sesquiplicarius-Corporal
Sextus Vatia-Cavalryman 9th Legion
signifier-The soldier who carries the standard
Spurius Ocella-Decurion 9th Legion
Sura-Pannonian warrior and deserter
tonsor-Roman barber
Tuathal-Iceni warrior
Trierarch-Captain of a Roman warship
Via Claudia-Watling Street (A5)
Via Nero-Dere Street (Al)-Eboracum North
Via Hades-Road to Hell (A1)
Venta Icenorum-Castor St Edmunds near Norwich
Vicus pl vici-Roman settlement close to a fort
Vindonissa-Roman legionary fortress on Swiss border
Wolf (Lupus Ulpius Felix)-Pannonian

Other books
by
Griff Hosker

If you enjoyed reading this book, then why not read another one by the author?

Ancient History

The Sword of Cartimandua Series
(Germania and Britannia 50 A.D. – 130 A.D.)
Ulpius Felix- Roman Warrior (prequel)
Book 1 The Sword of Cartimandua
Book 2 The Horse Warriors
Book 3 Invasion Caledonia
Book 4 Roman Retreat
Book 5 Revolt of the Red Witch
Book 6 Druid's Gold
Book 7 Trajan's Hunters
Book 8 The Last Frontier
Book 9 Hero of Rome
Book 10 Roman Hawk
Book 11 Roman Treachery
Book 12 Roman Wall
Book 13 Roman Courage
The Aelfraed Series
(Britain and Byzantium 1050 A.D. - 1085 A.D.)
Book 1 Housecarl
Book 2 Outlaw
Book 3 Varangian
The Wolf Warrior series

(Britain in the late 6th Century)
Book 1 Saxon Dawn
Book 2 Saxon Revenge
Book 3 Saxon England
Book 4 Saxon Blood
Book 5 Saxon Slayer
Book 6 Saxon Slaughter
Book 7 Saxon Bane
Book 8 Saxon Fall: Rise of the Warlord
Book 9 Saxon Throne
Book 10 Saxon Sword
The Dragon Heart Series
Book 1 Viking Slave
Book 2 Viking Warrior
Book 3 Viking Jarl
Book 4 Viking Kingdom
Book 5 Viking Wolf
Book 6 Viking War
Book 7 Viking Sword
Book 8 Viking Wrath
Book 9 Viking Raid
Book 10 Viking Legend
Book 11 Viking Vengeance
Book 12 Viking Dragon
Book 13 Viking Treasure
Book 14 Viking Enemy
Book 15 Viking Witch

Bool 16 Viking Blood
Book 17 Viking Weregeld
Book 18 Viking Storm
Book 19 Viking Warband
Book 20 Viking Shadow
Book 21 Viking Legacy
Book 22 Viking Clan
The Norman Genesis Series
Hrolf the Viking
Horseman
The Battle for a Home
Revenge of the Franks
The Land of the Northmen
Ragnvald Hrolfsson
Brothers in Blood
Lord of Rouen
Drekar in the Seine
Duke of Normandy
The Anarchy Series
England 1120-1180
English Knight
Knight of the Empress
Northern Knight
Baron of the North
Earl
King Henry's Champion
The King is Dead
Warlord of the North
Enemy at the Gate
Fallen Crown
Warlord's War
Kingmaker
Henry II
Crusader
The Welsh Marches
Irish War
Poisonous Plots

The Princes' Revolt
Earl Marshal
Border Knight
1190-1300
Sword for Hire
Return of the Knight
Baron's War
Magna Carta
Welsh War
Henry III
Struggle for a Crown
England 1367-1485
Blood on the Crown
To Murder a King

Modern History

The Napoleonic Horseman Series
Book 1 Chasseur a Cheval
Book 2 Napoleon's Guard
Book 3 British Light Dragoon
Book 4 Soldier Spy
Book 5 1808: The Road to Corunna
Waterloo
Lucky Jack
American Civil War series
Rebel Raiders
Confederate Rangers
The Road to Gettysburg
The British Ace Series
1914
1915 Fokker Scourge
1916 Angels over the Somme
1917 Eagles Fall

1918 We will remember
them
From Arctic Snow to Desert
Sand
Wings over Persia

**Combined Operations
series**
1940-1951
Commando
Raider
Behind Enemy Lines
Dieppe
Toehold in Europe
Sword Beach
Breakout

The Battle for Antwerp
King Tiger
Beyond the Rhine
Korea

Other Books
Carnage at Cannes (a
thriller)
Great Granny's Ghost
(Aimed at 9-14-year-old
young people)
Adventure at 63-
Backpacking to Istanbul

For more information on all of the books then please visit the author's web site www.griffhosker.com where there is a link to contact him. Or you can Tweet me at @HoskerGriff

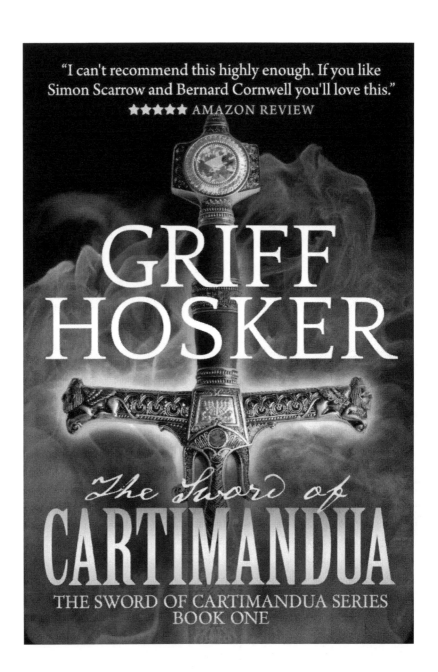

"I can't recommend this highly enough. If you like
Simon Scarrow and Bernard Cornwell you'll love this."
★★★★★ AMAZON REVIEW

GRIFF
HOSKER

The Sword of
CARTIMANDUA
THE SWORD OF CARTIMANDUA SERIES
BOOK ONE

The opening of the Sword of Cartimandua

Prologue

Stanwyck A.D. 50

Claudius might have been Emperor of the largest Empire the world had ever seen but he still hated the rain. This outpost of the Empire was a foul, wet, disease ridden cesspit. In addition he had a wicked and persistent cold; he never had a cold in Rome. He sneezed noisily and glowered angrily at the slave by his side. "Well? Why are we still waiting?" His famous stammer disappeared when he addressed servants or was angry and on this wet and dismal morning he was not at his best.

"I was assured, divine one, that she would be here presently."

He shuddered at the title; like his Uncle Tiberius and his father Germanicus he despised the very notion that a mortal could become a living god. He had hoped that both the horrendous journey across the interminable land of Gaul, the ferocious ocean leading to this end of the world and the barbaric people he had so far met would make the journey worthwhile. The kings and queens who had been presented to him were all barbarians and the not so divine Claudius was glad that his Praetorians were on hand for he did not trust one of them.

Claudius was about to make some barbed comment about divinity when he heard the three blasts on the buccina which heralded the arrival of Queen Cartimandua, leader of the Brigantes. Even Claudius was impressed by the striking young woman who confidently manoeuvred her chariot between the waiting lines of legionaries. He had heard stories of her beauty but he was not prepared for both her presence and power; she seemed to dwarf her surroundings. Her jet-black hair framed an incredibly white face. Her deep-set violet eyes seemed to leap out from her face and her lips, obviously coloured by the crushed body of a scarab beetle, surrounded by remarkably white teeth looked like luscious plums. The Queen was, Claudius realised, everything he had heard and more. He found it hard to countenance that a young woman who looked as though she had only seen a handful of summers as a woman should rule the most powerful tribe in Northern Britannia and had done so, successfully, for over seven years. The way she handled a chariot showed that she was a warrior as did the skulls adorning the outside of the chariot. He could make out, just behind the chariot, the wretch who was being dragged in chains. Although he had never seen him, the Emperor knew it was Caractacus the leader of the Britons in their fight against Rome. Caractacus was the charismatic leader who had sought refuge with the most powerful ruler in the North of these islands, Cartimandua. Caractactus he was also the ex-lover of the rapacious young Queen and had been used and then discarded. If there was one thing that Claudius admired it was someone who could scheme, plot and survive as well as he had. She certainly had been a confident young queen who took over the rule of her land, Brigantia when her father was murdered. She ruled the largest tribal lands in Britannia; spanning the country from coast to coast. Claudius realised that she was wise beyond her years; she had seen the power of the Roman war machine and come to an accommodation rather than conflict. Perhaps that was why she ruled this enormous land of wild men and even wilder places. The Emperor of Rome himself would need to be careful about the promises he made.

"Welcome Queen."

"All Hail Claudius." Claudius was impressed that her Latin was flawless, this was an educated woman. "I bring you a gift. "She gestured with her arm and her bodyguards brought out Caractacus, the putative King of the Britons, and his face displayed just how much he hated the woman who had betrayed him. The queen to whom he had turned in the hope that, united, they could defeat the monster that was Rome. Instead she had ensured the safety of Brigantia and her high place in the Emperor's favour. "It is Caractacus. He was your enemy and now he is mine." Her guards dragged the bound warrior to be symbolically thrown at the feet of the Emperor. Before Claudius could speak, he always gathered his thoughts before uttering anything important; Cartimandua drew from a scabbard in her chariot, the most magnificent sword Claudius had ever seen. Although a cerebral rather than military man Claudius admired beauty and functionality and this magnificent weapon fulfilled both as well as anything he had seen before. Its steel blade was so highly polished it was almost silver, with a line of gold trickling sinuously along its length. It was half as long as the tall Queen's body and looked as though it needed two hands to hold it, although the warrior queen held it in one. The handle was adorned with a red jewel, the size of a grape and Claudius surmised that it must be a ruby, an incredibly rare ruby. The black ebony hilt was engraved with what appeared to be pure gold. "Would it please the Emperor for me to despatch this rebel and part his sorry head from his body?"

"N-n-no Queen. I wish to take him back to Rome so that the whole Empire can see the power of the Emperor and the Brigante." Her cold callous attitude to execution impressed the Emperor. She had no problem with carrying out the act herself, something the Emperor knew he could not do. He could order a murder or an execution as easily as he ordered supper but he could not soil his hands. Claudius turned to a grizzled centurion who stood at his side. "Gerantium, untie the prisoner and have your men take him away then join the Queen and myself inside my tent for we have much business to discuss."

As they entered the pavilion especially erected for the occasion Claudius began to wonder if this island was as wild as he had thought. Although the buildings were primitive and some of the actions of its people somewhat barbaric he could see a sophisticated level of politics which made him think it might become civilised one day. In this young queen he had seen someone who could have held her own with the senate. She was confident, she was cruel, she was calculating and she was charming. The old Emperor shook his head to free himself from the spell he was falling under. He felt happier now with this island for the northern part would be secure with an ally. He had no doubt that Queen Cartimandua would remain in power and the Emperor determined to support her in that. He was glad that she did not live in Rome for if she did he would fear for his throne.

Printed in Great Britain
by Amazon

57676301R00144